SHARPER KNIVES

SHARPER KNIVES

CHRISTOPHER FOWLER

WARNER BOOKS

A *Warner* Book

First published in Great Britain in 1992 by Warner Books

Copyright © Christopher Fowler 1992

The moral right of the author has been asserted.

A CIP catalogue record for this book
is available from the British Library.

ISBN 0 7515 0152 2

Typeset by Leaper & Gard Ltd, Bristol
Printed in England by Clays Ltd, St Ives plc

Warner Books
A Division of
Little, Brown and Company (UK) Limited
165 Great Dover Street
London SE1 4YA

For Sarah and Michael

'Without hope we'd all need sharp knives.'
Robert R. McCammon

Contents

Touching Darkness

As I sit down to begin writing this book, Jeffrey Dahmer, the Milwaukee serial killer, is having his trial nationally televised. Aren't we living in exciting times? According to the producer of the show, they're concentrating on the issue of the madness rather than the cannibalism. Well, that makes *me* feel a whole lot better. From the footage I've seen, he looks like a regular guy. Perhaps he and Dennis Nilsen could flatshare when they get out. *Whoa* — I'm sorry, that was politically incorrect.

Which brings me to my point.

The two hundred year history of the horror story is littered with accusations of offensiveness. Victorian chroniclers of the supernatural sought to produce a thrill of fear with shocking tales of madness and murder, and if there were outraged gasps from the reading public, so much the better.

But murder, as we have seen in police documentaries, is never thrilling. It's usually rather sad and squalid, with the guilty more to be pitied than reviled. Authors simply took the concept of violent death and twisted it to their own ends, adding hauntings and vengeance and all the other staple ingredients of the canon.

Which was fine, until something awful happened.

Real life became more horrible than fiction.

We're living in a time when Dahmer, the killer who saved a victim's heart in his refrigerator 'to eat later', is appearing on TV sandwiched between ads for fish fingers. We're unshockable now. We go to movies and instead of cheering for the cops we root for the murderer. Hannibal Lecter and Henry Lee Lucas — tinseltown stars. Frankenstein and the Wolfman — washed-up kiddie fare.

The New York annual murder rate has now topped the two thousand mark. On 21 July 1991 in that fair city, some guy shot a street vendor dead for — get this — not having cherry flavoured ice-cream. During the race-riot torching of Los Angeles, a looter interviewed on TV explained that he was 'having a lot of fun'.

How did all this happen? When were we forced to abandon hope and arm ourselves with sharp knives? If you had to put an exact time on it, try 12.30 p.m. on 22 November 1963. That shattering afternoon at Dealey Plaza gave us a glimpse into the abyss. It was the moment with which no eerie fiction in the world could begin to compare.

And it got worse. King and Lennon shot to death, Nixon a crook and the AIDS apocalypse, horrors piling upon one another to produce a new concept — Post Modern, which is another word for cynicism.

So the problem is, where to go from here? Movie horror opted for teenage gross-out and found itself in a dead end. Literary horror fragmented; some returned to traditional chills, now a genre as cosy as the locked-room mystery or the country house whodunnit. Some brave new directions collapsed before they became established.

Me, I'm going for the Post Modern Worst-Scenario anxiety tale. There's a rich vein to be tapped here, so let's see what we have. (Thumbs through pages.) Hmmm. Thirteen grim tales and one with a happy ending. The moods are varying shades of black and the monsters are human. That seems about right.

In writing classes they often tell you to work from experience. If these stories had been produced that way, I'd be insane by now. But we're all a little mad in this fast-living, low-attention, sound-sampled, media-buzzed rob-stab-burning end of the century. Perhaps that's what happens when you can finally touch the darkness.

And after all, these ideas have to come from some-where.

So, if you pass me in a London Street and are tempted to ask 'Hey, where did you get your sharper knives from?' you'll already know the answer.

From you, dear reader.

From you.

Christopher Fowler
Soho, August 1992

On Edge

A brazil nut, thought Thurlow, of all the damned things. That'll teach me. He leaned back tentatively in the plastic chair and studied the posters which had been taped to the walls around him.

Confidential HIV testing.

Unwanted Pregnancies.

Mind That Child He May Be Deaf.

He thought: no wonder people avoid coming here. Sitting in the waiting room gave you a chance to consider your fate at leisure.

He checked his watch, then listened. From behind a distant door came the whine of an electric drill. Determined to blot the sound from his brain, he checked through the magazines on the table before him. Inevitably there were two battered copies of *The Tatler*, some ancient issues of *Punch* and a magazine called *British Interiors*. With the drill howling faintly at the back of his brain, he flicked idly through the lifestyle magazine. A pied-à-terre in Kensington decorated in onyx and gold. A Berkshire retreat with a marble bas-relief in the kitchen depicting scenes from *The Aeneid*. The people who lived in these places were presumably drug barons. Surely their children occasionally knocked over the bundles of artfully arranged dried flowers, or vanished into priest's holes to be lost within the walls?

As he threw the magazine down in disgust the drill squealed at a higher pitch, suggesting that greater force had been used to penetrate some resistant obstacle.

A damned brazil nut. Next time he'd use the crackers instead of his teeth. God, it hurt! The entire molar had split in half. Torn skin, blood all over the place. He was

7

sure there was still a piece of nutshell lodged between the gum and the tooth, somewhere deep near the nerve. The pain speared through his jaw like a white-hot knife every time he moved his head.

The receptionist — her name was something common that he never quite caught — had sighed when she saw him approach. She had studied her appointment book with a doubtful shake of her head. He had been forced to point out that, as a private patient, his needs surely took precedence over others. After all, what else was the system for? He had been coming here regularly for many years. Or to put it more accurately, he had arranged appointments in this manner whenever there was a problem with his teeth. Dr Samuelson was away on a seminar in Florida, apparently, so he'd be seeing someone new, and he might have to wait for a while. With the pain in his tooth driving him crazy, Thurlow didn't mind waiting at all.

There were two other people in the room. He could tell the private patient at a glance. The woman opposite, foreign-looking, too much gold, obviously had money. The skinny teenaged girl in jeans and a T-shirt had Council House written all over her. Thurlow sniffed, and the knife rocketed up into his skull, causing him to clutch at his head. When the pain had subsided once more to a persistent dull throb, he examined his watch again. He'd been sitting here for nearly forty minutes! This was ridiculous! He rose from his seat and opened the door which led to the reception desk. Finding no one there, he turned into the white-tiled corridor beyond. Somebody would have to see him if he kicked up a fuss.

In the first room he reached, a fat woman was pinned on her back with her legs thrown either side of the couch while the dentist hunched over her, reaching into her mouth like a man attempting to retrieve keys from a drain. In the second room he discovered the source of the drilling. Here, an exhausted teenaged boy gripped the armrests of the chair with bony white knuckles while his dentist checked the end of the drill and drove it back into his mouth, metal grinding into enamel with the wincing squeal of a fork on a dry plate.

'You're not supposed to be back here, you know.'

Thurlow turned around and found a lean young man in a white coat looking crossly at him.

'I've been waiting for nearly an hour,' said Thurlow, feeling he had earned the exaggeration.

'And you are ...?'

'Mr Thurlow. Broken tooth. I was eating a brazil nut ...'

'Let's not discuss it in the corridor. You'd better come in.'

Thurlow would have been annoyed by the brusqueness of the dentist's manner had he not heard the upper class inflections in his voice, and noted the smart knot of his university tie. At least this way he would be dealt with by a professional.

Thurlow entered the room, removed his jacket, then waited by the red plastic couch while the dentist made an entry in his computer.

'I normally have Dr Samuelson,' he explained, looking about.

'Well, he's not here, he's ...'

'I know. Florida. All right for some. You're new, I suppose. You're very young.'

'Everyone looks young when you start getting older, Mr Thurlow. I'm Dr Matthews.' He continued tapping the keyboard, then raised his eyes to the screen. 'We haven't seen you for a check-up in well over a year.'

'Not for a check-up, no,' said Thurlow, climbing onto the couch.

'I had a thing, a lump.' He waggled his fingers at his cheek. 'I thought it was a cyst.'

'When was the appointment?' Matthews was clearly unable to find the reference on his screen.

9

'I didn't have one. Anyway, it wasn't a cyst. It was a spot.'

'And the time before that?'

'I lost a filling. Ginger-nuts. Same thing the year before that. Peppermints.'

'So you haven't seen the hygienist for a while?'

'And I don't need to see one now,' said Thurlow. 'They always try to fob you off with dental floss and sticks with rubber prongs on. What is this anyway, going on about the check-ups? Are you on commission?'

Dr Matthews ignored his remark and approached the couch. As Thurlow made himself comfortable, the dentist slipped a paper bib around his neck and fastened it.

'Don't you have an assistant?'

'I used to, but she didn't like my methods so I murdered her,' said Matthews. 'Ha ha.' He adjusted the chair from a control pad by his foot, then switched on the water-rinse pump. 'I always make jokes. It takes the edge off. Mouth open please.' He swung a tray of dental tools over Thurlow's chest.

Thurlow opened wide, and the light from the dentist's pencil torch filled his vision. He watched as the hooked probe went in, tapping along the left side of his molars, and glimpsed the little circular mirror at the corner of his vision. Saliva quickly began to build in his mouth. The tapping continued. He knew he would have to swallow soon. Quickly sensing his unease, Matthews placed a spit-pump in the corner of his mouth. It made a loud draining sound, like water going down a sink.

Suddenly Thurlow felt the sharp point of the probe touch down on the bare nerve in his split tooth. It was as if an electric current had been passed through his head. If it had remained in contact for a second longer he would have screamed and bitten the tool clean in half. Matthews observed the sudden twitch of his patient's body and quickly withdrew the instrument.

'I think we can safely say that we've located the problem area,' he said drily, shining the torch around, then lowering the large overhead light. 'That's pretty nasty. Wouldn't be so bad if it was an incisor. It's split all the way from the crown to the root. The gum is starting to swell and redden, so I imagine it's infected. I'll have to cut part of it away.'

Thurlow pulled the spit-pump from his mouth. 'I don't want to hear the details,' he said. 'It's making me sick.' He replaced the pump and lay back, closing his eyes.

'Fine. I'll give you a jab and we'll get started.' Matthews prepared a syringe, removed the plastic cap from the tip and cleared the air from the needle. Then he inserted it into the fleshy lower part of Thurlow's left gum. There was a tiny pop of flesh as the skin surface was broken and the cool metal slipped into his jaw, centimetre by centimetre. Thurlow felt the numbing fluid flood through his mouth, slowly removing all sensation from his infected tooth.

'As you're squeamish, I'll give you an additional valium shot. Then I can work on without upsetting you.' He rolled back Thurlow's shirt sleeve and inserted a second syringe, emptying it slowly. 'It's funny when you think of it,' he said, watching the calibrations on the side of the tube. 'Considering all the food that has to be cut and crushed by your deciduous and permanent canines, in-cisors and molars, it's a miracle there's anything left in your mouth at all. Of course, humans have comparatively tiny teeth. It's a sign of our superiority over the animals.'

Thurlow finally began to relax. Was it the drug that was making him feel so safe and comfortable in Matthews' hands, or merely the dentist's air of confident authority? He hummed softly as he worked, laying out instruments in familiar order while he waited for the drugs to take effect. A feeling of well-being crept over Thurlow. His arms and legs had grown too heavy for him to move. His

11

heart was beating more slowly in his chest. The lower half of his face was completely numb. Suspended between sleep and wakefulness, he tried to identify the tune that Matthew was humming, but concentration slipped away.

The dentist had placed two other metal instruments in his mouth; when did he do that? One was definitely there to hold his jaws apart. Although the overhead light was back-reflected and diffuse, it shone through Thurlow's eyelids with a warm red glow. There was a metallic clatter on the tray.

'I'm going to cut away part of the damaged gum tissue now,' said Matthews. Hadn't he demanded to be spared the details? The long-nosed scissors glinted against the light then vanished into his mouth, to clip through flesh and gristle. His mind drifted, trying not to think of the excavation progressing below.

'I don't think there'll be enough left to cap,' said Matthews. 'The one next to it is cracked pretty badly, too. What the hell was in that nut?'

When the drill started, Thurlow opened his eyes once more. Time seemed to have elapsed, for now there seemed to be several more instruments in his mouth. The drill howled on, the acrid smell of burning bone filling his nostrils. However, thanks to the effect of the valium dose, he remained unconcerned. The drill was removed, and Matthews' fingers probed the spot. There was a sharp crack, and he held up the offending tooth for Thurlow to see, first one half, then the other.

'You want this as a souvenir? I thought not. Now, to do this properly I should really clear out your root canal and drive a metal post into the gum,' he said. 'But that's a long, painful process. Let's see how we can work around it without tearing your entire jaw off. Ha ha.'

The drill started up again and entered his mouth. Thurlow could not tell which of his teeth it was touching,

12

but by the familiar burning smell he guessed it was drilling deep into the enamel of a molar.

'That's better,' said Matthews. 'I can see daylight through the hole. Now that we have room to manoeuvre, let's bring in the big guns.' He produced a large semi-circular metal clip and attached it to the side of Thurlow's lower lip. A new instrument appeared before the light, a large curved razorblade with a serrated tip, like a cheese-grater with teeth. The dentist placed it in his mouth and began drawing it across the stump of the damaged molar. The rasping vibrated through Thurlow's head, back and forth, back and forth, until he began to wonder if it would ever stop.

'This is no good, no good at all.' He withdrew the instrument, checked the blunted tip and tossed it onto the tray in disgust. 'I need something else. Something modern, something — technological.' He vanished from view, and Thurlow heard him thumping around at the side of the room. 'One day,' he called, 'all dentistry will be performed by laser. Just think of the fun we'll have then!' He returned with a large piece of electrical equipment that boasted a red flashing LED on top. Matthews' grinning face suddenly filled his vision.

'You're a very lucky man,' he said. 'Not many people get to have this baby in their mouths.' He patted the side of the machine, from which extended a ribbed metal tube with a tiny rotating steel saw. When he flicked it on, the noise was so great that he had to shout. 'You see, the main part of the tooth is made of a substance called dentine, but below the gumline it becomes bone-like cement, which is softer...'

He missed the next part as the saw entered his mouth and connected with tooth enamel. One of the pipes wedged between his lower incisors was spraying water onto the operating zone, while another was noisily sucking up saliva. His mouth had become a hardhat area.

13

Suddenly something wet and warm began to pour down his throat. Matthews turned off the saw and hastily withdrew it. 'Shit,' he said loudly, 'that's my fault, not watching what I was doing.' He reached behind him and grabbed up a wad of tissue, which he stuffed into Thurlow's mouth and padded at the operation site, only to withdraw it red, filled and dripping. 'Sorry about that, I was busy thinking about what I fancied for tea tonight.' Now there seemed to be something lodged in Thurlow's oesophagus. Through the anaesthetic he began to experience a stinging sensation. Bile rose in his throat as he started to gag.

'Wait, wait, I know what that is.' Matthews reached in his gloved hand and withdrew something, throwing it onto the tray. 'You've been a brave boy. A hundred years ago this would have been a horribly painful experience, performed without an anaesthetic, but thanks to modern techniques I'll have you finished in just a few more hours. Ha ha. Just kidding.'

He reached back to the tray and produced another steel frame, this one constructed like the filament wire in a lightbulb. Carefully unscrewing it, he arranged the contraption at the side of his patient's mouth. Thurlow was starting to feel less calm. Perhaps the valium was wearing off. Suppose his sensations returned in the middle of the drilling? Yes, he could definitely feel his jaw now. A dull pain had begun to throb at the base of his nose. The dentist was stirring something in a small plastic dish when he saw Thurlow shifting in his chair.

'Looks like I didn't give you a large enough dose,' he said, concerned. He removed the plastic cap from another syringe and jabbed it into Thurlow's arm.

'There,' he said, cheerfully depressing the plunger. 'Drug cocktail happy hour! You want a little umbrella in this one?' Thurlow stared back at him with narrowed eyes, unamused. Matthews grew serious. 'Don't worry, when

14

you wake up I'll have finished. I think you've been through enough for one day, so I'm giving you a temporary filling for now, and we'll do that root canal on your next appointment.'

As he began to spoon the cement into Thurlow's mouth on the end of a rubber spatula, Thurlow felt himself drifting off into an ethereal state of semi-wakefulness.

While he floated in this hazy dream-state, his imagination unfettered itself, strange visions uncoiling before him in rolling prisms of light. The humming of the dentist became a distant litany, a warm and familiar soundtrack, like the work-song of a seamstress. Colours and scents bled into one another, jasmine and disinfectant. He was home and safe, a child again. Finally these half-formed memories were replaced by the growing clarity of the present, and he realised that he was surfacing back to reality.

'Oh good,' said Matthews as his eyes flickered open. 'Back in the land of the living. For a minute I thought I'd overdosed you. Ha ha. We're just waiting for the last bit to dry.' He reached into Thurlow's mouth and probed around with a steel scraper, scratching away the last of the filler. Thurlow suddenly became aware of the restraining strap fixed across his lap, holding him in place. How long had that been there?

'You know, we had a nasty case of "tooth squeeze" in here last week, ever hear of that? Of course, you can't answer with all this junk in your mouth, can you? He was an airline pilot. His plane depressurised, and it turned out he had an air bubble trapped beneath a filling. When the cabin atmosphere decreased, the air expanded. His tooth literally blew up in his mouth. Bits were embedded in his tongue. What a mess.' Matthews peered into his mouth, one eye screwed tight. 'It happens to deep sea divers, too, only their teeth implode. And I've seen worse. There was one patient, a kid who rollerskated face-first into a drinking fountain ...' Mercifully, he lost his train of thought. 'Well,

15

that last batch seems to have done the trick.'

The sensation was slowly returning to Thurlow's mouth. Something was very sore, very sore indeed. He raised his hands, hoping to see if he could locate the source of the pain, but Matthews swatted them down. 'Don't touch anything for a while. You must give it a chance to set. I still have some finishing off to do.' The pain was increasing with every passing second. It was starting to hurt very badly, far worse than when he had arrived for treatment. Something had gone wrong, he was sure of it. He could only breathe through his nose, and then with difficulty. He tried to speak, but no sound came out. When he tried to pull himself upright, Matthews' arm came around the chair and pushed him back down. Now the dentist stepped fully into his view. Thurlow gasped.

It looked as if someone had exploded a blood transfusion bag in front of him. He was dripping crimson from head to foot. It was splashed across his chest and stomach, draining from his plastic apron to form a spreading pool between his feet. The white tiled floor was slick with blood. Streaks marred the walls in sweeping arcs, like rampant nosebleeds. Thurlow's head reeled back against the rest. What in God's name had happened? Pain and panic overwhelmed him as his hands clawed the air and he fought to stand, chromatic sparkles scattering before his eyes as the remnants of the drug affected his vision.

'You shouldn't be up and about yet,' said Matthews. 'I've not finished.'

'You're no dentist,' Thurlow tried to say, the white-hot knives shrieking through his brain, but his words came out as a series of hysterical rasps.

The dentist seemed to understand him. 'You're right, I'm no dentist.' He shrugged, his hands held out. *So sue me.* 'I always wanted to be one but I couldn't get my certificate. I can't pass exams. I get angry too easily. Still, it's a vocation with me, a calling. I know what I'm doing is

16

right. I'm simply ahead of my time. Nearly finished.'

He thrust his hand into his patient's mouth and made a tightening motion. A starburst of pain detonated between Thurlow's eyes. The dentist held his head back against the rest while he pulled at something. There was a ting of metal, and he extracted a twisted spring. On one end a small silver screw was embedded in a bloody scrap of bright red gum.

'You don't need this bit,' said Matthews jovially. He picked up a Phillips screwdriver and inserted it in Thurlow's mouth, happily ratcheting away, as if he was fixing a car. 'I like to think of this as homeopathic medicine,' said the dentist, 'except that I'm more of an artist. I went to art school but I didn't pass the exam because — you guessed it —' he nodded his head dumbly, *silly old me*, 'I got angry again. They took me out of circulation for a while.' He removed the screwdriver and peered inside, smiling. 'Still, every now and again I get to try out a few of my ideas. I go to a particular area and search through the Yellow Pages, then I visit all the private dentists they list. Sometimes I find one with a vacant operating room, and then I just wait for custom. I look the part, you see, white coat, smart tie, good speaking voice. And I keep the door locked while I work. No one ever tries to stop me, and nothing would ever come out in the papers if they did, because private dentists are too scared of losing their customers. You'd never think it could be that simple, would you?'

He went to the desk beside the operating chair and detached a large circular mirror. 'But let's face it, when was the last time you asked to see a dentist's credentials? It's not like the police. Let's see how you turned out.'

Thurlow could barely breathe through the ever-increasing pain, but as the dentist tilted the mirror in his direction, the next sight that met his eyes almost threw him into a faint.

17

'Good, isn't it?' said Matthews. 'Art in dentistry.'

Thurlow's face was unrecognisable. His lips had been cut and peeled back in fleshy strips, then pinned to his cheeks with steel pins. Most of his teeth had been filed into angular shapes, some pointed, others merely slanting. His upper gums had been opened to expose the pale bone beneath. A number of screws had been driven into his flayed jaw, and were attached to cables. The last two inches of his tongue — the lump he had felt in his throat — were missing completely. He watched as the leaking stump jerked obscenely back and forth like a severed reptile. Around his mouth a contraption of polished steel had been fitted to function as an insane brace, a complex network of wires and springs, cogs and filaments. The skin beneath his eyes had turned black with the pummelling his mouth had taken.

'I know what you're thinking,' whispered Matthews. 'It's special, but not spectacular. You haven't seen the best bit yet. It's not merely art, it's — kinetic dental futurism. Watch.'

Matthews reached up and turned a silver handle on the left of Thurlow's jaw. The springs and wires pulled taut. The cogs turned. Thurlow's mouth grimaced and winked, the flaps of his lips contorting back and forth as his face was twisted into a series of wide-mouthed grins and tight, sour frowns. On a separate spring, the end of his tongue flickered in and out of his own ear. The pain was unbearable. Fresh wounds tore in his gums and cheeks as the mechanism yanked his mouth into an absurd rictus of a laugh. Matthews released his grip on the silver handle and smiled, pleased with himself.

'Is there somebody in there?' The receptionist was calling through the door.

'This stuff won't catch on for years yet,' said the dentist, ignoring the rattling doorknob behind him. He tilted the mirror from side to side before Thurlow's horrified face. Finally, he set the mirror down and released the

18

restraining strap from the operating couch. Blinkered by the heavy steel contraption that had been screwed into his jaw, Thurlow was barely able to stand. As he tipped his head forward the weight pulled him further, and blood began to pour from his mouth. He wanted to scream, but he knew it would hurt too much to pull open his mouth without the help of the contraption. The receptionist began to bang on the door.

'Don't worry,' said the dentist with a reassuring smile. 'It'll seem strange at first, but you'll gradually get used to it. I'm sure they all do eventually.' He turned around and looked out of the window. 'That's the beauty of these old buildings; there's always a fire escape.' He unclipped the security catch on the casement and pushed it open, raising his legs and sliding them through the gap. Blood smeared from his saturated trousers onto the white sill. 'I nearly forgot,' he called back as Thurlow blundered blindly into the door, spraying it with his blood. 'Whatever you do — for God's sake — don't forget to floss.'

His laughter echoed hard in Thurlow's ears as a descending crimson mist replaced his tortured sight.

19

Norman Wisdom
And
The Angel Of Death

Diary Entry # 1   Dated 2 July

The past is safe.

The future is unknown.

The present is a bit of a bastard.

Let me explain. I always think of the past as a haven of pleasant recollections. Long ago I perfected the method of siphoning off bad memories to leave only those images I still feel comfortable with. What survives in my mind is a seamless mosaic of faces and places that fill me with warmth when I choose to consider them. Of course, it's as inaccurate as those retouched Stalinist photographs in which comrades who have become an embarrassment have been imperfectly erased so that the corner of a picture still shows a boot or a hand. But it allows me to recall times spent with dear friends in the happy England that existed in the fifties; the last era of innocence and dignity, when women offered no opinion on sexual matters and men still knew the value of a decent winter overcoat. It was a time which ended with the arrival of the Beatles, when youth replaced experience as a desirable national quality.

I am no fantasist. Quite the reverse; this process has a practical value. Remembering the things that once made me happy helps to keep me sane.

I mean that in *every* sense.

The future, however, is another kettle of fish. What can possibly be in store for us but something worse than the present? An acceleration of the ugly, tasteless, arrogant times in which we live. The Americans have already developed a lifestyle and a moral philosophy entirely modelled on the concept of shopping. What is left but to manufacture more things we don't need, more detritus to be thrown away, more vicarious thrills to be selfishly experienced? For a brief moment the national conscience flickered awake when it seemed that green politics was the only way to stop the planet from becoming a huge concrete turd. And what happened? Conservation was hijacked by the advertising industry and turned into a highly suspect sales concept.

No, it's the past that heals, not the future.

So what about the present? I mean right now.

At this moment, I'm standing in front of a full-length mirror reducing the knot of my tie and contemplating my frail, rather tired appearance. My name is Stanley Morrison, born March 1950, in East Finchley, North London. I'm a senior sales clerk for a large shoe firm, as they say on the quiz programmes. I live alone and have always done so, having never met the right girl. I have a fat cat called Hattie, named after Hattie Jacques, for whom I have a particular fondness in the role of Griselda Pugh in Series Five, Programmes One to Seven of *Hancock's Half Hour*, and a spacious but somewhat cluttered flat situated approximately one hundred and fifty yards from the house in which I was born. My hobbies include collecting old radio shows and British films, of which I have an extensive collection, as well as a nigh-inexhaustible supply of amusing, detailed anecdotes about the forgotten British stars of the past. There's nothing I enjoy more than to recount these lengthy tales to one of my ailing, lonely patients and slowly destroy his will to live.

I call them my patients, but of course they aren't. I merely bring these poor unfortunates good cheer in my capacity as an official council HVF, that's a Hospital Visiting Friend. I am fully sanctioned by Haringey Council, an organisation filled with people of such astounding narrow-minded stupidity that they cannot see beyond their lesbian support groups to keeping the streets free of dogshit.

But back to the present.

I am rather tired at the moment because I was up half the night removing the remaining precious moments of life from a seventeen-year-old boy named David Banbury who had been in a severe motorcycle accident. Apparently he jumped the lights at the top of Shepherd's Hill and vanished under a truck conveying half-price personal stereos to the Asian shops in Tottenham Court Road. His legs were completely crushed, so much so that the doctor told me they couldn't separate his cycle leathers from his bones, and his spine was broken, but facial damage had been minimal, and the helmet he was wearing at the time of the collision had protected his skull from injury.

He hasn't had much of a life, by all accounts, having spent the last eight years in care, and has no family to visit him.

Nurse Clarke informed me that he might well recover to lead a partially normal life, but would only be able to perform those activities involving a minimal amount of agonisingly slow movement, which would at least qualify him for a job in the Post Office.

Right now he could not talk, of course, but he could see and hear and feel, and I am reliably informed that he could understand every word I said, which was of great advantage as I was able to describe to him in enormous detail the entire plot of Norman Wisdom's 1965 masterpiece *The Early Bird*, his first colour film for the Rank Organisation, and I must say one of the finest examples of post-war British slapstick to be found on the face of this spinning planet we fondly call home.

On my second visit to the boy, my richly delineated account of the backstage problems involved in the production of an early Wisdom vehicle, *Trouble In Store*, in which the Little Comedian Who Won The Hearts Of The

Nation co-starred for the first time with his erstwhile partner and straight-man Jerry Desmonde, was rudely interrupted by a staff nurse who chose a crucial moment in my narration to empty a urine bag that seemed to be filling with blood. Luckily I was able to exact my revenge by punctuating my description of the film's highlights featuring Moira Lister and Margaret Rutherford with little twists of the boy's drip-feed to make sure that he was paying the fullest attention.

At half past seven yesterday evening I received a visit from the mentally disoriented liaison officer in charge of appointing visitors. Miss Chisholm is the kind of woman who has pencils in her hair and 'Nuclear War — No Thanks' stickers on her briefcase. She approaches her council tasks with the dispiriting grimness of a sailor attempting to plug leaks in a fast-sinking ship.

'Mr Morrison,' she said, trying to peer around the door of my flat, presumably in the vain hope that she might be invited in for a cup of tea, 'you are one of our most experienced Hospital Helpers' — this part she had to check in her brimming folder to verify — 'so I wonder if we could call upon you for an extracurricular visit at rather short notice.' She searched through her notes with the folder wedged under her chin and her case balanced on a raised knee. I did not offer any assistance. 'The motorcycle boy ...' She attempted to locate his name and failed.

'David Banbury,' I said, helpfully supplying the information for her.

'He's apparently been telling the doctor that he no longer wishes to live. It's a common problem, but they think his case is particularly serious. He has no relatives.' Miss Chisholm — if she has a Christian name I am certainly not privy to it — shifted her weight from one foot to the other as several loose sheets slid from her folder to the floor.

'I understand exactly what is needed,' I said, watching

26

as she struggled to reclaim her notes. 'An immediate visit is in order.'

As I made my way over to the hospital to comfort the poor lad, I thought of the ways in which I could free the boy from his morbid thoughts. First, I would recount all of the plot minutiae, technicalities and trivia I could muster surrounding the big-screen career and off-screen heartache of that Little Man Who Won All Our Hearts, Charlie Drake, climaxing with a detailed description of his 1966 magnum opus *The Cracksman*, in which he starred opposite a superbly erudite George Sanders, a man who had the good sense to kill himself when he grew bored with the world, and then I would encourage the boy to give up the fight, do the decent thing and die in his sleep.

As it happens, the evening turned out quite nicely.

By eleven-thirty I had concluded my description of the film, and detected a distinct lack of concentration on behalf of the boy, whose only response to my description of the frankly hysterical sewer-pipe scene was to blow bubbles of saliva from the corner of his mouth. In my frustration to command his attention, I applied rather more pressure to the sutures on his legs than I intended, causing the crimson blossom of a haemorrhage to appear through the blankets covering his pitifully mangled limbs.

I embarked upon a general plot outline of the classic 1962 Norman Wisdom vehicle *On The Beat*, never shifting my attention from the boy's eyes, which were now swivelling frantically in his waxen grey face, until the ruptured vessels of his leg could no longer be reasonably ignored. Then I summoned the night nurse. David Banbury died a few moments after she arrived at the bedside.

That makes eleven in four years.

Some didn't require any tampering with on my part, but simply gave up the ghost, losing the will to go on. I went home and made myself a cup of Horlicks, quietly rejoicing

27

that another young man had gone to meet his maker with a full working knowledge of the later films of Norman Wisdom (not counting *What's Good For The Goose*, a prurient 'adult' comedy directed by Menahem Golem which I regard as an offensive, embarrassing travesty unworthy of such a superb family performer).

Now, standing before the mirror attempting to comb the last straggling wisps of hair across my prematurely balding pate, I prepare to leave the house and catch the bus to work, and I do something I imagine most people have done from time to time when faced with their own reflection. I calm myself for the day ahead by remembering the Royal Variety Performance stars of 1952. The familiar faces of Naughton & Gold, Vic Oliver, Jewel & Warriss, Ted Ray, Winifred Atwell, Reg Dixon and the Tiller Girls crowd my mind as I steel myself to confront the self-centred young scum with whom I am forced to work.

It is no secret that I have been passed over for promotion in my job on a number of occasions, but the most terrible slap-in-the-face yet performed by our new (foreign) management was administered last week, when a boy of just twenty-four was appointed as my superior! He likes people to call him Mick, walks around smiling like an idiot, travels to work wearing a Walkman, on which he plays percussive rubbish consisting of black men shouting at each other, and wears tight black jeans which seem specifically designed to reveal the contours of his genitalia. He shows precious little flair for the job, and has virtually no knowledge whatsoever of the pre-1960 British radio comedy scene. Amazingly, everyone seems to like him.

Of course, he will have to go.

Diary Entry # 2 Dated 23 August

Mick is a threat no more.

I simply waited until the appropriate opportunity arose, as I knew it eventually should. While I watched and listened, patiently enduring the oh-so-clever remarks he made to the office girls about me (most of whom resemble prostitutes from Michael Powell's excessively vulgar and unnecessary 1960 film *Peeping Tom*) I comforted myself with memories of a happy, sunlit childhood, recalling a row of terraced houses patrolled by smiling policemen, uniformed milkmen and lollipop-ladies, a place in the past where Isobel Barnet was still guessing contestants' professions on *What's My Line*, Alma Cogan was singing 'Fly Me To The Moon' on the radio, cornflakes had red plastic guardsmen in their packets and everyone knew his place and damned well stayed in it. Even now when I hear the merry tickle of 'Greensleeves' heralding the arrival of an ice-cream van beset by clamouring tots I get a painful, thrilling erection.

But I digress.

Last Tuesday, while shifting a wire-meshed crate in the basement workroom, Mick dislocated his little finger, cutting it rather nastily, so naturally I offered to accompany him to the casualty ward. As my flat is conveniently situated on the route to the hospital I was able to stop by for a moment, trotting out some absurd excuse for the detour.

After waiting for over an hour to be seen, my nemesis was finally examined by Dr MacGregor, an elderly physician of passing acquaintance whose name I only remember because it is also that of John Le Mesurier's character in *The Radio Ham*. My experience as an HVF had familiarised me with basic casualty procedures, and I knew that the doctor would most likely inject an antibiotic into the boy's hand to prevent infection.

The needles for the syringes come in paper packets, and are sealed inside little plastic tubes that must only be broken by the attending physician. This is to prevent blood-carried infections from being transmitted.

It was hard to find a way around this, and indeed had taken dozens of attempts over the preceding months. The packets themselves were easy enough to open and reseal, but the tubes were a problem. After a great deal of practice, I found that I was able to melt the end of a tube closed without leaving any trace of tampering. To be on the safe side I had prepared three such needles in this fashion. (You must remember that, as well as having access to basic medical supplies — those items not actually locked away — I also possess an unlimited amount of patience, being willing to wait years if necessary to achieve my goals.)

While we waited for Dr MacGregor to put in an appearance, the boy prattled on to me about work, saying how much he 'truly valued my input'. While he was thus distracted, it was a simple matter for me to replace the loose needles lying on the doctor's tray with my specially prepared ones.

A little while ago I throttled the life out of a very sick young man whose habit of nightly injecting drugs in the toilet of my local tube station had caused him to become ravaged with terminal disease. I would like to say that he died in order to make the world a safer, cleaner place, but the truth is that we went for a drink together and I killed him in a sudden fit of rage because he had not heard of Joyce Grenfell. How the Woman Who Won The Hearts Of The Nation in her thrice-reprised role as Ruby Gates in the celebrated *St Trinians* films could have passed by him unnoticed is still a mystery to me.

Anyway, I strangled the disgusting urchin with his own scarf and removed about a cupful of blood from his arm, into which I dropped a number of needles, filling their capillaries with the poisoned fluid. I then carefully wiped each one clean and inserted it into a tube, neatly resealing the plastic.

Dr MacGregor was talking nineteen to the dozen as he inserted what he thought was a fresh needle into a vein on the back of Mick's hand. He barely even looked down to see what he was doing. Overwork and force of habit had won the day. Thank God for our decaying National Health Service, because I'd never have managed it if the boy had possessed private medical insurance. My unsuspecting adversary maintained an attitude of perky bravery as his finger was stitched up, and I laughed all the way home.

Mick has been feeling unwell for several weeks now. A few days ago he failed to turn up for work. Apparently he has developed a complex and highly dangerous form of Hepatitis B.

As they say, age and treachery will always overcome youth and enthusiasm.

Diary Entry # 3 Dated 17 October

The hopeless liaison officer has returned with a new request.

Yesterday evening I opened the door of my flat to find her hovering on the landing uncertainly, as if she could not even decide where she felt comfortable standing.

'Can I help you?' I asked suddenly, knowing that my voice would make her jump. She had not caught me in a good mood. A month ago, Mick had been forced to resign through ill-health, but my promotion had still not been announced for consideration.

'Oh, Mr Morrison, I didn't know if you were in,' she said, her free hand rising to her flat chest.

'The best way to find out is by ringing the doorbell, Miss

Chisholm.' I opened the door wider. 'Won't you come in?'

'Thank you.' She edged gingerly past me with briefcase and folders, taking in the surroundings. Hattie took one look at her and shot off to her basket. 'Oh, what an unusual room,' she said, studying the walnut sideboard and armchairs, the matching butter-yellow standard lamps either side of the settee. 'Do you collect Art Deco?'

'No,' I said tersely. 'This is my furniture. I suppose you'd like a cup of tea.' I went to put the kettle on, leaving her hovering uncomfortably in the lounge. When I returned she was still standing, her head tilted on one side as she examined the spines of my post-war *Radio Times* collection.

'Please sit down, Miss Chisholm,' I insisted. 'I won't bite.' And I really don't because teethmarks can be easily traced.

At this instigation she perched herself on the edge of the armchair and nibbled at a bourbon. She had obviously rehearsed the speech which followed.

'Mr Morrison, I'm sure you've read in the papers that the health cuts are leaving hospitals in this area with an acute shortage of beds.'

'I fear I haven't read a newspaper since they stopped printing The Flutters on the comic page of the *Daily Mirror*,' I admitted, 'but I have heard something of the sort.'

'Well, it means that some people who are required to attend hospital for tests cannot be admitted as overnight patients any more. As you have been so very helpful in the past, we wondered if you could take in one of these patients.'

'For how long?' I asked. 'And what sort of patient?'

'It would be for two weeks at the most, and the patient I have in mind for you —' she churned up the contents of her disgusting briefcase trying to locate her poor victim's folder — 'is a very nice young lady. She's a severe diabetic, and she's in a wheelchair. Apart from that, she's the same as you or I.' She gave me a warm smile, then quickly looked away, sensing perhaps that I was not like other people. She handed me a dog-eared photograph of the patient, attached to a medical history that had more pages than an average weekly script of *The Clitheroe Kid*, a popular BBC radio show which for some reason has never been reissued on audio cassette.

'Her name is Saskia,' said Miss Chisholm. 'She has no family to speak of, and lives a long way from London. Ours is one of the few hospitals with the necessary equipment to handle complex drug and therapy trials for people like her. She desperately needs a place to stay. We can arrange to have her collected each day. We'd be terribly grateful if you could help. She really has nowhere else to go.'

I studied the photograph carefully. The girl was pitifully small-boned, with sallow, almost translucent skin. But she had attractive blonde hair, and well defined features reminiscent of a young Suzy Kendall in Robert Hartford-Davies' patchy 1966 comedy portmanteau *The Sandwich Man*, in which Our Norman, playing an Irish priest, was not seen to his best advantage. What's more, she fitted in perfectly with my plans. A woman. That would certainly be different.

I returned the photograph with a smile. 'I think we can work something out,' I said.

Diary Entry # 4 Dated 23 October

Saskia is here, and I must say that for someone so ill she is quite a tonic. The night she arrived, I watched as she struggled to negotiate her wheelchair around the flat without damaging the paintwork on the skirting boards, and despite many setbacks she managed it without a single protestation. Indeed, she has been here for two days now, and never seems to complain about anything or anyone. Apparently all of her life she has been prone to one kind of disease or another, and few doctors expected her to survive her childhood, so she is simply happy to be alive.

I have installed her in the spare room, which she insisted on filling with flowers purchased from the stall outside the hospital. Even Hattie, never the most amenable of cats, seems to have taken to her.

As my flat is on the second floor of a large Victorian house, she is a virtual prisoner within these walls during the hours outside her hospital visits. At those times the ambulance men carry her and the folded wheelchair up and down the stairs.

On her very first night here I entered the lounge to find her going through my catalogued boxes of BBC comedy archive tapes. I was just beginning to grow annoyed when she turned to me and asked if she could play some of them. No one had ever shown the least interest in my collection before. To test her, I asked which shows she would most enjoy hearing.

'I like Leslie Phillips in *The Navy Lark*, and the Frazer Hayes Four playing on *Round The Horne*,' she said, running a slim finger across the spines of the tape boxes. 'And of course, *Hancock's Half Hour*, although I prefer the shows after Andre Melee had been replaced by Hattie Jacques.'

Suddenly I was suspicious.

This tiny girl could not be more than twenty-two years of age. How could she possibly be so familiar with radio programmes that had scarcely been heard in thirty years?

'My father was a great collector,' she explained, as if she had just read my thoughts. 'He used to play the old shows nearly every evening after dinner. It's one of the few lasting memories I have of my parents.'

Well naturally, my heart went out to the poor girl. 'I

know exactly how you feel,' I said. 'I only have to hear Kenneth Williams say "*Good Evening*" and I'm reminded of home and hearth. They were such happy times for me.'

For the next hour or so I sounded her out on other favourite film and radio memories of the past, but although there seemed no other common ground between us, she remained willing to listen to my happy tales and learn. At eleven o'clock she yawned and said that she would like to go to bed, and so I let her leave the lounge.

Last night Saskia was kept late at the hospital, and I was in bed by the time the heavy tread of the ambulance man was heard upon the stair. This morning she asked me if I would like her to cook an evening meal. After some initial concern with the hygiene problems involved in allowing one's meal to be cooked by someone else, I agreed. (In restaurants I assiduously question the waitresses about their sanitary arrangements.) Furthermore, I offered to buy produce for the projected feast, but she insisted on stopping by the shops on her way home from the hospital. Although she is frail, she demands independence. I will buy a bottle of wine. After being alone with my memories for so long, it is unnerving to have someone else in the apartment.

And yet it is rather wonderful.

Diary Entry # 5 Dated 24 October

What an enthralling evening!

I feel as if I am truly alive for the first time in my life. Saskia returned early tonight — looking drawn and pale, but still vulnerably beautiful, with her blonde hair tied in a smart plait — and headed straight into the kitchen, where she stayed for several hours. I had arranged a ramp of planks by the cooker so that she could reach the hobs without having to rise from her chair.

Hattie, sensing that something tasty was being prepared, hung close to the base of the door, sniffing and licking her chops. To amuse Saskia while she cooked I played dialogue soundtracks which I had recorded in my local cinema as a child during performances of *Passport To Pimlico* and *The Lavender Hill Mob*, but the poor quality of the tapes (from a small reel-to-reel recorder I had smuggled into the auditorium) was such that I imagine the subtleties of these screenplays were rather lost to her, especially as she had the kitchen door shut and was banging saucepans about.

The meal was a complete delight. We had a delicious tomato and basil soup to start with, and a truly spectacular salmon en croute as the main course, followed by cheese and biscuits.

Saskia told me about herself, explaining that her parents had been killed in a car crash when she was young. This tragedy had forced her to live with a succession of distant and ancient relatives. When the one she was staying with died, she was shunted into a foster home. No one was willing to take her, though, as the complications arising from her diabetes would have made enormous demands on any foster-parent.

As she talked she ate very little, really only toying with her food. The diabetes prevents her from enjoying much of anything, but hopefully the tests she is undergoing will reveal new ways of coping with her restricted lifestyle.

The dining table is too low to comfortably incorporate Saskia's wheelchair, so I have promised to raise it for tomorrow's dinner, which I have insisted on cooking. I was rather nervous at the prospect, but then I thought: if a cripple can do it, so can I.

Saskia is so kind and attentive, such a good listener. Perhaps it is time for me to introduce my pet topic into the dinner conversation.

Diary Entry # 6   Dated 25 October

Disaster has struck!

Right from the start everything went wrong — and just as we were getting along so well. Let me set it out from the beginning.

The meal. I cooked a meal tonight that was not as elaborate as the one she had prepared, and nothing like as good. This was partly because I was forced to work late (still no news of my promotion), so most of the shops were shut, and partly because I have never cooked for a woman before. The result was a microwaved dinner that was still freezing cold in the centre of the dish, but if Saskia didn't like it she certainly didn't complain. Instead she gave a charming broad smile (one which she is using ever more frequently with me) and slowly chewed as she listened to my detailed description of the indignities daily heaped upon me at the office.

I had bought another bottle of wine, and perhaps had drunk a little too much of it by myself (Saskia being unable to drink for the rest of the week), because I found myself introducing the subject of him, Our Norman, The Little Man Who Won All Our Hearts, before we had even finished the main course. Wishing to present the topic in the correct context I chose to start with a basic chronology of Norman's film appearances, beginning with his thirteen-and-a-half-second appearance in *A Date With A Dream* in 1948. I had made an early decision to omit all but the most essential stage and television appearances of The Little Man for fear of tiring her, and in my description of the films stuck mainly to the classic set pieces, notably the marvellous 'Learning To Walk' routine from *On The Beat* and the ten-minute 'Teamaking' sequence from the opening of *The Early Bird*.

I was about to mention Norman's 1956 appearance with Ruby Murray at the Palladium in *Painting The Town* when I became distinctly aware of her interest waning. She was fidgeting about in her chair as if anxious to leave the table.

'Anyone would think you didn't like Norman Wisdom,' I said, by way of a joke.

'Actually, I'm not much of a fan, no,' she said suddenly, then added, 'Forgive me, Stanley, but I've suddenly developed a headache.' And with that she went to her room, without even offering to do the washing up. Before I went to bed I stood outside her door listening, but could hear nothing.

I have a bad feeling about this.

Diary Entry # 7 Dated 27 October

She is avoiding me.

It sounds hard to believe, I know, but there can be no other explanation. Last night she returned to the flat and headed directly to her room. When I put my head around the door to see if she wanted a late night cup of cocoa (I admit this was at three o'clock in the morning but I could not sleep for worrying about her) it seemed that she could barely bring herself to be polite. As I stepped into the room, her eyes widened and she pulled the blankets around her in a defensive gesture which seemed to suggest a fear of my presence. I must confess I am at a loss to understand her.

Could she have led me on, only pretending to share my interests for some secret purpose of her own?

Diary Entry # 8 Dated 1 November

At work today we were informed that Mick had died. Complications from the hepatitis, annoyingly unspecified, but I gained the distinct impression that they were unpleasant. When one of the secretaries started crying I made a passing flippant remark that was, I fear, misconstrued, and the girl gave me a look of utter horror. She's a scruffy little tart who was sweet on Mick, and much given to conspiring with him about me. I felt like giving her something to be horrified about, and briefly wondered how she would look tied up with baling wire, hanging in a storm drain. The things we think about to get us through the day.

At home the situation has worsened. Saskia arrived tonight with a male friend, a doctor whom she had invited back for tea. While she was in the kitchen the two of us were left alone in the lounge, and I noticed that he seemed to be studying me from the corner of his eye. It was probably just an occupational habit, but it prompted me to wonder if Saskia had somehow voiced her suspicions to him (assuming she has any, which I consider unlikely).

After he had gone, I explained that it was not at all permissible for her to bring men into the house no matter how well she knew them, and she had the nerve to turn in her chair and accuse me of being old-fashioned!

'What on earth do you mean?' I asked her.

'It's not healthy, Stanley, surrounding yourself with all this,' she explained, indicating the alphabetised film and tape cassettes which filled the shelves on the wall behind us. 'Most of these people have been dead for years.'

'Shakespeare has been dead for years,' I replied, 'and people still appreciate him.'

'But he wrote plays and sonnets of lasting beauty,' she persisted. 'These people you listen to were just working comics. It's lovely to collect things, Stanley, but this stuff was never meant to be taken so seriously. You can't base your life around it.' There was an irritating timbre in her voice that I had not noticed before. She sat smugly back in her wheelchair, and for a moment I wanted to smother

her. I could feel my face growing steadily redder with the thought.

'Why shouldn't these people still be admired?' I cried, running to the shelves and pulling out several of my finest tapes. 'Most of them had dreary lives filled with hardship and pain, but they made people laugh, right through the war and the years of austerity which followed. They carried on through poverty and ill-health and misery. Everyone turned on the radio to hear them. Everyone went to the pictures to see them. It was something to look forward to. They kept people alive. They gave the country happy memories. Why shouldn't someone remember them for what they did?'

'All right, Stanley. I'm sorry — I didn't mean to upset you,' she said, reaching out her hand, but I pushed it away. It was then that I realised my cheeks were wet, and I turned aside in shame. To think that I had been brought to this state, forced to defend myself in my own home, by a woman, and a wheelchair-bound one at that.

'This is probably a bad time to mention it,' said Saskia, 'but I'm going to be leaving London earlier than I first anticipated. In fact, I'll be going home tomorrow. The tests haven't taken as long as the doctors thought.'

'But what about the results?' I asked.

'They've already made arrangements to send them to my local GP. He'll decide whether further treatment is necessary.'

I hastily pulled myself together and made appropriate polite sounds of disappointment at the idea of her departure, but inside a part of me was rejoicing. You see, I had been watching her hands as they rested on the arms of her wheelchair. They were trembling.

And she was lying.

Diary Entry # 9 Dated 2 November

I have much to relate.

After our altercation last night, both of us knew that a new level in our relationship had been reached. The game had begun. Saskia refused my conciliatory offer of tea and went straight to her bedroom, quietly locking the door behind her. I know because I tried to open it at two o'clock this morning, and I heard her breath catch in the darkness as I twisted the knob from side to side.

I returned to my room and forced myself to stay there. The night passed slowly, with both of us remaining uncomfortably awake on our respective beds. In the morning, I left the house early so that I would not be forced to trade insincere pleasantries with her over break-fast. I knew she would be gone by the time I returned, and that, I think, suited both of us. I was under no illusions — she was a dangerous woman, too independent, too free-minded to ever become my friend. We could only be adversaries. And I was dangerous to her. I had enjoyed her company, but now she would only be safe far away from me. Luckily, I would never see her again. Or so I thought. For, fast as the future, everything changed between us.

Oh, how it changed.

This morning, I arrived at work to find a terse note summoning me to my supervisor's office. Naturally I assumed that I was finally being notified of my promotion. You may imagine my shock when, in the five-minute interview which followed, it emerged that far from receiving advancement within the company, I was being fired! I did not 'fit in' with the new personnel, and as the department was being 'streamlined' they were 'letting me go'. Depending on my attitude to this news, they were prepared to make me a generous cash settlement if I left at once, so that they could immediately begin 'implementing procedural changes'.

I did not complain. This sort of thing has happened many times before. I do not fit in. I say this not to gain sympathy, but as a simple statement of fact. Intellect always impedes popularity. I accepted the cash offer. Disheartened, but also glad to be rid of my vile 'colleagues', I returned home.

It was raining hard when I arrived at the front gate. I looked up through the dank sycamores and was surprised to find a light burning in the front room. Then I realised that Saskia was reliant on the council for arranging her transport, and as they were never able to specify an exact collection time, she was still in the house. I knew I would have to use every ounce of my control to continue behaving in a correct and civilised manner.

As I turned the key in the lock I heard a sudden scuffle of movement inside the flat. Throwing the door wide, I entered the lounge and found it empty. The sound was coming from my bedroom. A terrible deadness flooded through my chest as I tiptoed along the corridor, carefully avoiding the boards that squeaked.

Slowly, I moved into the doorway. She was on the other side of the room with her back to me. The panels of the wardrobe were folded open, and she had managed to pull one of the heavy-duty bin-liners out of the floor. Somehow she sensed that I was behind her, and the wheelchair spun around. The look on her face was one of profound disturbance.

'What have you done with the rest of them?' she said softly, her voice wavering. She had dislodged a number of air fresheners from the sacks, and the room stank of lavender.

'You're not supposed to be in here,' I explained as reasonably as possible. 'This is my private room.'

I stepped inside and closed the door behind me. She looked up at the pinned pictures surrounding her. The bleak monochrome of a thousand celebrity photographs

42

seemed to absorb the light within the room.

'Saskia. You're an intelligent girl. You're modern. But you have no respect for the past.'

'The past?' Her lank hair was falling in her eyes, as she flicked it aside I could see she was close to tears. 'What has the past to do with this?' She kicked out uselessly at the plastic sack and it fell to one side, spilling its rotting human contents onto the carpet.

'Everything,' I replied, moving forward. I was not advancing on her, I just needed to get to the bedside cabinet. 'The past is where everything has its rightful place.'

'I know about your past, Stanley,' she cried, pushing at the wheels of her chair, backing herself up against the wardrobe, turning her face from the stinking mess. 'Nurse Clarke told me all about you.'

'What did she say?' I asked, coming to a halt. I was genuinely curious. Nurse Clarke had hardly ever said more than two words to me.

'I know what happened to you. That's why I came here.' She started to cry now, and wiped her nose with the back of her hand. Something plopped obscenely onto the floor as the sack settled. 'She says you had the worst childhood a boy could ever have. Sexual abuse, violence. You lived in terror every day. Your father nearly killed you before the authorities took charge. Don't you see? That's why you're so obsessed with this stuff, this trivia, it's like a disease. You're just trying to make things all right again.'

'That's a damned lie!' I shouted at her. 'My childhood was perfect. You're making it up!'

'No,' she said, shaking her head, snot flying from her nose. 'I saw the marks when you were in the kitchen that first night. Cigarette burns on your arms. Cuts too deep to ever heal. I thought I knew how you must have felt. Like me, always shoved around, always towered over, always scared. I didn't expect anything like this. What were you thinking of?'

43

'Are you sure you don't know?' I asked, advancing toward the cabinet. 'I'm the kind of person nobody notices. I'm invisible until I'm pointed out. I'm in a private world. I'm not even ordinary. I'm somewhere below that.'

I had reached the cabinet, and now slowly pulled open the drawer, groping inside as she tried to conceal her panic, tried to find somewhere to wheel the chair.

'But I'm not alone,' I explained. 'There are many like me. I see them begging on the streets, soliciting in pubs, injecting themselves in alleyways. For them childhood is a scar that never heals, but still they try to stumble on. I end their stumbling, Saskia. Miss Chisholm says I'm an angel.'

My fingers closed around the handle of the carving knife, but the point was stuck in the rear wall of the drawer. I gave it my attention and pulled it free, lowering the blade until it was flat against my leg. A sound from behind made me turn. With a dexterity that amazed me, the enfuriating girl had opened the door and slipped through.

I ran into the lounge to find her wheelchair poised before the tape archives and Saskia half out of the seat, one hand pincering a stack of irreplaceable 78s featuring the vocal talents of Flanagan and Allen.

'Leave those alone!' I cried. 'You don't understand.'

She turned to me with what I felt was a look of deliberate malice on her face and raised the records high above her head. If I attacked her now, she would surely drop them.

'Why did you kill those people?' she asked simply. For a moment I was quite at a loss. She deserved an explanation. I ran my left thumb along the blade of the knife, drawing in my breath as the flesh slowly parted and the pain showed itself.

'I wanted to put their pasts right,' I explained. 'To give them the things that comfort. Tony Hancock. Sunday roast. Family Favourites. Smiling policemen. Norman Wisdom. To give them the freedom to remember.'

I must have allowed the knife to come into view, because her grip on the records faltered and they slid from her hands to the floor. I don't think any smashed, but the wheels of her chair cracked several as she rolled forward.

'I can't give you back the past, Saskia,' I said, walking towards her, smearing the knife blade with the blood from my stinging thumb. 'I'm sorry, because I would have liked to.'

She cried out in alarm, pulling stacks of records and tapes down upon herself, scattering them across the threadbare carpet. Then she grabbed the metal frame of the entire cabinet, as if trying to shake it loose from the wall. I stood and watched, fascinated by her fear.

When I heard the familiar heavy boots quickening on the stairs, I turned the knife over and pushed the blade hard into my chest. It was a reflex action, as if I had been planning to do this all along. Just as I had suspected, there was no pain. To those like us who suffered so long, there is no more pain.

Diary Entry # 10 Dated 16 November

And now I am sitting here on a bench with a clean elastic bandage patching up my stomach, facing the bristling cameras and microphones, twenty enquiring faces before me, and the real probing questions have begun.

The bovine policewoman who interrogated me so unimaginatively during my initial detainment period bore an extraordinary resemblance to Shirley Abicair, the Australian zither player who performed superbly as Norman's love interest in Rank's 1954 hit comedy *One Good Turn*, although the *Evening News* critic found their sentimental scenes together an embarrassment.

I think I am going to enjoy my new role here. Newspapers are fighting for my story. They're already comparing me to Nilsen and Sutcliffe, although I would rather be compared to Christie or Crippen. Funny how everyone remembers the name of a murderer, but no one remembers the victim.

If they want to know, I will tell them everything. Just as long as I can tell them about my other pet interests.

My past is safe.

My future is known.

My present belongs to Norman.

Dale And Wayne Go Shopping

'There's nothing else for it,' she said, raising her hands in apology. 'We have to go to the store.'

'Christ, Dale, isn't there another way?' asked Wayne. He walked to the refrigerator, yanked open the door and peered inside. At the back of the bare shelves he found an almost empty jar of peanut butter and two curled slices of packet ham, so dark and stale that they looked like jerky. In the icebox there was half a pint of mildewing pistachio flavoured ice-cream and a bottle of amyl nitrate. 'I mean, it ain't as if we're gonna be holding any dinner parties in the next few days. We can get by on takeouts.'

'Wayne, my guts can't handle any more pizza.'

'Then we'll get burgers.'

'I don't know what they put in them these days. Last time we ate at BurgerShack I nearly died, remember?' She pulled a bothersome strand of blonde hair from her face and tied it back. The heat in the apartment was dishevelling them both. 'Besides, I have a recipe I want to try out. Let's just do it without thinking about it, then it'll be over quicker.'

'I guess you're right,' Wayne conceded as he selected a long-bladed knife from the kitchen rack and slid it under the belt of his jeans. 'I just wish the sun was a little higher. We could always try somewhere different this time.'

'We know the layout of the Pricefair, Wayne. And it's real near for us. We'll be safer there. See what else we need, honey.' Her blue eyes studied his for a moment before flicking away. As her husband checked the kitchen cupboards, Dale chose a short wooden-handled knife with a broad blade and tucked it point down in her side pocket. Then they left the stifling apartment and walked around

49

the back of the block to the van.

It was little more than a three-minute drive to the vast supermarket at the corner of Grove and 23rd. They parked as near to the building's main entrance as they could. As usual, the lot was almost empty.

'Jeezus, it's gonna be dark soon. I don't like this,' said Wayne, searching around. 'Leave the van unlocked, just in case we have to make a run for it.'

They walked across the lot in perfect step, low-slung sunlight yanking their shadows tall across the cracked tarmac. Brightly coloured special offer posters filled the gold-reflecting windows of the store. No details of the interior could be seen from outside.

'Oh Christ, this is it.' Wayne dug his hand into his pocket and touched his silver dollar. 'Make me lucky today.' He looked over at Dale. 'Make us both lucky. Now you touch it.'

Dale touched the dollar.

'Ready?'

'Ready as I'll ever be.'

They stood at the threshold of the supermarket, drawing one last deep breath before breaking the electronic beam which shot the glass doors wide before them.

'Okay, where's the list?' called Wayne as Dale ran for a trolley.

'In my hand.' She raised a fist so he could see. 'Eggs,' she shouted back. 'We need eggs. Go quickly. I'll meet you there.'

Above them, Henry Mancini's 'Theme From A Summer Place' played on the Muzak system. Wayne dashed into the first section, the steel-tipped heels of his cowboy boots skidding on the tiled floor. He knew where the eggs were, end of the shelf on aisle one, but in front of him was the first sign of trouble. An elderly woman in a heavy woollen coat, burning pretty fiercely. She must have been on fire for some time, because her charred body had collapsed in on itself, and the floor was blackened all around her. Wayne moved cautiously past the crackling pyre. The woman looked like an immolated buddha. Her wire basket had fallen to one side, unfortunately devoid of produce. She'd barely had time to pick up a carton.

That was the problem with the eggs. Sometimes they were booby-trapped with this napalm-like stuff that stuck to your skin and stayed alight for hours.

He reached up and grabbed the box beside the one she had removed, figuring it was unlikely that two cartons next to each other would both be tampered with. Cautiously he raised the lid and checked inside. One dozen fresh farm eggs. A good start.

'Make sure you get Free Range,' called Dale, sliding into view at the tip of the second aisle. 'It's easier on the hens.'

'A whole lot easier on them than us,' muttered Wayne, deciding not to take the risk of switching the cartons. Ahead, Dale's trolley slewed to one side and slammed into a rack of tinned fruit. A can of cling peaches fell to the ground with a bang, followed by a second. Wayne and his wife dropped to the floor with their hands over their ears, but nothing happened.

Dale climbed to her feet and hefted one of the cans into the trolley. 'A nice little bonus,' she said, grinning at him. 'Let's get on.' They had no way of knowing what the noise might have attracted while they were hanging around. She consulted the items on the list. 'Butter and cheese.'

'Oh, not the cold cabinet,' complained Wayne. They both remembered seeing a man torn limb from limb in the yoghurt section last month. They carefully wheeled the trolley past a pair of black-shirted punks who were randomly stabbing at the back and neck of a cowering man, and arrived at the cold cabinet. The Muzak had now changed to 'Lara's Theme' from *Dr Zhivago*.

'This is so unhygienic,' complained Dale, pointing at

51

the various packaged cheeses. 'You'd think they'd clean it out every night.' A black pool of blood lay scabbing over between packets of Edam and Cheddar. Blood spattered most of the products on the shelves. The reason for the mess quickly became obvious. A man with no head lay half out of the cabinet, the ragged stump of his neck glutinously leaking onto the frozen pastries. Some kind of razorblade device had swung down on him when he'd reached in for a pound of margarine. Trying not to look at the twisted form beside her, Dale pointed out the brand of butter she needed as Wayne darted his hands in and scooped it up.

'And grab that cheese,' she said, waving her hand at a block of Emmenthal. 'Don't take the front one. There's some kind of wire hanging out of it.' The front cheeses were indeed wired up, probably to the mains electricity supply. One touch would burn the skin clean off your bones. Wayne leaned gingerly forward and checked at the back of the shelf, but it was overrun with hairless baby rats, plump pink forms that wriggled away, scattering to the touch. 'Could you make do with a piece of Stilton?' he asked.

'Actually, that would be nicer for what I had in mind,' said Dale. 'Is it safe?'

'Nothing is safe anymore,' he replied, grimacing as he flicked the tiny blind rodents aside to reach a chunk of shrink-wrapped Stilton. 'What's next?'

'Bleach.'

'Oh, *great.*' He tossed the cheese into the trolley. It was becoming hard to steer because the front wheels had been standing in blood, and were now rolling crooked crimson tracks across the cream plastic floortiles. Above them, the tannoy system was playing the theme from *Born Free.*

The Household Items aisle was notoriously dangerous even by Pricefair standards. A group of drugged-out kids were standing in front of the shelves, popping the tops from economy sized bottles of bleach and chugging

52

them down. It was a manhood thing, a kind of dare. Lots of kids were doing it now. One child of no more than eight or nine had fallen to the floor and was convulsing as the acidic liquid seared its way through his internal organs.

Two of the taller children moved menacingly toward them brandishing opened bleach bottles. Wayne could see that their lips were badly burned. One of them swung his bottle, spraying bleach at Dale. She ducked behind the end of the aisle as the liquid splashed around her. With a shout, Wayne withdrew his knife and ran at one of the larger children, a girl, slashing a cheek, then an arm. As she screamed and fell back he grabbed a large plastic bottle from the shelf and threw it to his wife. Dale caught it in a seasoned swing as if accepting a Bronco pass. Then Wayne was running, sliding out of the aisle, safe in the knowledge that he could not be followed because the Bleachers would never risk surrendering their home turf.

The centre of the store was quiet enough. Here the spoor of violence had grown stale. They passed a half-rotted corpse folded up in a lawn lounger in the Garden Furniture section, black body fluids leaking through the multicoloured fabric. The scene had an ugly peace about it. At least there were no signs of recent disturbance. In Jams & Jellies, sticky gossamer nets of brown crawly things pulsed with life on the shelves between the pots. An old Jim Reeves song was now tinkling from the ceiling speakers. Something with a lot of legs ran past Dale and vanished under Special Offer Soups, brushing the backs of her legs as it went.

'For God's sake let's get out of here,' said Wayne, pulling the cart to a halt. 'We got everything we need.'

'We don't, Wayne. I still have to get some other stuff.' She tapped the paper with her index finger. Wayne looked over her shoulder at the list.

'You can cross those frozen diet dinners off,' he said, grimacing. 'I saw a man lose his nuts trying to get a Weight-

Watchers meal outta the cabinet.'

Over on aisle six the air conditioning ducts set in the ceiling had been blocked up with something alarmingly bulky and human-sized, and the rising temperature caused sweat to sheen their faces. Dale smudged damp hair from her eyes and sighed. 'Okay, we'll just get some dessert. Please, Wayne, it's been so long since we had a nice cake. A black forest gâteau, maybe.'

'Well ... all right.'

The Cakes & Pastries freezer was suspiciously devoid of life. As they wheeled their errant trolley to the far end of the store they could see someone leaning over into the refrigerated cabinet, pushing and shoving at the cartons within.

'I don't like the look of this,' whispered Wayne. 'Slow down.' As they approached the cabinet, they could see that the figure was convulsing, knees jerking back and forth beyond muscular control, shoes banging and skittering against the wall of the freezer unit.

'Hey, mister, you okay?' called Dale. There was no reply.

Suppressing a shudder of alarm, Wayne looked over into the dessert compartment. One of the gâteau boxes had exploded in a tangle of metal coils. He quickly pushed Dale away. 'You don't wanna see this, honey, believe me.' But he could not resist another look himself. The wires had sprung from the booby-trapped box to pierce its victim's face in a hundred different places, gripping flesh and bone with springs of steel.

'Okay, *that* does it, we're out of here,' shouted Wayne, grabbing his wife by the arm and hauling her and the trolley off in the direction of the checkout.

'Wait,' cried Dale, pulling back. 'We're passing right by Savouries. I want some ketchup, and a pack of those little silver balls you put on cakes.'

As the song on the tannoy changed to The Doors'

'Light My Fire' rearranged for xylophone, they ran past the Savouries section, where a pair of leather-jacketed teenagers were sawing the head from a squatting female shopper with a large kitchen-knife. Wayne noticed that the knife worked pretty well considering it was still in a bubble pack. 'I think you can forget the ketchup,' he said.

A bored-looking girl sat playing with her hair at the express-lane till. Dale and Wayne yanked the runaway trolley to a stop beside her and began throwing their purchases onto the conveyor belt. Dale could tell that the checkout girl was stoned out of her mind by the way her eyes kept involuntarily rolling up into her head until only the whites showed.

'We gotta find a new place to shop,' said Wayne.

'Yeah,' his wife agreed. 'I miss the friendliness of the local corner stores.' The girl at the till managed to run each product over the barcode laser but had most of them the wrong way up, so that half of the prices failed to register. Her hair was matted with overperming, and a thin strand of drool hung suspended between her lips and her sweater. Suddenly she jerkily hoisted the bleach and shouted 'Pricecheck on this item', in a slurred screech before letting the bottle slide from her hand. As Wayne deftly caught it, she coughed and blew a chunk of nose-blood onto the register.

Trying not to look, Dale stood the eggs on the conveyor belt. The checkout girl turned her attention to the carton and stared at it with bulging eyes.

'This yours?' she asked in amazement.

'I figure so,' replied Dale sarcastically, 'seeing as we managed to get it off the shelf.'

Wayne stopped filling the takeout bag. 'What's the problem?' he asked.

'Eleven items,' slurred the girl, pressing a button beneath the till. 'This is the express lane. Ten items only.'

'Then we'll put one ba —' Wayne managed to say before

the bullet shattered his skull and his body was punched into a backward somersault, landing him in the end aisle.

As Dale's voice rose in a scream another burst of gunfire came, shattering her arm and shoulder, tearing open her neck in a powerful geyser of blood as she spun around with her hands raised and toppled to the floor.

The Pricefair manager, a ginger-haired boy of twenty-one, dropped the scorching pistol back into his overall pocket and turned to the checkout girl.

'I told you before, Charlene,' he admonished, 'Warn 'em before you start ringin' stuff up. I gotta reset the total each time.'

Above them, the overture from *Mary Poppins* began to play.

Contact High

1. SIGHT

She stormed from Jack's flat with such anger in her heart that she was almost killed crossing Hammersmith Broadway, the driver barking obscenely at her as she ran for the safety of the far kerb.

Cheryl remembered casting a sour glance at the squatting tramp in the corner of the station forecourt, looking for someone to blame, then feeling ashamed for doing so. The action of digging out £1.20 change and buying her ticket calmed her down a little more, so that she was able to close off her thoughts from the evening's events.

As she walked through the barrier and descended the steps for the Eastbound Piccadilly Line train, she became convinced that it was entirely Jack's fault. She just wished she hadn't retaliated to the point of hitting him.

It was a bitterly cold night, the stars jagging out of the black city sky like shards of blue glass. The wind skittered along the platform, whipping dust-devils of wastepaper by the benches, but there appeared to be no waiting room open. Worse still, it looked as if there had been no train for some time. The platform was crowded even though the pubs were still open.

Months later she tried to remember every detail clearly, but her mind was preoccupied, and only impressions remained. A giant hoarding beyond the tracks; some ridiculous-looking girl selling a new hairspray. A couple kissing on a red metal bench, both very young, probably with nowhere else to go.

And the man, of course.

Slim and ski-tanned, about five feet ten inches tall, standing a couple of feet from the edge of the platform. Looking down the line with a frown on his face, giving the bitter little look some commuters get when their schedules are thrown out. She did not really know why she noticed him. She supposed he was attractive, but all she recalled after was that he had nicely cut hair, dark and short. He wore a heavy grey overcoat and carried a briefcase, probably on his way home after working late in some fluorescent box above their heads.

As she waited, her mind filled with thoughts of Jack, who she assumed had by now slammed the front door of his flat and gone downstairs to sit seething at the corner table in his local. The argument was nothing new, one of those annoying stalemates, like the Irish question, a battle nobody could win. Seven months ago she had agreed to go out with Jack on the condition that he understood her commitment to Denny. Now, he seemed to be using the boy as an excuse not to see her. The novelty of having an instant family was fast wearing off for him. The relationship didn't seem likely to last into an eighth month.

She couldn't remember what made her look back at the man in the grey overcoat. He was extracting a paperback, trying to close his briefcase. She was standing perhaps ten feet behind him, to the right. Although she couldn't hear it there was obviously a train approaching, because people were moving nearer the edge of the platform.

She became aware that someone was pushing through the forward-facing crowd to the far left of her vision. She had an impression of bulk and height and irate energy. He was six feet three at least, a dark face framed with curly black hair shaved away at the sides, a glowing cigarette and an impatient stride similar to her own a few minutes ago. As he passed by, his cool grey eyes flicked over her disinterestedly. He pulled a cigarette carton from his pocket, shook it and threw it aside. An emerald ring glinted on his hand.

What followed was the one thing she saw very clearly, as if it had taken place in slow motion. The tall man had reached the one in the grey overcoat, who was in his path and still buckling the case shut, standing with one knee slightly raised. To get past him, one of them would have to move a foot or so. The taller man reached down and grabbed the other's hand in a firm clasp, then released it and moved swiftly on, shifting away into the expectant crowd. The man in the grey overcoat stared after the retreating figure, who glanced angrily back at him, then at her watching them both. Cheryl had the odd feeling of witnessing something she should not have seen, as if she had been present at a secret ritual.

Suddenly the man in grey shot out his arms and seized the back of his neck, his briefcase tumbling forward onto the track. He began to scream, a high-pitched wail that cut the icy air and stilled the platform chatter. Everyone was turning to look at him. The train was pulling in now, and for one awful moment she thought he was going to jump in its path, but the silver carriage ran smoothly past.

It was then that he leapt, too late of course, so he simply slammed into the side of the passing steel wall and dropped down between the platform edge and the racing train. Some people screamed and the train braked hard, screeching to a halt before reaching its correct stopping point at the end of the platform. Even before it had fully reached a standstill, she knew that he had probably been killed instantly. There was a thin smear of blood along the side of the carriage, dropping from a height of several feet to below the platform edge. A scrum formed around the area where the man, or what was left of him, presumably lay, but something made her push her way back to where he had been standing. To where he had been touched.

It was the handclasp that bothered her, even though she

did not recognise it then. She stopped at the spot and looked down, expecting nothing and finding instead the cast aside cigarette box, 20 Silk Cut, the cellophane outer wrapper still in place, a business card slipped behind it. She did that with her own cigarette pack sometimes, if she had no purse with her. How could she not bend down to pick it up? She slipped it into her coat pocket and guiltily left the platform just as the first policeman arrived.

The central heating was turned too high. It was poisoning her dreams. She pushed back the cover and rose from the bed, glancing at the clock. 4.13 a.m. She found her dressing gown and donned it, switching on the hall light. Her mouth tasted brackish. Toothpaste had failed to remove the taste of the red wine she had drunk with Jack. She caught sight of herself in the hall mirror and grimaced. Her thin blonde hair felt lank and dirty, the effect of the four tube trains she had taken to and from Jack's flat. Why had he spoiled it, just when things were progressing smoothly?

She looked in on Denny and found him hanging halfway out of bed as usual. Gently tucking him back beneath the blankets, she wondered how the boy would feel about not seeing Jack again. What was the point of seeing him? He just wanted sex without any of the responsibility. He wasn't even prepared to acknowledge the fact that she had a six-year-old child. She closed the bedroom door behind her and shut her eyes, tired of marking time with men like Jack.

A flash — the grey overcoat against a speeding steel wall. A few hours ago she had seen a man die, or at least become very badly injured. He'd had some kind of fit. An attack of epilepsy, or perhaps he'd been stung by a wasp. The tall man who had grabbed his hand could have injected him with a lethal drug, like the Russian spy who was jabbed with the poisoned umbrella a few years ago. Whatever the method, she was seized with the overwhelming impression that he had somehow caused the other man's death.

Which was when she realised that her hands were shaking. She should have stayed at the station to talk to the police. But they would have thought it odd. What could she have said? It wasn't as if the tall man had given him a shove. He'd simply held his hand. She went to the kitchen counter and found the cigarette packet, pulled out the card and read it.

Bellamy & Forshaw Ltd. Sounded like a tailors. *Michael Devery, Managing Director.* Somewhere in the darkened street below a cat was crying, making a noise like an abandoned baby. She knew she would have to ring the number in the morning. She couldn't help herself, never had been able to. Journalism in the blood, just like Dad.

Yeah, he'd been right about that. She lit a cigarette, shook out the match and tossed it into the sink. Five nerve-deadening years on a political tidbit column in the local paper. Alderman attends Dunkirk honour ceremony. Local councillor in parking row. Big time stuff. *You don't have what it takes to be a good newswoman, you're too shy. I'm telling you this for your own good.* That's what he'd always told her. *Having an overactive imagination isn't enough. It takes guts. You'll make someone a wonderful wife instead. Be happy with that.* Well, we tried that option, she thought, and we managed to screw it up.

'I hope you're watching, Dad,' she said, shaking the cigarette packet and tossing it onto the counter. 'This one's for you.'

'I'm holding for Mr Devery,' she said again, blowing smoke away from the mouthpiece of the phone. Muzak resumed, a song from *South Pacific.* 9.47 a.m. on the kitchen clock. Misha, her best and oldest friend, had called by to take Denny to school. She looked over at the stack of dirty washing up in the sink, checked her nails for chips, examined the card again. The music cut out.

'What can I do for you?'

She set down the cigarette and sat up. 'Michael Devery?'

'That's right.' A cultured, pleasant tone.

'I'm sorry about this. My secretary took a call from you and set it down on my pad, and I'm returning it without knowing quite who you are or what you wanted.'

'Well, who are you?'

'My name is Cheryl Brunton. I'm a journalist.' *Of sorts.*

'I don't have any —' A brief pause. 'Wait, this wouldn't be about the Reynolds dismissal, would it?'

Shit, now what? What would Dad have done? What the hell did Bellamy & Forshaw do for a living, make shoes? Sell antiques? She should have checked with the switch-board. *Dismissal.* It sounded like a lawsuit. Try that. 'You mean the court action?'

'Yes, but it hasn't actually reached the court yet, so I don't think I can talk to you about it.'

That was a lucky shot. Try another one. 'Wait a minute, Bellamy & Forshaw, don't you have an associate, a tall man with curly black hair shaved at the sides, wears an emerald ring, what's his name now?'

A silence. Uh oh.

'What is this?' Suddenly aggressive. Her mouth dried. She tried to think of something to say, her fingers flexing with impatience. She couldn't get it.

'Do you know this man?' Tension in his voice.

'We've met, in a manner of speaking.'

'Is he a friend of yours? Are you acting for him?'

'No, I just wondered —'

'I think you'd better cut the bullshit and tell me why you're calling.'

'I wanted to know. Can you hurt someone just by touching them? Just by holding their hand?' She couldn't stop herself. It just came out.

'Where are you?'

'Me — I —' She pulled the receiver away from her. Sweet

Jesus. She looked at the phone, gingerly returned it to her ear. She could hear him breathing.

'Where did you get this number?'

'I — found it. He had it.'

'When was this?'

'Last night.'

'What time?'

'Around nine-thirty.'

Another silence. 'Hammersmith Station.'

'That's right.'

'Miss — Brunton.'

'Yes.'

'Do you know what a Contact High is?'

'No. But I saw what he did.'

'Then I have to meet you, wherever you are, right now.'

'Listen, I —' She never expected to get in this deep, this fast. 'How do I know you aren't —'

'I'm not going to hurt you, if that's what you're worried about.'

'I don't know that.'

'Meet me somewhere in the West End, where there are plenty of people about. That suit you?'

'All right. The Trocadero, in Piccadilly. The café downstairs.'

'How long do you need to get there?'

She looked down. She was still in her dressing gown. 'An hour.'

'I'll meet you in an hour. If you see him again, just start running. You run, and you run. Understand?'

'I understand.'

The line went dead.

There was a twenty-minute wait for the next Northern Line train, and when it arrived it was packed to the roof. She squeezed herself in and kept against the far wall of the carriage, watchful for any sight of the tall man. She had dressed for the low outside temperature in jeans, a heavy sweater and a scarf, and was soon perspiring in the swaying crush. Disgorged at Leicester Square, she was acutely aware of the difficulty in avoiding contact with those around her. Tourists and late-running office workers jostled for places on the escalator, bumped like railway couplings at the automatic barriers, criss-crossed tracks on the stairs to the street.

The café was always deserted. She presumed other people found the Trocadero as depressing as she did, and stayed away. She crossed the white-tiled floor and scanned the tables ahead, wishing she'd remembered to bring her glasses. Nearby, a fountain feebly piddled blue-dyed water into a basin. Unusually, several of the tables were occupied. She should have asked what he looked like.

He spotted her first.

Rising from a chair half-hidden by large plastic ferns, he beckoned her to his table. He was wearing pale calfskin gloves, and did not offer to shake her hand.

'Miss Brunton.'

'Please, call me Cheryl.' She sat in the chair he indicated, and waited while he filled an empty cup with coffee. Devery was in his mid-to-late thirties, a close-cropped beard rising to high cheekbones and serious brown eyes, stylishly dressed in a broad-shouldered black suit and rollneck sweater. He looked like an executive for an upscale record company.

'I didn't mean to jump at you on the phone,' he said, pushing the cup across. 'I was concerned that you might hang up. It's happened before. How did you get our number?'

She studied him carefully, wondering whether he could be trusted. *A man has lost his life. Don't take anything he says lightly.* 'He'd put your card inside his cigarette pack.'

'I don't understand. How did you come by it? Perhaps it would help if you told me the full story.'

66

Whether or not she had intended to, she found herself describing everything she had seen — or thought she had seen. Devery listened quietly and intently, watching her face, his gloved hands remaining flat on the table. She dug out a cigarette and lit it, inhaling nervously.

'So, is that possible?' she asked finally. 'You sounded as if you knew.'

He looked away at the shoppers travelling listlessly on walkways beneath the dead light of the shopping dome. 'You said you were a journalist.'

'That's right.'

'You lied about the reason for your call.'

'Yes.'

'Before we go any further you'd better give me your home address.'

'You can have the phone number.' She wrote it on the back of a Safeway receipt and slid it across the table. 'Can you tell me what's going on?'

'To do that you'll have to come with me, and then you'll be involved. Are you married?' He pointed to the slim diamond ring she wore.

'Divorced. I have a young boy.'

'Then I can't take you.' He removed the bill from the table and examined it.

'Why not?' She knew there was a story here, and that selling it would be her key to the world of real journalism.

'He could hurt the child. I'm not authorised to take that kind of risk.' He pulled off his right glove and fished around in his pocket for change.

'What do you mean? I don't understand.'

'You've seen what he can do. If you ever see him again, you must call me at once. Right now we've nothing further to discuss.' He rose to leave.

'What's to stop me from talking to the police?' she said, annoyed with his dismissive attitude.

'Nothing. Thank you for coming to see me. You did the

right thing to call.' He pulled his glove back on and turned away.

'Wait.' She ran after him. 'I can still get this published.'

He paused and looked back at her. 'You have no facts.'

'I can give them a damned good theory. I'm an eye witness, remember?'

'Did he see you? I mean, a really good look?'

'He stopped and stared.'

He thought for a moment. 'Then you're no safer out than in. Perhaps you'd better come with me after all.'

'How much time will this take?' she asked, pleased at a chance for a story but concerned that Misha would be bringing Denny home to an empty flat at three.

'I don't know. If you give me the address of the school, we'll have your boy collected.'

'He's been told never to go with a stranger,' she said as they climbed the escalator to ground level. 'Anyway, a friend of mine is collecting him.'

'We'll figure something out. Right now we'd better get you off the street.'

A taxi took them to a nondescript sixties office block in the grey backstreets of Clerkenwell. Neither of them spoke during the journey. It seemed that no topic could be broached without considerable explanation, and neither of them felt like making small talk. As they alighted, she read the nameplate over the door. Bellamy & Forshaw Ltd. 'What do you do here?' she asked, but received no reply. Again, Devery removed a single glove to pay the driver, refitting it immediately after. He ushered her through a set of darkened glass doors, then arranged a visitor's badge for her at the commissionaire's desk, situated in a depressing, underlit lobby. The hallway was lined with framed government notices, the floor tiles an ugly mismatch of faded red and institutional green.

They passed through three more sets of wooden

portholed doors, down three more corridors, past endless closed offices, beyond which could be heard the muffled tick-tacking of word processors, the mechanics of bureaucracy. Finally he led her into a large, bright room filled with computer equipment, and pulled out a chair for her. She sat and looked around, noting the cages lined along the far wall. Most contained sleeping hamsters. One or two had rabbits inside. There were two other people in the room, an old man hunched over a computer console, and a young Chinese student busy filling notepads with strings of numbers.

'Tell me, how much of an open mind do you have, Cheryl?' asked Devery, seating himself on the edge of a desk, more relaxed now than he had been in the street. 'Do you believe in ESP?'

'Some, perhaps. Twins seem to sense things.'

'How about, let's see,' he searched around for an example, 'telekinesis?'

'Moving things with the mind? I'm not sure.'

'Okay. Let me give you a little history lesson about what we're dealing with here. I'll try to keep it simple. In 1982, around about the time when the AIDS virus was first being taken seriously, scientists stepped up their experiments with DNA ...'

'Is that what this place is?' she interrupted. 'A government science lab?'

'Not really. We mostly handle the research and funding, although some of the simpler experiments take place here. At the time when large-scale DNA sampling was becoming common, a new pattern was noticed in certain subjects.'

'Human subjects?'

'Yes. If you'll let me continue?' Silenced, she sat back. 'Tests were carried out on kidney tissue by a research group in Munich, and their Scanning Force Microscopy Unit turned up something odd; a rogue enzyme. Some people, very few — our closest estimate so far is one in

69

seventy thousand – produce an enzyme with unprece-
dented properties. When sudden changes occur that affect
the central nervous system, the enzyme is produced,
causing subtle changes in the construction of body
fluids. In some cases it alters glandular excretions, particularly sweat. The interesting thing is, it's toxic. Contact-
lethal.'

'How could that be?' she asked, intrigued. It sounded
like a perfect biological weapon.

'In order to survive in the human system the enzyme
creates a kind of virus, taking over healthy cells and
converting them for its needs. It does this very quickly
indeed. When it meets an outside fluid, say sweat in the
palm of another person's hand, its invader cells send a
DNA-encrypted code through the new host that knocks
out the central nervous system and enters the brain,
causing instantaneous neutralisation.'

'Death.'

'That's right.'

'Just by touching someone.'

'Yes. A kind of reverse Midas touch. Only the most
microscopic amount of fluid is needed to act as a new host
for the rogue cells. This man you saw could have touched
the back of your hand, and you may have thought his
touch was quite dry, but by the time you'd considered the
question you'd be dead.'

'But people don't just go around killing everyone they
meet,' she protested. 'Something like this is too big to
keep secret for long. Surely I'd have read about it in the
papers by now.'

'That's the most extraordinary part. The research is still
in its infancy, but we're starting to think some people have
always had this enzyme. It's just that the ability to kill has
remained dormant until now. We think it's brought on by
new higher levels of stress. It's only been found in city
dwellers so far.'

70

He rubbed his hand through his hair, anxious to explain. 'This is a vast, exciting field of research, and only a corner of it is being explored. For example, different levels of enzymatic interference appear to have different effects. A light touch can induce headaches, nausea, vomiting. But it's not all harmful, either. A certain way of holding someone can produce a, uh, heightened sense of pleasure. We call that a Contact High.'

'You have it, don't you? This — disease.' She pointed to the gloves.

'Yes, I do. But please don't call it a disease. It's something far more special, and we hope that eventually it can be harnessed to become a useful medical tool. You see, with a little practice it can be controlled.'

'Then why do you wear the gloves?'

'Because unlike most people walking around in the streets, I've been made aware of my capabilities,' he replied. 'I know what I can do, and when it's likely to happen. I can't always guarantee my mood, so I don't want to take any undue risks.' As he spoke, he crossed to one of the cages at the end of the room and withdrew a small black rabbit, stroking its ears with the back of his hand. Setting it down on the desk, he slipped off his right glove and placed his hand over the rabbit's head, holding it lightly in place. Moments later the animal sagged, its head dropping.

'It's asleep,' he explained. 'That's about all I can do in a calm state. I have to be emotionally destabilised for anything more than this. My abilities are still in a very early stage of growth.'

'You mean you have to make yourself angry before you can cause physical injury?'

'That's right. But the man you encountered doesn't have to do that. He's a born natural, our star pupil. Or rather, he was. We found him in one of the random volunteer groups a few days ago. The needle went off the

71

graph when we tested him. Unfortunately, he proved to be mentally unstable, a borderline psychotic. After an argument, he elected not to stay with us.'

'You mean you made him aware of his power, and now he's out there running around, hurting anyone he chooses? If you're on the side of law and order, why aren't you co-operating with the police?'

'The police wouldn't be able to do anything even if the research could be declassified in time to tell them. The only way to bring him in is through civilian interception, I'm certain of that.'

'You'd better be right,' said Cheryl. 'Otherwise you'll be allowing the deaths of innocent people.'

'That's why I need you to co-operate with me, for everyone's sake,' said Devery, reaching out to her. His right hand was still free of its glove. She instinctively shied away.

'It's okay, I can't hurt you,' he said, 'but you're right to look nervous. I'll put the glove back on.' He slid the leather over his fist and smiled at her.

'What do you want me to do?' she said, warily eyeing his hands.

'His name is José Pescano,' he said, 'I want you to help me bring him in.'

She looked past Devery, out at the hallway beyond the door, where two Chinese men were wheeling a trolley laden with labelled jars. An odd smell drifted through; formaldehyde. From somewhere beyond the laboratory wall came the muffled whine of an electric saw.

'I could get hurt,' she said, her eyes still on the doorway.

Devery smiled quickly. 'We're here to see that you don't. For a start, we'll move you and your son into the research station's guest rooms for a while. There should be minimal disruption to your daily routine.' *Right.* She watched the banks of computer equipment on the other side of the room, where red numerals rolled silently in stacks. There was something wrong here. *Too much money on show. Look around. Wang. IBM. All the latest technology.* Devery was wearing a three hundred pound jacket. *You don't make that kind of money working for British government research.*

'I presume you don't know where to look for this Mr Pescano, otherwise you'd have brought him in yourselves. What makes you think I'll have any more luck?'

'We'll allow you to release some information to him, make him understand —' Devery drifted off, his thoughts clearly somewhere else.

'I can't stay here, Mr Devery. This is a government institute, isn't it?'

'Affiliated.' Another reassuring smile. 'Staying here will be the safest thing for you. Someone can bring your boy here.' Very wrong. *Trust your instincts.*

'Then I'd better go and collect some things to wear.'

'There's really no need.'

He doesn't want you to leave. You have to get out now. Keep him talking.

'Tell me more about Pescano.'

'We tried the Fulham address he entered on the volunteer form, but he hasn't been back there. Pescano mentioned to one of the logging students that he sometimes works in a restaurant in the King's Road, but she isn't able to recall the name of it. Something to do with ducks, she said. We haven't found it yet, but we're still checking.' As he spoke he raised the telephone receiver beside him, dialled two digits and waited. 'Obviously we have to find him quickly, before he can injure anyone else.' He turned his attention to the receiver. 'Ah, John, I wonder if you'd like to meet our newest recruit. Bring Graham up here with you.'

'I really should call someone,' said Cheryl, pushing herself forward to the edge of the chair.

'I can do that for you.' The smile again. *Go now. Now.* She rose to her feet. 'First, could you show me the way to the bathroom?'

'Of course.' He rose and led the way from the laboratory. They walked side by side down the hall, through one pair of swing doors to a wide stairwell. Devery pointed at the door directly ahead. He's going to wait outside, she thought, dismayed. I'll never be able to climb out of the toilet window. We're two floors up. Nothing for it but to take the stairs. Without thinking further, she began to run downwards.

'Cheryl!' he called in alarm. 'Don't be stupid!' Then he began to run after her.

The sign on the landing below indicated that this was the first floor. She continued down, taking the steps in pairs, with Devery closing in behind. The door at the bottom could only be opened by punching a series of digits into a keypad, but a Chinese lab technician was just passing through it. She slammed into him with all the momentum she had gained on the stairs, knocking him aside. As she passed through the door she pulled it shut behind her, hoping that the keypad would delay him. The hallway ahead was deserted, and led to a barred exit at the side of the building. Forcing open the steel bar set off a deafening electronic alarm, but with one push she was out in the alley and away down the street, running as fast as she could.

The restaurant was painted green and gold, and looked expensive. She remembered reading about it, but had never eaten here. The Wilde Goose. *Something to do with ducks.* It was not due to open until 6.00 p.m., but by shielding her hands against the glass she could discern a pair of figures moving about inside. She checked her watch. 2.15 p.m. Denny would be coming home from school in three quarters of an hour. One of the men saw her silhouette and opened the door. A heavy-set Italian wiped his hands on his apron and offered a gesture of apology. 'Is not open yet.'

'I know. I wanted to ask you about one of your employees.' As she spoke, she saw Pescano's head and shoulders pull sharply back behind the counter. Pushing past the protesting chef, she ran to the rear of the darkened restaurant.

'Wait, José! I want to help you. I know it was you I saw at the station.'

He filled the doorway, his dark bulk turning slowly towards her.

He was only a few feet from the back door. If she lost him now she was sure she would never find him again. 'One of the institute's spies,' he said softly, taking a step forward.

'No, I swear. Devery told me you were crazy, dangerous, but I knew he was lying.'

'How?'

'I'm not sure. Instinct. Maybe I've seen too many conspiracy movies. Please, you must tell me what really happened at the station.'

Pescano moved slowly towards her. His deep-set eyes were shadowed, intense. He looked like a man hounded from sleep. 'He was one of Devery's surveillance men. They work in pairs. I took out one. The other attacked me as I left the station.'

'What happened to him?'

'You don't want to know.' He held his large, bare hands lightly at his sides. 'I don't understand why you're here, but you shouldn't have come.'

'Neither should you. If Devery could have remembered the name of the restaurant, he'd have caught you by now.'

'I needed money. I can't go back to my flat.'

'I can help you, José.'

'I have to get out of the city.'

75

As he walked into the light, she saw that he was beautiful.

2. TOUCH

The taxi coasted sharply around the corner of Sloane Square, but Pescano was careful to remain on his side of the bench seat. Throughout the journey, he stared straight ahead and kept his hands clasped between his knees. He smelled as if he badly needed a bath. His physical bulk beside her was both unsettling and sensual, strength in abeyance. She didn't want to think how she would explain his presence to Denny.

'It's a private research establishment for the military,' he said. 'In all of their testing so far, I'm only the fourth one they've ever found. Devery says that a couple have been discovered in America, and there's supposed to be a whole group of people who can do this in Germany but they're hiding somewhere, and no one's sure of their abilities. It seems that none of us has quite the same power. It may depend on our environmental background. Devery was the first, and they offered him a directorship, giving him the task of liaising with newcomers. I guess they thought we'd respond better if we were brought in by our own kind.'

'What do you think they have planned for you?'

'Taking out civilian targets, I guess. It's a foolproof form of assassination.' He dropped his head into his hands, ran thick fingers through his dirty hair. 'I was doing a series of tests for them when I saw some documents, military orders. When I discharged myself, they tried to stop me. Told me they'd kill me. I've got nowhere to go. They'll be watching the airports.'

'At least we won't be stopped by the police,' she said, trying to sound positive. 'It sounds as if Devery's operating way beyond the law.'

He cleared a patch of window and looked out. 'Where are we?'

'Belsize Park. I have to pick up my son.' The cab turned off the hill into a side street.

They'd be at the flat in a moment. There was about forty pounds in the tea caddy, and she had her credit cards on her. She'd drop Denny back at Misha's, get José onto a northbound train, then collect her son. That seemed safest.

'Just here.' The cab pulled over and she alighted, digging into her purse for change.

He watched her, awkward.

'I don't have much cash. They'd cleared the tills at the restaurant, but Sergio the chef lent me a little. I've been hiding in the subway all night.'

'That's okay. I have enough to get us through. I hope we're in time. It won't take them long to work out my address from the telephone number.' I'll never get another chance like this, she thought, passing coins to the driver. It'll make quite a story if he manages to come out of it alive.

Misha was just leaving as they ran along the third-floor hall of the block of flats. The young Japanese girl was surprised and puzzled to see her friend arriving with a large, dirty-looking man loping behind her.

'Misha, where's Denny?' she asked anxiously, looking towards the flat.

'He's in his room playing Nintendo. I wondered where you were.'

'Thanks for collecting him. I have to go out again.'

'No problem if you want him to stay with me.'

'Listen, if you see anyone calling here, stay well away from them. If they ask whether you've seen me, you have to say no.'

'Are you in some kind of trouble?' asked Misha, worried. 'You can stay at my place.'

'I thought of that, but it's too risky being in the same building. I'll figure something out.' She was anxious to get out of the corridor, where they were easy targets. 'Do me a favour and call Jack, would you? Tell him I've gone abroad or something. Just in case they find a way of checking with him.'

'You don't have to come with me,' said Pescano. 'I can look after myself.'

'I'm aware of that. I've seen you, remember?' She turned back to Misha. 'It's best that no one knows where we are. I'll be back in a couple of days, or I'll get in touch with you somehow.'

Inside the flat, she bundled some clothes into a holdall and pulled a sweater onto Denny, who was not pleased to be torn from his SuperHunchback game. She handed José a bag containing jeans and a sweatshirt that Jack had left at the flat.

'Where are we going? He smells,' he said, pointing to Pescano and holding his nose.

'It's a little holiday,' she said, grabbing toiletries and dropping them into the sidepockets of the bag. 'Like when we go to visit Grandma, only more fun.'

Pescano stood by the window watching the street. It was growing dark, and rain had begun to spatter the windows. 'Pack the boy a good coat,' he said. 'I'll carry him.'

'No, I'll take him,' she said quickly. 'You bring the bag.'

'There's a car turning into the street. We have to go.'

They ran down the concrete fire escape stairs to the car park beneath the block, where Cheryl's green Deux Chevaux was parked. 'I think you'd better drive,' she said, depositing Denny in the rear of the car. 'That's if you can get inside. I'm a bit of a tortoise on the road.'

He pushed back the seat as far as it would go and

lowered himself into the driving seat. As the little car exited from the ramp beside the building, she saw three men alighting from a black Mercedes double-parked before the block.

'We'd better stay away from the major stations,' said Pescano. 'They're bound to be watching them. It's safer to drive.'

'Mum, where are we going?' asked Denny, bumping about on the seat as Pescano crashed the gears.

'I don't know, darling,' she said, throwing him a nervous smile. 'Isn't this exciting?'

Denny looked at his mother as if she'd taken leave of her senses.

She hadn't quite done that, but she had reached a decision. The three of them would travel together.

Moments she remembered: the Deux Chevaux coughing to a halt in a layby on the M1. Pescano fixing the engine with a kit from the boot, bent beneath the hood, his body half obscured in the descending rain.

The uneasy hotel clerk in Nuneaton, who eyed them oddly and gave them a cramped room at the far end of the building. Pescano swathed in steam, emerging from the bathroom with wet hair and a clean, smiling face.

Denny and Pescano playing roadgames on the way to Manchester, singing as they cautiously passed a police barricade surrounding a traffic accident.

Arriving in Harrogate, Denny asleep, Pescano still motionlessly staring through the windscreen, hands at ten to two, the car engine overheating and cracking as they coasted into the motel park.

'We'll run out of land eventually.'

She looked up at the night, a density of stars unseen in London, a sky like spilled salt on black velvet. Denny was curled into his dreams on the single bed in the adjoining room. They had booked a family suite to arouse less suspicion. The motel was a faded sixties relic, too dull to draw attention, too inefficiently run for the staff to remember them.

The night was bitterly cold, the windowpane radiating chill air, almost painful to the touch. Pescano sat wrapped in a towel on the far side of the double bed studying an Ordnance Survey map.

'Scotland will be safer. We have to do something about the car. The cylinder head is damaged.'

'I could leave the 2CV here. Jack lent it to me as a runaround. He warned me that it didn't have much life left in it. We can rent a car.'

'Then we should leave early tomorrow.' He looked over at the dirty bundle in the corner of the bathroom. 'I don't have any clean clothes.'

'Check the bag I gave you,' she said, pointing to the holdall. 'The sweatshirt should fit. I don't know about the jeans.'

They were short in the leg, but better than the clothes he had been wearing. She and Pescano emerged into the night air and walked to the car park trailing their breath, Cheryl marvelling at the silence of the countryside. Her father had rarely taken her outside London. She had seen too little of him in the last days of his life. Her fault, too busy with her own failing marriage, too late to make amends now.

They filled a carrier bag with identifying items from the car, then José wheeled it backwards to the broad drainage ditch at the end of the fallow fields beyond the motel. The Citroën slid softly into a tangle of brambles, its colour helping to disguise it beneath the bracken.

'You must be tired,' she said, watching as he climbed from the ditch.

'No time to be tired.' He rose and stood beside her, the furrowed fields stretching off in lunar modulation. 'Perhaps they'll forget about me. Spend their time developing the others.'

'You really had no idea that you had this power?' she asked. 'I mean, before you volunteered for Devery?'

'None at all.'

'How do they manage to bring it out in people?'

'First they see if you fit an existing psychology profile. Then you do aptitude tests. Hypnotic suggestion with pentathol-morphine based drugs and a hypnotherapy course. An injection of some weird new synthetic hormone. They pay you £75 a day, and you sign a waiver saying that they can pump whatever they want into your system.' He held out his hands and examined the moonlit palms in wonder. 'And now it's there all the time, and I can't turn it off. How can I live when I can't trust my own touch?' He turned to her and held out his hand.

Neither of them moved. Cheryl studied the splayed fingers, the broad palm, the thick wrist stemming from the sleeve of Jack's faded blue shirt. He was a physically daunting man, handicapped by his own strength, a prisoner within his own body. How could you survive with everyone frightened of you? How could you not become the thing you most feared to be?

Without being consciously aware that she was doing so, she reached out her hand and brushed his fingertips with her own. Their palms met, fingers entwining. She could feel his body shaking slightly, a tremor beneath the skin, warmth and a slight petillance. She hardly dared to exhale. He stepped towards her and raised his other hand to her shoulder.

The night was still and silent, but within their bodies a powerful energy coursed, a whirling core of violence. It was a molecular hurricane which grew through their meeting lips in the hot moisture of their open mouths. He opened her coat, folding it about him, raising their clothes so that her breasts were free to press against his warm bare chest, and a scalding tingle began to scratch at her like thawing frostbite. As they lay down between the ridges of freezing hard earth, the fusion within their bodies heated their skin with a million stinging pinpricks.

Even before he had fully entered her, she experienced the most powerful sensation she had ever felt in her life, as if her molecular structure was somehow changing to accommodate a newly heightened emotional scale.

Each thrust of his body brought a fresh sparkling wave of forced growth within her. Exhilarated, she wanted to scream into the sky, to spiral up through clouds into the bitter ether, to strip away the shell of her body and be born into a new shape, to look down at the frozen azure planet in the benign radiance of his embrace, never to descend.

She had not realised she was crying until he wiped her cheek. As the cold night closed in around them, he carefully rebuttoned her coat and helped her from the ground. He looked every bit as shocked as she imagined she did. They made their way back to the motel in silence, drained of emotion.

Her sleep was dark and dreamless, lost in the desolate void of the night sky. She awoke late, to the insistent tugging of her son. Denny in his superhero pyjamas, pulling at her and pointing at the door. 'Mum, there's someone knocking.'

She sat up, momentarily disorientated, and checked the room. The other side of the bed was empty. The pair of them were alone. 'José, is that you?' She pulled a T-shirt from the chair and slipped it over her head, rising from the mattress. No answer came from the hall. Crossing to the door, she slipped on the burglar chain and unlocked the door. José was standing outside with a tray of coffees. A bag of doughnuts hung from his mouth. She released the chain and allowed him in, removing the bag.

'Sorry,' he said, 'I couldn't carry them. Did you sleep well?'

She looped her arm around Denny, drawing him to her. 'Like a newborn child.'

'Good. We have a long day ahead.'

They ate breakfast and washed, prepared to leave. It was a little before nine, and the sky had grown over with a dense bracken of cloud. They were leaving the room, discussing the direction in which to head, when they heard running footsteps in the next corridor. Devery and another man appeared in the hall ahead of them, slowing to a walk.

'I don't want either of you to be foolish about this,' said Devery, raising his hands in a gesture of peace. 'I just want the institute to continue with your research and help you come to terms with this — gift.'

'I've already come to terms,' replied José, stepping ahead of her and the child. 'Leave us alone.'

'You know I can't do that. We're dealing with something we don't yet understand. It began as an extreme rarity, an aberration, but now seems to be proliferating. This is the most important discovery of the century, more important than the rights of any single individual.'

Devery and his sidekick had advanced until they were standing less than six feet from them in the narrow corridor. 'We have to understand what's happening, José, and we can't afford to have any loose cannons on deck. Your ability could well be altering the way you think. All kinds of psychoses could evolve. You can't look after yourself. Cheryl, you must see that there's no point in running away.'

'Then tell me you're not interested in the military potential of all this,' she said, lifting Denny and holding him to her.

'Obviously there's enormous military interest in something this extraordinary —' he raised his voice above their protestations '— as a peacekeeping initiative. And as an effective deterrent.'

'An assassination tool.'

'I wouldn't have put it like that.'

José glanced back at her, checking their position, and thought for a moment. 'I'll tell you what,' he said, raising his eyes to Devery's. 'If you want to take me back, you'll have to use force.'

Devery smiled. 'I am prepared for that eventuality.'

He waved his sidekick forward. The close-cropped, heavy-set young man was certainly no research scientist. His expression was blank as he advanced, like a brain-damaged boxer. Cheryl saw that José had removed his right glove. As Devery's soldier made a clumsy lunge, he slapped his palm hard against his opponent's throat, searing the nerves which caused muscular contractions and instantly closing the young man's windpipe. He fell to his knees with a bone-cracking thud, then toppled onto his back with his hands clawing at his shirt collar.

'Very impressive,' said Devery calmly, lifting a small military-issue revolver from the holster beneath his jacket. 'I'm glad to see that you still have such control over your ability. Sorry to use such a crude form of coercion, but you're too valuable to lose. We've yet to find someone else with your level of power. Let's go to the car now.'

He ushered them forward to the end of the corridor, towards the main staircase. As Devery pushed through the swing doors he walked straight into a pair of maids wheeling a trolley full of laundry. José needed no further opportunity. He shoved Devery hard in the chest, knocking his arm high. The director fell back against the trolley, which tipped over, causing the maids to shout in anger and surprise. As Cheryl ran past with the boy crying at her breast, José touched the sprawled body lightly on the forehead.

'I've put him to sleep. I don't know how long it will

last,' he said, rejoining them at the bottom of the stairs. He shepherded them through the lobby and into the car park, searching for Devery's vehicle.

The black Mercedes stood idling at the edge of the misty fields, the driver bent over the raised boot, rummaging around inside. José approached him from behind, running lightly forward across the tarmac, and seized his bare neck. Within seconds, the driver's body had shaken itself to the ground in an uncontrollable fit, and they were inside the automobile. José pulled out of the car park, tyres squealing on the wet drive, and quickly left the dual carriageway, taking them into the verdant maze of backroads that led into deep countryside.

'You used your credit card to pay for the room,' he said, looking over at her. 'They traced the location through their mainframe.'

'I won't be able to do that again,' she said, still trying to catch her breath. 'My bag's back in the corridor. There's some cash in my purse. That's all we have.'

'They won't give up,' he said quietly. 'If they've received a government sanction for the project, they have the entire military network at their disposal.'

'Then we'll have to hide well,' she said, removing a set of maps from the glove compartment and unfolding them.

3. FEELING

After that, they were more careful.

They avoided large towns and areas with military connections, always travelling at night, only using the backroads. José successfully managed to exchange the Mercedes through a dubious vehicle operator in Manchester, and received some cash to balance the trade-in. The little Renault had been sprayed a nondescript grey, and quickly became their second home.

In Scotland they found a lonely stone cottage at the foot of the Grampians, and took over the rental. Trapped by the weather in the three rooms of the little house, Denny grew bored and fractious until José purchased some books and a small portable television. The cottage was warm and secure, but they never dared to cease their vigil, always checking the winding road for strangers, always watching the sky for surveillance helicopters. Finally winter began to relinquish its icy grip on the hills, and the streams unfroze. Cheryl passed the time by writing up the events which led to their flight, and watched from the kitchen window as the countryside slowly returned to life.

'You don't suppose it's safe to go into town yet?' she asked José, who was seated with Denny finishing his supper.

'No, I don't,' he replied, 'and I thought we weren't going to discuss it in front of You-Know-Who.'

'He may as well get used to the idea. This is starting to feel like a life sentence.'

In bed that night they made love with a chemical intensity that modified itself through her pores, through the shifting fluid in their palms and mouths and genitals. With each passing day, José's abilities and his capacity to modulate them became subtler, more controlled. After, she watched his face in the strip of pale moonlight which fell across the bed and smiled. 'We should leave the country,' she said, half to herself. 'There must be somewhere we can go. Denny needs an education.'

'Do you miss your old life badly?' he asked.

'Not particularly. Things hadn't fallen into place before. Funny, I feel more settled now, just when nothing is. Do you miss anything?'

'From my old life? There was nothing to miss. My family moved from Madrid to England when I was two, but they were never comfortable here. When my mother died, my father returned home. You're right, we should leave England. The airport and port authorities will have our descriptions; we'll have to use an alternative method of travel. I have my passport with me. Will you be able to get hold of yours?'

'I think so.' She moved closer, resting her head on his shoulder. 'We could go to Germany. There are other people like you there. I have some distant relatives in Frankfurt — I'm the only one who knows about them. We'd be safe for a while. I could get the story published. Someone will have to investigate.'

'You think so?'

'I'm sure of it.'

'Then Germany's where we'll go. As soon as we can get hold of your passports.'

One day in March they drove into Aviemore, and she decided it was time to risk a call to Misha. Her friend was amazed and delighted to hear from her, but warned her not to return to London.

'There are all kinds of people looking for you here,' she explained. 'No mention of your disappearance in the papers, though, which seems odd. Your flat was burgled just after you left, really ransacked. Now there's a re-possession order on it. Two guys went to see Jack and demanded to know where you were, but he couldn't tell them anything. He came complaining to me. Honestly Cheryl, we've been worried sick about you.'

'Listen, Denny and I are fine,' she said, 'but we're going to need your help.'

'Hey, we sat next to each other at school, didn't we? You got me my flat. You know I'll do anything I can.'

'Good. Because this is going to be a tricky one.'

Through a complex system of drops and false forwarding-addresses, Cheryl was eventually able to collect everything she needed. The only major risk she took was closing her bank account from Aberdeen, but there was no way to trace her whereabouts beyond the city, and they were desperate for money with which to pay for their crossing. José befriended a man who owned boats moored near Peterhead, and arrangements were made to travel to the French Coast. On the day they were due to close up the cottage and make for the coast, Denny and José loaded the car while she rang Misha to say goodbye.

'I want to come and see you,' Misha said tearfully. 'I'm going to miss you and Denny so much.'

'I can't tell you where we're leaving from, you know that,' replied Cheryl. 'It would only put you in danger.'

'But nobody's asking about you anymore. Even the police have stopped calling me.'

'I can't, Misha. We're starting a new life as a family. I can't afford to jeopardise that.'

'Couldn't I come with you?'

'It's hard enough for the three of us to travel together ...'

'You're never coming back. I know.' There was a sad silence. 'I want to see you, Cheryl. You're my only family. I hate to say this, but you owe me. I nursed your poor father and you said —'

'I know, I would always be there for you, but can't you see that this is different?' She looked out of the window. Denny was trying to push a tube bag filled with his toys into the back seat of the car.

'No, it's not different. I really need this, Cheryl.'

She thought for a moment. The boat was leaving late tonight to catch the tide. If Misha could be there an hour before midnight there would be no time for anyone to follow her. 'All right,' she agreed against her better judgement. She could not spell out the exact location in case Misha's phone was tapped. 'My father had to break off his honeymoon because he was sent to cover a big bribery scandal. Do you remember the name of the town where they sent him?

'Yes, of course.'

'The dock is six miles North of there, two words, same initials as the name of your ex-boss at Griffins.'

'I've got it —'

'Don't say it. I'll wait on the quay for exactly ten minutes, no more, do you understand?'

'I understand. Thank you.'

José was calling to her. The car's engine was running, and Denny was waving from the back seat. She knew better than to mention what she had done, and prayed that no harm would come of it.

The coast was bleak and forbidding, wreathed in mist, the sea as still and grey as a corpse. A beam from the unmanned lighthouse further along the coast scanned the distant gloom. At the edge of the shingle beach, four small boats were moored from a concrete jetty. José explained that they always made the crossing in a flotilla, as the frequent bad weather could place a single boat in jeopardy.

There was a small café near the boathouse where fishermen and workers from the nearby engine repair shop sat with whisky and tea, and the three of them went there to wait. The old woman behind the counter made a fuss over Denny while she and José talked with the seamen, whose clandestine attitude suggested that smuggling was behind the flotilla's frequent irregular trips.

10.50 p.m. She checked her watch, then slipped her hand into José's, an electric tingle filling and warming her arm all the way to her shoulder. He had allowed that to happen. José rarely wore the gloves now. Maintaining control had become an automatic reflex for him. She leaned over and whispered in his ear. 'I'm going outside for some air. I won't be long.'

'I'll come with you.'

She looked across at Denny, being patted on the head and offered chocolate biscuits. 'All right.'

They walked down to the shoreline arm in arm and watched the lighthouse beam flaring through the mist. 'Every day I'm surprised that I can love someone as much as I love you,' she said. 'I thought I'd used up that capacity. Had it spoiled for me by other people.'

'I always want to be with you,' he said softly. 'You're the one who gives me strength, not this.' He raised his hand.

'Then that's how it will always be. Wherever we decide to go in the world.'

As they kissed, she heard the faint sound of a car arriving. 'Let's walk back. Don't be angry with me. We have a surprise guest.'

He looked at her in puzzlement. 'What do you mean?'

'Misha wanted so much to say goodbye. I've known her all my life and I may never see her again, so I said she could come up and —'

'You did *what*?' he shouted suddenly, frightening her. In the next moment he was off, dashing across the shingle in the direction of the café.

Even before she had managed to catch up with him, she knew that something terrible had happened. The seamen had vacated the room, and the door was standing wide open, warm air bleeding into the night.

'Denny!'

The boy had gone. The café was deserted. The chair where he had been sitting lay on its side. She ran back out, around to the front of the building. José was standing very still, his back turned towards her. In front of him stood Devery, holding the boy tightly in his arms.

'Good evening,' he said, his tone calm and measured. 'It looks as if I just made it in time. I'm afraid your skipper's taken off. I mentioned the possibility of him carrying

90

contraband cargo and he changed colour.'

'If you hurt the boy I'll see you dead,' said José.

'That won't be necessary as long as you co-operate. Get in the car.'

'Where's Misha?' she asked. 'What have you done with her?

'She's under detention. Official Secrets Act, I'm afraid. You must have known that we'd be monitoring her phoneline. It was embarrassingly easy to work out where you were. Your father was a famous reporter. The stories he filed are catalogued quite thoroughly. Into the car now. We have a long drive ahead.'

She could see a figure seated at the wheel, the driver José had disabled at the motel, waiting for them to enter. Devery held the boy high in front of him like a shield as she passed.

José outstretched his hands. 'Give me the boy first.'

'Not until you're both inside.'

Reluctantly, she climbed into the back seat. José turned to face the car door, waiting for her to slide across. As he bent down to enter, he raised his right leg and kicked back hard, catching Devery in the genitals. As he fell backwards José pulled the boy free and threw him into the car. The driver jumped him from behind, his hands clasped over José's throat. Moments later he began screaming as the enzymatic change took hold of his system, and he dropped to the ground, blood gushing from his nose.

Devery had risen to one knee, the revolver in his hand. 'This time you're not getting out,' he said, his breath ragged, 'no more running away.'

José walked slowly towards him. He had only another yard to go when Devery fired, the blast punching a hole into his chest and knocking him off his feet. Cheryl screamed, hurling herself from the car, slamming Denny back inside. José lay on his back in pained surprise, his hand rising to the gaping wound which was pumping dark fluid across his chest.

'You don't need to be kept alive any more,' said Devery, rising to his feet. 'We can still experiment on you when you're dead. Now there are others just as powerful as you.'

She felt hot blood rising in her face, her neck and shoulders, an anger denser than any she had felt before as she hurled herself at the surprised institute director, her hands slapping hard against the sides of his face. He tried to break her grip, but the heat from her fingers began to blister his skin. As Devery started to scream, his nose poured black blood and his cheeks split open, exposing muscles and gums.

The gun fell from his hands as she pressed harder still. She could hear the blood rushing and popping in his veins as its temperature was raised to boiling point, felt the bones beneath her fingers start to disintegrate as Devery's body ruptured in a thousand places, destroying itself from within. Unable to contain the volatile fluids which coursed within it, his skin burst apart like an overripe plum, meat and liquid spilling in every direction from his collapsing shell. She turned away from the exploded body, sickened, the heat from her hands vaporising in the night air.

José was on his back, breathing in short, shallow gasps.

'You'll be all right.' She knelt at his side, cradling his head. 'I'll get help.'

'No, not all right.' His skin was frosted with icy sweat. The wound was too deep, too close to his heart. One look was enough to tell her that.

'You gave the touch to me,' she said softly. 'That's how it spreads. Through love.'

'I'm sorry.'

'I'm not. I might never have known I had it.' She stroked his face gently. 'I guess it just took a lot to make me angry.'

'Find the others. Go to Germany.' As he tried to raise his head, blood began to pool in his mouth.

She was crying, unable to think, losing him fast. 'I don't want to live without you.'

'Live for your son.' He focussed his eyes on hers. 'Touch me.'

As their lips met, his blood tingled on her skin like bitter alcohol. The sensation faded, taking away his life.

While she nursed the sleeping boy, two of the returning seamen buried José's body beneath the shingle. They refused to touch Devery and his driver, not that there was much of the director left to bury. There was still time for the flotilla to sail with the tide. The skipper, shamed by his earlier cowardice, sat silently on board.

She stood at the end of the quay with Denny at her side, the now familiar tingle filling her body and warming the palms of her hands. She had watched him as he learned to control his power. She could learn to do the same. She would write up the story and find a way to get it published.

'What's happened to José?' asked the boy. 'Isn't he coming with us?'

'He has to stay behind,' she said, taking the child's hand. 'But don't worry. In a way he'll be wherever we go. He's given us something wonderful.'

Ahead, the boats waited patiently on the sleeping grey sea.

Last Call For Passenger Paul

Passport. Tickets. Washbag. Walkman. Cassettes. Batteries ... no, no batteries. Paul pushed everything back into his flight bag and headed for the airport stationery shop, threading his way between hordes of holidaymakers and pyramids of suitcases. He'd need at least four Duracells for the trip. The ones in his Walkman were dead. He entered the stationery shop, passing racks of brightly-coloured trashy paperbacks, teatowels decorated with scenes of Buckingham Palace and St Paul's Cathedral, headsquares and cuddly toys. Outside, the public address system boomed loud and indistinct. Paul pulled a pack of batteries from the stand and paid for them with the last of his English money.

It was early August, and Heathrow airport was a scene of total chaos. Frazzled check-in clerks dealt patiently with mislaid tickets and last-minute arrivals, while passengers complained about missed connections and missing baggage. Queues extended across every concourse. Moslems unrolled prayermats in the corners and children chased each other around video machines and parents lay stretched out asleep on benches and in chairs, oblivious to the announcements detailing further delays and more cancellations.

Paul hitched his flight bag further onto his shoulder and aimed himself at the upstairs restaurant, past a congregation of confused nuns and a group of fifty elderly American tourists, each one neatly nametagged, all standing in the middle of the floor waiting to be told what to do next.

The restaurant was no quieter. There were no seats to be found, and tiny Pakistani ladies dragged vast green

97

plastic sacks from table to table, attempting to keep pace with mounting stacks of dirty crockery. Paul stood his bag down in a corner and fitted the batteries into his personal stereo. At twenty-eight, he was pretty much an old hand at dealing with crowded airports. His job as a CBS record executive saw to that, regularly requiring him to board the transatlantic flights for Chicago, Los Angeles and New York. This trip, however, was purely for pleasure. The last six months had been hellishly hectic, culminating two nights ago in a spectacular launch party from which Paul was still feeling the effects. Now he was preparing to board the next flight to Larnaca, Cyprus for two weeks of well-earned R&R.

Adjusting the volume on his Walkman, Paul walked through passport control and into the passenger lounge to await the arrival of his flight. On the column ahead of him the screens announced the first call for Cyprus. Paul decided to wait until the actual departure time was closer before heading for the gate. He sat back in the chair and closed his eyes for a moment, letting the music surround him completely. After working with rock bands every day of the week, he found his own tastes straying to Beethoven and Mozart in his leisure hours.

The voice on the PA system announcing the final call for flight 203 to Larnaca brought him back from Mozart's *Marriage of Figaro* with a start. Paul swung his bag back up on his shoulder, ran a hand through his cropped blond hair and made his way to the gate.

The flight was full, mostly with holidaymakers of the worst kind, it seemed. He leaned on the counter while the check-in girl stamped a boarding pass and handed it to him. Just as he thanked her and moved off, she called him back.

'Sorry, sir,' she smiled. 'You'll be needing this.' She pressed a small blue sticker onto his ticket and returned it. Paul looked at the sticker, which had a tiny figure printed on it. The ink had blurred, but it appeared to be a man riding on the back of another — St Christopher, perhaps? It was either a new computer symbol, or the airline had turned religious.

He hung back until the last passenger had moved out into the corridor before handing in his boarding pass. As he made his way onto the Tristar, he fingered the control button of his Walkman nervously. Actual flying did not bother him — taking off and landing did.

As soon as he had located his seat, he secured the belt in his lap, refastened his earphones and lay back. He planned to stay that way until they were in the air. There was an elderly man of presumably Turkish origin in the seat next to him, happily emptying the contents of a holdall into both his seat pocket and Paul's, oblivious to the revving engines outside. Paul shut his eyes and kept them that way until they were safely off the ground.

The first thing Paul saw from the window when he finally opened his eyes was Windsor Castle, far below and briefly glimpsed through racing clouds. He turned from the scuffed plastic porthole and looked around. The palms of his hands were slick with sweat. As the cabin levelled out and the seatbelt sign was turned off, he released the back of his chair, kicked off his trackshoes and began to relax. Two weeks away from the office with nothing to do except lie in the sun — it seemed too good to be true. He had been careful to tell no one where he could be reached. He knew only too well how likely it was that he would be called back to deal with a crisis otherwise.

A stewardess arrived with the drinks trolley, and Paul requested a gin and tonic, watching while the girl — tall and tanned, with strong white teeth — continued smiling as she filled the glass. The elderly Turk in the seat next to him had presumably become bored with rummaging around in the seat pockets and was already comatose, remaining so until woken for his meal. Paul ate and drank with a hearty appetite. After idly thumbing through the in-flight magazine as he sipped his brandy, he turned to stare out at the motionless azure sky and his eyelids began to fall. By the time the stewardess quietly slipped his meal tray away and folded his seat flap up, he was lost in a deep and dreamless sleep.

The first thing Paul became aware of upon awakening was the heat, even before he felt the hand shaking him. The steward's face swam before his eyes.

'Sir, wake up, sir, time to get off. All the other passengers have disembarked.'

Paul blinked and rubbed his eyes, then pulled the earphones from his head. The air in the cabin was stiflingly hot. He sat up and stared about at the empty seats surrounding him. Up ahead, two stewardesses stood by the galley entrance talking as the last of the passengers threaded their way through the exit door.

'Boy, I was out cold,' Paul said to the steward, smiling. His mouth felt hot and dry, the after-effect of drinking in an air-conditioned atmosphere. The heat surprised him. Already he could feel sweat forming between his shoulder-blades.

'Don't forget your hand luggage, sir,' said the steward, moving off.

Paul pulled his bag from beneath the seat and stood up. The cabin was empty now except for the crew. He checked his seat to make sure that he had not left anything behind, then stooped and peered out of the window. A large white concrete terminal, arched with the architecture of a harem, stood at the end of the blurred, dusty airstrip. Somehow, Paul had expected Cyprus to be prettier at first sight than this. He made his way down the aisle to the exit door, where a smiling stewardess waited to bid him farewell.

'We look forward to seeing you again soon, sir,' she said. 'Have a pleasant stay in Amman.'

He had almost passed through the doorway before he realised what the stewardess had said, and turned back to her, puzzled.

'Where?' he asked.

'Amman, sir,' said the stewardess, her smile fading as she realised something was wrong.

'This isn't Cyprus?'

'No, sir. We left Cyprus over an hour and a half ago.'

'Oh my God, I was supposed to get off there,' said Paul. 'Why didn't someone wake me?'

'I'll get the cabin director, sir, if you'll hold on for a moment.'

A tall, square-jawed man in a crisply cut blazer came over. 'What seems to be the problem?' he asked, in a deep, relaxed voice.

'I've gone past my stop,' said Paul, aware that he sounded like someone addressing a bus conductor. Just then, the stewardess who had served Paul his meal came over.

'I didn't wake this gentleman up because I thought Amman was his final destination,' she told the cabin director.

'Did you look at his boarding card?'

'Yes, it was in the seat pocket in front of him.'

'That wasn't mine,' explained Paul, producing his own. 'It must have belonged to the guy sitting next to me.'

'We were on the ground for over an hour,' said the cabin director, turning to the embarrassed-looking stewardess. 'Didn't you think to check?'

'I'm sorry, a lot of people were staying on. I had my hands full.'

'I'm afraid you'll have to sort this out in the terminal,' said the cabin director apologetically. 'It shouldn't take long to get you back to Cyprus. In fact, I think there's a flight later on this afternoon.' Paul sighed and hitched up his flight bag. He couldn't believe how dumb he could be, falling asleep like that. Outside, the temperature was astounding. Before he could reach the terminal building, his face was popping with beads of sweat, and the strap of his bag was leaving a wet bar of heat across his right shoulderblade. The vast white strip of concrete over which he walked glared up at him. Where the hell was Amman? He had a vague recollection that it was somewhere in Jordan. Was it safe here? Jesus, what a way to start a vacation!

Inside the terminal it was fresh and cool. He explained what had happened to the woman on the desk, who happened to be English and therefore quite amused by the situation, much to Paul's annoyance.

'Oh, it happens all the time, sir,' she said after checking his ticket and examining the small blue sticker. 'We often have people disembarking too early, grandads getting off at Singapore when they're supposed to stay on until Australia. It's just like the buses. We're always leaving passengers in strange places because the flights are full. And where their *luggage* turns up is nobody's business.'

Paul failed to see the amusement in this. 'Well, when can I get back to Cyprus?' he asked, already suspecting that he knew the answer. The concourse behind him was disturbingly free of passengers.

'That's the trouble, sir. Our direct flight to Larnaca has been cancelled today because of an aircraft fault.' Her smile was extremely apologetic.

'Does that mean I just have to hang around the airport until it gets fixed?' asked Paul with mounting irritation.

'Well, let's see.' The counter clerk consulted her timetable. She looked like a holiday courier, heavily tanned, with auburn hair swept back in a ponytail. 'What we could do is transfer you to an airline which does have a flight going out this afternoon. How about that?'

'Fine, fine,' agreed Paul. 'I just want to get there before nightfall.'

The clerk dutifully transferred his ticket to a local

airline, and arranged for his luggage to be forwarded.

So it was that, two hours later, Paul found himself boarding an Alia flight filled with Jordanian businessmen.

At the entrance to the aircraft, the stewardess checked his ticket and directed him to a business class seat. Obviously he had been upgraded in order to recompense in part for the inconvenience of having to switch airlines. Paul felt uncomfortable in these unfamiliar surroundings. As the plane reached its cruising altitude he found it impossible to concentrate on the pages of his paperback, and instead donned the earphones of his Walkman to relax with a soothing symphony. When he became aware of a voice speaking in a foreign tongue above the sound of the music, he turned down the volume on the Walkman to listen. Unfortunately, the announcement was not repeated in English, so he summoned a stewardess.

'What was that last message?' he asked.

'Owing to a problem at Larnaca airport we are having to put down in Adana,' said the stewardess. And then, in a lower tone, she confided 'I think they are bringing the hostages in to Larnaca. No other planes can come in or out for several hours.'

'Thank you, but where the hell is Adana?'

'It's in Turkey, near the coast.'

'Great, just great.' Paul was beginning to wonder if he would ever reach his destination. The papers had been full of news about the hostages for the last few days. They had been expected to be released at any moment, but they could not have picked a worse time, he thought uncharitably.

Adana turned out to have an even hotter and dustier airstrip than Amman. Its terminal building was old and filthy and crowded with the most extraordinary people. Despite reassurances from the Alia stewardess that his luggage would be forwarded, Paul doubted that it would ever find its way out of the airport, since it was quite obvious that no one here spoke any English.

Once inside, he fought his way over to the nearest flight desk and attempted to make himself understood to the clerk. By now he was hot, tired and angry, his sour shirt sticking to his back. The clerk, in hopelessly fractured English, attempted to placate him. Eventually Paul went to sit with the others from his flight on a long wooden bench by one of the gates. The terminal was packed. There were old men in shawls asleep on the floor, and tired women clutching huge bundles of clothing, and at one point a mange-ridden mongrel hobbled over to where Paul sat and peed against his flight bag.

After he had rinsed off some of the sweat and changed into a crumpled but fresh T-shirt in the washroom, he returned to his seat to find his fellow passengers swarming through two gates onto a pair of newly arrived planes.

The mad scramble for seats was alarming. Paul tried to gain the attention of one of the passing passengers, a woman he had seen on his previous flight. He waved his ticket before her in a desperate effort to attract her assistance. She was obviously torn between helping him and rushing onto the flight herself.

'Larnaca?' he shouted above the babble of the tannoy. 'Larnaca airport is open again, yes?'

The woman stared at his ticket, with the little blue sticker fixed to its corner, and suddenly seemed to comprehend. 'Yes!' she cried. 'You want Larnaca, next gate, hurry, now!'

'Thank you! Thank you very much!' Paul grabbed her arm gratefully, but the woman pulled away in alarm. Quickly he made his way over to the second of the gates and held his ticket before the man at the door. Around them swarmed girls with wicker baskets, ancient men with their belongings bundled into sacks, and children of every size and description. There seemed to be nobody issuing boarding passes. The man at the door glanced at the ticket, then nodded and waved Paul through and onto the aircraft.

He hadn't had a chance to look at the outside of the plane, but inside, the cabin seemed narrow and cramped. Paul found himself without a seat allocation, and after failing to reach either of the stewardesses, seated himself next to a fat Turkish woman bouncing a child on her knee. There seemed to be a 'first come, first served' policy regarding the seating arrangements.

Eventually the cabin doors were closed, the stewardesses managed to find everyone a seat, and the plane jiggled along the runway in the direction of the afternoon sun. If Paul had been nervous about taking off before, this time he was petrified. The overhead lockers creaked and juddered as the aircraft revealed its stress points in the airstreams of the sky. Children began crying and old men wandered from their seats, attempting to light their pipes until the stewardesses insisted on extinguishing them.

Paul slumped back in the uncomfortable seat and plugged into his Walkman once more in an effort to shut out the surrounding noise of the children playing in the aisles. He wanted to ask someone how long the flight would take, but was loath to become involved in a linguistic wrestling match with any of his fellow travellers. He was seated in an aisle seat this time, in an area which may or may not have been designated as a smoking zone for all the notice anyone was taking around him. As he tried to let the music blot out all other sounds, he imagined the problem of relocating his luggage, and was glad that he had not packed anything of value.

Beyond the cabin window afternoon was slowly turning into evening, and the sky was filled with heliocentric hues. The edges of the scudding clouds were flashed with red and purple as, far below, the sea glittered with dying light. There was nothing to do now but wait.

✳

105

The aircraft was approaching the runway below at an alarming angle. On both sides of the cabin people were craning out of their windows to see the airport terminal. When Paul managed to locate it, his stomach dropped. This could not be Larnaca. Against the dusty orange walls of the low concrete building ahead lounged two armed policemen. In the distance stood a truck, filled with what looked like goats, and further afield the lights of a small town twinkled against low velvet hills. As the plane taxied to a standstill, he read the cracked sign along the wall of the airstrip.

Ajdabiquh.

They had landed in North Africa. There could be no other explanation. This time Paul contained his rage until he was inside the terminal building, threw his bag onto the counter of the first official he could locate and demanded to know what was going on. The official, a young customs clerk, spoke no English, and after five minutes of shrugging and face-pulling, went to fetch his superior. He returned with a broad, heavy-set African wearing flamboyant gold insignia.

'Do you speak English?'

'Certainly, sir. Now what seems to be the trouble?'

'I've just arrived on this flight ...' Paul indicated the candy-striped aircraft standing on the runway outside, 'and I was told that our destination was Larnaca.'

'Well, whoever told you that was wrong, sir,' said the senior official in a simple, placating tone. He looked at the sweating young man with interest.

'Is there any way that I can get back to Larnaca tonight?' asked Paul. He wiped his forehead with an unsteady hand, refusing to let his paranoia rise to the surface.

'I don't know about that, sir. We have no scheduled flights going there from here ...'

'Here being where?'

'This is Libya, sir.'

'So how am I going to get back?' he demanded, panic creeping into his voice. Outside, darkness had fallen, and the runway lights had come on.

'Can I see your ticket for a moment, sir?' The senior official reached out a broad pink palm. Why not? thought Paul. Everybody else has, and handed it to him.

The two men behind the counter examined Paul's ticket closely. The young clerk pointed to the corner of the ticket and said something to his superior, who slowly nodded his head in agreement.

'I think we may be able to help you,' he said as he returned the ticket. Paul found himself following the two men through the sand-blown terminal towards one of the far exit doors. He had to virtually run to keep pace with them as they chattered on in their native tongue, completely ignoring him. Paul's sole consolation, he told himself, was that he was seeing places he would never otherwise see. And, he mentally added, they were places he'd never bother trying to see again.

The outside of the terminal building was lit with grey tin lights which swung crazily in the warm night breeze. Here, on a low bench along a wall, were four other travellers, one of whom appeared to be of European extraction. The senior official pointed to a smartly suited pilot who was crossing the tarmac from a small passenger plane.

'He is a charter pilot. He will take you to your correct destination,' said the senior official. 'These other people have been misrouted as well. You should be in Larnaca before midnight. I am sorry you have had such a bad journey.'

'Me too, but thanks for your help, at least,' said Paul. 'I thought I was never going to find anyone who spoke English. Are you sure this pilot knows where he's going?'

'Don't worry, he knows. This sort of thing happens all the time. Enjoy your trip.' He turned to explain what he had just said to the junior clerk, who let out a snort of laughter.

107

The pilot walked along past the bench to Paul, took his ticket from his hand, checked the destination and returned it. The officials re-entered the terminal, leaving Paul and the other four passengers alone outside. The pilot beckoned them forward, and they crossed the tarmac to the steps of the plane. Paul manoeuvred himself so that he was walking by the middle-aged white man he had seen on the bench, and took the opportunity of introducing himself. The man turned out to be a French businessman named Bernard. He spoke a fractured form of English, and was able to explain to Paul as they climbed the aircraft steps that he too had been redirected, and had boarded his flight in Paris at nine-thirty that morning.

Paul was relieved to find a kindred spirit, and decided to sit next to him for the flight. Inside the aircraft, which Paul reckoned would have seated about thirty people, there was no stewardess to be seen. He pushed his flight bag under the seat and sat down by the Frenchman. Within moments, the co-pilot closed the cabin door, the engines revved, and the plane shot up into the night sky, circling the airport once before heading south.

'This cannot be right,' said Bernard. 'We are heading in the wrong direction. We should be going north.' He peered from the window into the blackness beyond.

'You mean Cyprus is to the north?' asked Paul, sensing that something strange was going on. Behind them, the three other passengers were peering from the windows.

'Cyprus?' said Bernard. 'You mean Athens.'

'What?' Paul's eyes widened. He could not believe his ears. 'We're not going to Larnaca?'

'Not to my knowledge. I am supposed to be in Athens. I thought this was where we were heading, but we are going south. Look.' He drew out his travel folder and opened it to reveal a small map of central Europe and Africa.

'Here, the airport we just left faces north, but we took

108

off to the south. We are heading down into Chad.'

'This can't be happening,' said Paul shakily. 'Let me see your ticket.' Bernard pulled out his ticket and handed it across. There in the corner was the same square blue sticker that was affixed to Paul's.

'Do you know what this means?' he asked, pointing to the sticker.

'No, I have no idea.'

Paul examined it closely under his seat light. It definitely showed two men, one of whom appeared to be seated on the other's shoulders. He passed the ticket back and stared helplessly out of the window as the aircraft buzzed on through the cloudless night.

Paul looked at his watch. It read a quarter to twelve. The plane had just come to a stop. Beyond the runway lights, nothing could be seen. The other passengers were looking from one window to another, confused. One of them, a young black girl, was crying. Paul walked back to her seat and took the ticket from her hand. It too had a blue sticker on it.

'What the hell is going on here?' he shouted as the main cabin door suddenly opened from the outside with a dull bang. Grabbing his flight bag from beneath the seat, Paul strode to the front of the plane and trotted down the floodlit steps. The ground beneath his trackshoes was not tarmac, but earth. Beyond the perimeter lights marking the airstrip, there was nothing. Passing in front of the aircraft, Paul spotted a squat, dimly lit building ahead, the only one on an unbroken desert horizon.

'Come on!' he turned and called to the others, but nobody appeared in the cabin doorway. Why were they so reluctant to leave the plane?

As Paul headed towards what he presumed was the terminal building, the cool desert air ruffled his hair and calmed him slightly. He heaved the flight bag back onto

109

his shoulder, and paused to toss the dead batteries from his Walkman into the long grass which rustled drily several feet from the runway.

A hundred yards from the terminal, he realised with mounting horror that it had been completely burnt out. Bats flitted around the cracked bones of rafters which could be seen against open sky through its huge windows. And yet there were moving lights inside. Paul redoubled his pace.

He reached the entry door, which was ajar, and looked back at the plane. One of the remaining passengers was standing in the cabin doorway, hesitating before descending the steps. Turning back to the terminal door, he reached forward and pulled it open.

The building was just a concrete shell. Several fires burned on the remains of the tiled floor. Groups of men stood clustered around the fires, drinking and laughing. They were dressed in brown ragged cloaks, as if part of a tribe of desert nomads. Against the far wall, just beyond the largest fire of all, the flickering light revealed a sight which made Paul reel.

On a long wooden pole attached to the wall, several bodies hung by their feet. They were naked, and each one had been slit from waist to chin. Beneath their heads the ground was caked with dry brown blood. Paul stumbled back against the door, which banged against the wall and startled the men before him to attention.

There were cries of delight around the gutted room, and several of the men rushed forward to seize Paul's arms. Two of them pulled his flight bag away and tore it open, as the others propelled him across the floor towards the far wall. It was then that Paul noticed that the brown cloaks worn by the tribe members were made of human skin.

One of the tribe, a large, grinning man with gold teeth, revealed a long, hooked knife in his waistband. As Paul

110

shouted, the men holding him ripped the shirt from his back and threw him to the floor.

Before him, painted on the wall ahead, was a huge blue square, a grand version of the sticker attached to his plane ticket. It depicted a man not carrying another on his shoulders but someone donning the complete skin of another human being. The man with the gold teeth advanced towards Paul with the glittering culling knife in his hand.

'Why?' screamed Paul. 'Why me?'

Gold-Teeth leaned forward until Paul's sweat-sheened face was right beneath him.

'Your airline owes us for our land,' he hissed, then turned and called to the elders of the tribe. 'See! Nice blond boy, soft white skin make very special coat!' Gold teeth smiled spectacularly and nodded to the men surrounding Paul. They fell on him as the elders started the bidding.

They never did figure out what the Walkman was for.

The Legend of Dracula
Reconsidered As A Prime-Time TV Special

JOURNAL OF J.H.

16 July — NYC

I figured with a name like mine it was the best thing to do, kind of like an omen, y'know? I started it while I was at school — just about the only thing I *did* start at school apart from a fuckin' fight. I got maybe seventy, seventy-five pages finished before they threw me out. Most of the guys in my year were taking advanced business studies, high-risk trading in non-government approved chemicals, how to improve your yield by cutting your shit with powdered laxative. Lemme tell you, I stayed out of *that* stuff 'cause I'm a white boy and I just don't got the connections. So if I didn't live down to the neighborhood expectations, sue me — I walked outta school with bigger plans.

I wanted — I *want* — to write. I knew that much when I was five. Not classical stuff, 'cause let's face it a guy like me ain't ever gonna get to college given the fact that if my Ma ever got hold of enough money without turning tricks or robbing a bank, only the latter of which is unlikely, she'd blow it on a trip to Vegas to see Wayne Newton before she turned it over to me. So I figure I have to do it the other way around, which is write something first then sell it to the Big Boys. And hence the thing about my name, which is Harker, John Harker like the guy in *Dracula*, which gives me what to write about.

See, a guy with a pothole in his head can figure out the future is in media. You got more leisure time, you got more technological hoozis to play with, satellites and hi-definition and sixty 'leven channels, you're gonna need more programming to put out on the air. These network

115

guys are strip-mining the past for black-and-white sitcoms no one watched the first time around 'cause they were so crummy, anything they can slam out into the ether, build themselves some ratings and get a station profile, get advertisers knocking at their door with thirty-second spots for haemorrhoid ointment, and a guy like me, written off in the third grade as one of the Future Losers of America, stands a real chance of selling them something. First a pilot, then a series, then ninety-eight shows stripped weeknights coast to coast, bouncing off into space for the rest of eternity. Immortality, man. Immortality.

But first things first. I just finished writin' a sure-fire script, a new version of *The Legend Of Dracula* told from my viewpoint, John Harker's angle on the battle with the Lord of the Undead, and let me explain here that this script cost me on account of I got caught writing it in the store and they threw me out, so as of today I got no job.

Which means, according to this Self Help book I'm readin', it's time to take stock of myself.

I got my health, my height and my happiness (if a lifestyle scenario which excludes fun, sex and money can be called that). I got an apartment in Queens. I'm renting with these two guys who're never home, but findin' the rent keeps me working my butt off half the night at the store, only now I don't have that job.

So I'll get another, no big deal, and meanwhile it allows me the time to go through the phonebook calling the networks to find out who's the big cheese in each organisation that I can send my script to. The script's a second draft for a feature-length TV movie, but it's all there, they can make out what it's about, so I outlay a fucking grotesque amount of money on photocopying and postage and send off twenty-three separate envelopes in the Manhattan area.

And then I sit back and wait.

Which is what I'm doin' now.

116

9 August – NYC

A guy can die from waiting.

After sending those packets I'm really glad I didn't splash out on a radiopager 'cause to be absolutely frank my phone has not been ringing off the wall. At first I think maybe they don't like the subject matter, it's kind of ghoulish although there is what you'd call a subtext on the human condition, and the subtext is the reason for doing it.

I mean Dracula's been done to death, backwards, forwards, male, female, black, white, straight, gay, musical, comedy, soap, kid's stuff, and every version available on tape, CD, LP, VHS or Beta. See, I got this theory. Times have changed; we don't die in the bosom of the family no more, we die in the arms of efficient strangers. It's 'cause we've become scared of death. And the more scared we get, the more sanitised we make the process of decay, the more we sugar up the Dracula legend to give us a palatable handle on dying.

So Dracula's been turned into some kind of upscale Eurotrash salesman, and he's everywhere, soft drinks, breakfast cereal, you name it. New York has vampires up the wazoo, but the Undead have been totally emasculated. They're clowns now, an' that sure takes the sting out of death.

So my script, my own *Legend Of Dracula*, puts that life-draining shock of mortality back where it should be. It returns physical gravity to the material, provides us with a fear of death so real and deep and strong that we have to embrace it, and through catharsis allow it to exist in our lives once more.

Listen to me, I'm sitting on the john thinking my script is gonna change the fucking world and the truth is I can't get a network executive to read it. Not one reply so far, can you *believe* that?

Time for me to shit or get off the pot. So I ring around,

try and get to speak to these guys.

Now, I ain't so naive to think I can just zip through the chain of command and reach Mr Key-Decision-Maker straight off the bat, but I figure that sending out the script gives me a talking point, an edge even, and out of twenty-three packages one must have eventually landed on the right desk. I start at the top of the list an' I call each one: NBC, ABC, CBS, HBO, Ted Turner, Cable, and not only can I not reach the busy-busy PA bitches with the English accents, I cannot get beyond the fucking switchboards of these places.

I presume my script reached one of your readers, I hear myself saying, to which some girl wearing a plastic headset asks me if it was a solicited manuscript, and if it wasn't can I come and collect it 'cause they don't get returned no more on account of so many being received and cluttering up the place.

I just thought I'd start at the top. Start with the Big Guns, y'know? I never really expected it to get picked up at that stage. Time to move down the list to the smaller independent companies, people who handle specialist material. No need for somethin' like this to have big names in; it's the idea that counts. I sit and compile a new list and do the same thing again with the photocopies and the mailings, 'cause if I give this up I sure as hell ain't got anything else to look forward to. Only it used up all my money, and I'm still lookin' for a job. So I go to see Frankie at the AcuPak Night Storage way down on 3rd, but it don't pan out. I thought you said you'd always have a job for me, Frankie, I say, but he grinds his cigarette on the floor of the stockroom and looks dumbly at me. Everywhere's cuttin' back, John, he replies. There's a recession on, ain't you heard?

Yeah, I heard all right. Which is why I just left Queens for this unairconditioned shithole apartment on Bleeker that's cheap on account of the guy who owns it is a total

burned-out fuckup and his lover needs someone there to
keep a watch on him and stop him from sticking stuff in
his arms every chance he gets. So now each night I have to
close the bedroom door to block out the sound of Tina
Turner singing *Break Every Rule* for the four millionth time
before I can concentrate on getting the script out. This
time I will get it to the right people.

I have faith.

Probably 'cause that's all I have.

20 September — NYC

What is it about Robert De Niro's name? I cannot *believe*
this shit. Once again, no replies through the mail but then
I can't be sure if Mr Manic Depressive Disco-Dolly don't
reach the mailbox before me and set fire to the post. (I
empty uppers and downers out the bathroom cabinet as
fast as he puts 'em in, but I can't always be sure what he's
taking 'cause he lies about it. Right now he's dancing
around in the next room to some old Diana Ross album.
He's not happy — it's a high. It's 11.00 a.m. By my
estimation he's peaking about twelve hours too early.)

This time I figure why wait longer and start calling
around almost immediately, and now I get a new kind of
standard reply. I mean, it's obvious that small TV
companies can't afford a fancy Upper East Side address,
but just because De Niro put TriBeCa Films in a street full
of warehouses don't mean every two-bit TV exec in town
should evoke his name like a fucking talisman. Well, they
say, we're small but we're very selective, situated near
Bobby (Get this, *Bobby* De Niro, as if the exec goes over his
place for cocktails) De Niro's place.

I'm thinking listen, you could be workin' out of eastern
Turkey for all I care so long as you read the goddamn
script, and *this* is the crunch — for all the talk they give out,

usually about themselves and the saintlike regard the industry has for them, for all the smooth dialogue it emerges that none of them, not one, has read the damned thing. There's too much stuff coming in all the time. Too much loose paper around. Every dickhead with a desktop and an hour on his hands thinks he's got a script inside.

An' you know, maybe that includes me, but I still have faith in the script. That's what I tell myself as I type out the 'C' list and set about borrowing more postage money. My name is John Harker and I was born to battle the Prince of Darkness. And that's what I'm gonna do.

27 September — NYC

Well, the Disco Diva took a dive.

Yes, my room-mate managed to set fire to himself while enjoying the intoxicatin' effects of several noxious substances, which means he's in the hospital and I'm out of my watchdog job and out on the street. I think his lover was more pissed that the sound system got burned up than anything else. I don't even have the money to phone around the networks, 'cause these companies keep you on callwaiting systems for fuckin' hours, so I just did something I said I was never gonna do and that was, I sold a pint of blood. Under the circumstances, it seems appropriate.

It's hard conducting business from a callbox, but it's paying dividends. I start early, catch 'em before they got a chance to think. And guess what, someone has read the script and likes it. Two people, in fact. Both of them say they're interested. I got me a pair of meetings to take. Oh, I *like* the sound of that. Priorities first, though. At the moment I got nowhere to sleep, and no good clothes. It's still hot at night, I can rough it for a couple of days until something turns up, take the meetings — after all, they're

interested in the quality of writing, not whether I shop at
Armani — and maybe get an advance.

Round Two to the Harker family.

Good shall prevail.

2 October — NYC

I should know better by now.

The first meeting's at a place called Primetime Product,
situated, natch, near Bobby's building, and is taken in an
office the size of a basketball court by a guy who's coping
with premature baldness by growing a ponytail. He gives
me the once-over, wrinkles his nose as he lets me sit down
and hunts out the script. Then he asks me how I'd feel
about turning it into a half-hour sitcom featuring Dracula
as a funny superhero. I give the idea careful consideration,
then tell him I don't think it'll work, and remember, I say
this with an image of me sleepin' on a park bench in mind.
But he wants the bones without the meat and it really
won't work, a child of five could see that. End of meeting,
shown to the door, thanks for comin' in — and I have to
ask for the fuckin' script back because he's returning it to
the shelf behind his desk even as he's talking me out.

Sleepin' in the park is okay because the cops don't run you
in anymore — these days there's too many people an'
nowhere to put us all. I could have done without some
drunk puking his guts up on the next bench all night, but
right now it don't pay to be fussy, and besides I'm already
thinkin' of the next meeting. I got two shirts, one pair of
sneakers and one pair of shoes, one T-shirt and a pair of
ratty jeans, plus a nylon backsack containing a shave bag, a
blanket and the scripts. There's other stuff at my Ma's but
she's in Atlantic City underneath some loser and I don't got
the keys to her apartment.

Next day's a real hot one, so I go for a swim an' use my

last five bucks to get my shirt laundered so maybe I won't look like a total bum.

I get to PowerVision (I'd like to meet the guy who sits in a room thinkin' up these names) at twenty before the meeting, an' I'm still sittin' there at twenty after. The woman who sees me is dressed so severe that first of all I think she's wearin' a grey cardboard box. She looks at me funny even though I don't smell and my shirt looks great. Then she tells me she hasn't read the script but she's been instructed to buy it. Although I'm gettin' excited this alarm bell is goin' off inside me, and I ask what she would like to do with it.

And she says I want to give it to our writers to see what *they* can do. I ask her what she means. *I'm* the writer. I mean, if they like it what I've written, why get someone else to fuck with it? I guess I'm not supposed to speak at this stage 'cause she looks at me as if I just took a shit in her fruitbowl. Well, she says, the piece is way too down-beat. It can be Gothic, but it's got to be fun. We could liven up Dracula by giving him a wacky sidekick. I point out that there's one in the book we can use, and I see her flinch at the word *we*. Renfield, I say. He's an interesting character. What's he like? she asks. He's insane, I explain, and he eats flies. Not on television, she replies, not if we want a family audience. Also, the title has to go. We've already got a new title. *Fangs A Million.*

You can figure out the rest. At least this meeting lasted longer than the first one, mainly 'cause she was late gettin' it started.

On the way back I gave blood again, which gives me some ready cash, but I gotta tell you this is depressing the hell out of me. Tomorrow I'll maybe try to tap some guys I know for a loan. Then I guess I'll start calling again.

It's a setback for the Harker family as the Lord of the Undead goes into the lead. Where the hell is Van Helsing when you need him?

19 October — NYC

In the last couple of days the weather has turned. Central Park never looks fresh at the best of times. Even in spring the greenery has a kind of dusty look about it, an' now it's just brown. There's nothing lyrical you can write about autumn in this city. New England maybe but not here. I can't believe I'm still sleeping rough. It's gettin' too cold to stay out all night. I did one smart thing while it was hot — I kept out of the sun. You get a tan in New York, you automatically look like a bum unless you're wearing good clothes.

Nobody I know has any money to spare, but I ain't going to panhandle for it. That's what I told CeeCee, you offer a service or no deal. I was always taught that nobody rides for free. He laughed an' said that's exactly what he believes. CeeCee used to work at the coffeeshop on Bleeker, but he got canned and now he's started hustling again, which I figure you have to be pretty fuckin' desperate to do these days, and I ain't that desperate. Yet.

Trouble is I can't get welfare 'cause I ain't been out of work long enough, and in theory my Ma can still help. Of course, she's in a garter belt on her knees in some motel workin' off her blackjack bill at the Trump Casino, but try finding a sympathetic ear for that one. I been workin' on some revisions to the script, some improvements I think they'll go for. Trouble is I got no access to a typewriter. It's all written longhand, and the networks won't read longhand.

I got the blood thing down to a fine art by loaning out my card to a rota system. See, they won't let you give blood again until you've made it up fully, and they date-stamp your card, but a bunch of us go to different clinics with each other's cards. It shaves off a few days and don't harm you none so long as you keep eating.

I guess this is the low point of my life right now. It can

123

only get better from here. I even called around to my Ma but there was no one home. I've walked my ass off going to every single goddamned company on my list tryin' to get to see someone, anyone who could help. That's it; I've tried them all except the pornos, and out of the whole shebang I got me one decent new lead: I read that some rich NoHo gallery just financed a new TV company to develop independent projects for the cable nets, so I dropped a script around to them, called them back a week later and they want to see me tomorrow. I'll go along, but I ain't expecting a miracle. It's starting to get dark out here, and the park is looking more and more like Transylvania to me.

23 October — NYC

Max Barclay has the same number of letters in his name as Van Helsing, and the same powers. I feel like he just jumped on the refectory table and pulled down the drapes, blasting pure morning light across the prostrate figure of the Count. And in a way, that's what he's done. He's saving my fuckin' life is what he's doing. Let me go back three days.

WorldView TV turns out to be a pretty snappy joint, located in an area where the only thing that separates powerdressed corporate executives from bums lying in doorways pissing their pants is a foot of concrete and a window. Their receptionist is hip enough to once me over without calling security, which is a relief as I am sporting that 'just attacked in the park' look, then this beefy guy who may be a pro-football player comes up and shakes the bones outta my hand and tells me how he loves the script.

And how he wants to make it.

Just the way it is.

✳

An' that's where we are right now. It's gonna take a while to sort out the contract, but it's gonna happen. The bad news is, no loan until it does, but hey, it's always darkest before the dawn. That script is my stake, and now I've found someone with a hammer. Together we'll nail the son of a bitch.

27 October — NYC

No news yet.

Called Max today and we talked over problems with the script, all minor. He says he may be able to get some upfront money soon. I don't want him to know I'm still living in the park. It could fuck things up between us; he'll think I'm some kind of nut. I want this to be right. One day I'll be mixing drinks in my seventeen bedroom adobe-style Bel-Air ranch house telling kids how tough it was to break into showbiz, and at least I won't be lying.

My dawn will break.

11 November — NYC

I called Max and told him about my cashflow problem. It took a certain amount of pride swallowing, but I can't live like this much longer. He breezily suggested meeting over a drink but I can't let him see me, it's just too fuckin' humiliating. I got no clean clothes and no money. It is so fucking cold that even the seasoned park bums have all moved on, God knows where. Maybe they just froze up an' got covered over with leaves. Maybe that's what'll happen to me if I don't get a few regular meals soon.

Max says there's something he forgot to mention before, and that is he has to present the script to his board. There's no chance they'll turn it down so long as his recommendation stays, but it delays things. It ain't his

125

fault, he doesn't know what I'm goin' through here. And I ain't about to tell him any more than I have to.

18 November — NYC

Just when I thought my 'income' couldn't get any lower, some attitudinous dude at the clinic finally figured out what we've been doing with the donor cards. A few days back, the temperature went out the bottom end of the thermometer, so I moved down into the subway. The smells here are warm and bad. You can taste disease in the air. But the people are worse. Dangerous, like regular laws don't apply to them underground.

CeeCee says I can stay with him, it's a nice place, he can get me some duds an' a spending roll. All I have to do is take a couple of the extra johns from him. He says I got a good body, I could earn two, three hundred bucks a night. I told him things are bad but I'm just not ready for that kind of stuff.

I tell myself I'm the one with the moral strength. A Harker. A defender of the faith. So instead of waking in a soft bed, I look up at the city through a fucking grating.

30 November — NYC

I know the number so well I punch it out in my sleep: Wait. Give the extension. Wait. Max Barclay please. Wait. Last Tuesday I spoke to the PA again, Stephanie from London. Very polite. Max is in Hawaii for two weeks, didn't he tell me he was taking a vacation.

No he fucking didn't.

I try to explain I'm not badgering her, all I want is some reassurance, a sign of faith. I had — I *have* — faith in my script. Max says he has too but he don't ever prove it. It seems the board weren't entirely happy. There have to be a few small changes made. Okay, I'll wear the changes but let's get the contract through first, then we'll talk changes.

Changes. Dear God. I'm at CeeCee's apartment. When it started to snow an' the subway filled with crazies, the cops threw us back on the street an' I knew the time had finally come. I got no more blood to give. My weight was down to 120 pounds. I looked like a peeled stick. CeeCee's been good, at a price. I take no more than one john a night, and nothing too wild. If they won't wear a rubber they're out on their ass. I do it without thinking. I daren't let myself think. This is one part of my biography that's gonna stay in the drawer.

There's a new scene in the script.

By the dying light of the chamber's fire, the Count can be seen stepping forward. He stands a full head taller than the librarian. Gently, he takes Harker's face in his pale, tapered fingers and studies him, a spider examining a new kind of fly. The chill from his dead eyes sinks into Harker's bones. The young man is truly face to face with death. He feels the vampire's gaze killing off the cells in his body, and his brain starts to grow numb. He knows that if, at this moment, the Count chooses to let him die, he will indeed die. The numbness rapidly spreads. His will is drained away like blood leaking from a deep wound. Reason fades, to be replaced by a thrilling new sensation far beyond fear, an awakening ecstasy as Harker finally understands the night, the eternal night . . .

And the Count releases him, breaking off his gaze. He has granted his foe a steady, lingering look into the abyss. But the sight has made Harker stronger, because it has made death his friend. It has given him the power to free himself.

I hold on to that thought.

127

22 December — NYC

Max says I'm difficult, too idealistic, that nobody survives intact. I assume he's talking about the script. At least he's back from his vacation and we actually get to meet again now that I have some clothes. We drink red wine in a fashionable media joint on Amsterdam, surrounded by flickering TV monitors. Well, I say, this is the longest courtship I've had before somebody's fucked me, and he laughs. The contract's gonna be through after Christmas, he promises, when WorldView's legal department finally get to check everything out with the Bram Stoker estate, plus every other joker with a claim to the character who reckons they have exclusive copyright. It better come through, I say, 'cause right now what we have here is a failure to remunerate. He laughs again, tells me I'm really on form tonight.

If Max has noticed that I'm going quietly nuts waitin' for the green light, he ain't showing it. He wishes me a happy Christmas an' walks off into the snow with his scarf around his shoulders, that's how confident he is. Me, I don't wanna leave the bar. Leavin' the bar means leaving the warm an' going back to CeeCee's. Back to work. But at least I know now that I have the strength to get through it.

The Harker family will be avenged.

16 January — NYC

Why is it all the changes have to come from my side? He remains motionless, a silhouette on the ramparts, a shadow in the doorway. I adapt to survive. He lives on, unchanging, the eternal victor, the cape wrapped around his elegant form like a suit of armour. Impenetrable. Immovable.

It isn't fair.

CeeCee is dead. On Christmas Eve he went out to some fancy new club, and that was the last anyone saw of him. The cops say he got rolled by a john over at the Adonis around 2.00 a.m. Christmas morning. Ordinarily he wouldn't have died but he'd had a little booze and taken a few uppers, and the shock of hitting the ground did something to his neck. He never regained consciousness. The cops asked me if he had any family. It never occurred to me he even had a family.

Christmas morning. What a lonely time to die.

CeeCee always said I could stay on in the apartment. He knew I didn't like taking the johns. He wanted to help me so he said I could stay. He never told no one else. I went in his bedroom to pack up his stuff and it was like a little kid's. Teddy bears and movie star posters. The next night I came home and found the locks had been changed. I wish he'd told someone else I could stay.

I called Max to ask about the contract, but he wasn't there and the English PA wouldn't give me his home number. I found myself crying on the phone. Fucking pathetic.

Goin' back on the street was a shock. When I get ahold of Max I'm gonna ask him to put up or shut up. Hell, I'm gonna ask him if I can stay at his place while I'm writing the script. I should retitle the fuckin' thing *Out For The Count*, 'cause that's what I'm gonna be soon if he says no.

I'll do anything to get out of this situation, man.

Anything.

24 January — NYC

I am undead. That's how I think of it. Trapped in limbo. This is living death. Darkness reigns and Harker loses. Now and forever.

Fuck Max. Wherever he is, fuck him. He could have told me, he must have known. You don't leave a job without a little preparation. You don't just up and blow. The PA says he's gone out to LA, she don't know his whereabouts. She couldn't tell the truth if her fuckin' life depended on it. Lying is part of her job description.

The new guy's name is Feinstein.

I spoke to him after calling so many times he finally had to speak to me. He told me the first thing he did when he took over the job was freeze all of Max's projects. He needs to determine a budget floor and ceiling for next season, and he won't be rushed. It'll take some time to establish market windows. That's not to say the door is closed on my script. By this time I figure either he used to be a builder or he's incapable of gettin' through a sentence without using mediaspeak.

I tell him I am experiencing a downturn in my fiscal wellbeing at the moment and may not be alive by the time he gets around to perusing my masterpiece. Perhaps I can call him in a day.

Taken aback, he agrees. But not to a day. A week.

One week. Days, hours, minutes.

Nights.

I don't work on the script no more. I can't 'cause some asshole lifted my bag on the subway, and the last copy I had was in there. It's 3.00 a.m., way below freezing, and I'm hustling for johns on 42nd St.

Man, this is so far below my dignity, it's horrifyin'. I got a cold that won't go away, an' a dream that won't die. Better if it did. Better to let it go.

Maybe I been fightin' on the wrong side all this time. After all, my namesake met his end in the book, but it was just the beginning of the Count's career.

They say people are attracted to him because of the darkness.

The dark never seemed attractive to me until now.

31 January — NYC

Another couple of days, he tells me.

There are so many scripts to go through, and he must be fair to every one. Call him back at the end of the week and he promises to have an answer, this way or that. The PA tells him mine's one of the best scripts she's ever read, an' she's been in the business a long time.

I am standing in the phone booth listenin' to this.

It's so cold I can't tell where my feet end and the side-walk starts. I have two dollars in my pocket, a coldsore on my lip, and there are no johns on the street. I stayed a couple of nights at this guy Randy's apartment but it turns out he really wanted to beat me with a studded strap, so I got out. It was worth good money, but hey, I have my pride. That's a joke, by the way. There's a sticker on the coinbox in front of me, some broad offering guys an enema and I'm thinkin' well, at least it would warm me up. I feel weird, like I passed beyond some kind of barrier.

I can't give blood no more. They don't want it. They said it's gone bad. I got bad blood now. I told the doc I'd been bitten, but he didn't get it. Two more days. The dark before the dawn. This is gonna be an eleventh hour rescue, I can tell you.

You should never have tried to fight him, Jonathan.

2 February — NYC

A foot of snow around the callbox an' I got sweaty hands.

131

I got a pocket full of quarters which it turns out I need 'cause they leave me on callwait for ten minutes, during which I get to listen to three songs from *South Pacific*. Then he's not at his desk. It takes them a couple more minutes to locate him. I'm thinking this is good, this is a buildup of tension, this makes the news stronger.

Well, it does do that, at least.

I really didn't like it, he says. Not *sorry for fucking you around* or *maybe you'd like to write something else for us*. Just I *really* didn't like it. But that's not the best part. He leaves a small silence while I'm supposed to make grateful noises for his opinion. Then he says I should remember the network buzzwords, which are *Feelgood* and *Reassurance*. The public don't want to see this kind of thing, he says, it's way too depressing. They need to be told that everything's okay. I should bear that in mind next time.

I guess I could have screamed and shouted at him, but I just said quietly, there isn't gonna be a next time, and hung up.

At least it's over. I kind of feel better now. Not knowing was more painful than I'd realised. Yeah, I feel better now. I'm a little shaky walkin' out of the box, but the sun is shining. I should of asked him to return the script, but somethin' in me didn't want it back. The battle's ended. Dawn's here.

I gotta get myself a new jacket. This one's too thin. I'm freezin' my ass off. Pockets are ripped. Gonna get myself cleaned up. That's how I'll start. First the jacket. Then the life.

At least I took the bastard on, right?

Maybe I didn't win, but I sure as hell held him at bay once more.

Isn't that all you can ever do?

J.H.

132

New York Post   6 February

MAYOR SLAMS 42ND ST 'SIN PLAYGROUND'

A fresh call to clean up the 42nd St and Times Square areas has begun following the death of a young hustler in the early hours of yesterday morning.

John Harker, aged eighteen, intervened in a fight during which he was stabbed in the throat by an unknown assailant and left to bleed to death in the street. His pleas for help went unheeded and he died before reaching hospital. Police have so far been unable to trace his family, and are appealing for witnesses.

Mayor David Dinkins has called for an immediate crackdown on vice in the area, dubbing it a 'battleground where the forces of evil are nightly fought'.

DRAC'S BACK, AND WORLDVIEW'S GOT HIM!

Just when he seemed all played out, Dracula came back to wreak havoc with a record-breaking bite of the season's otherwise glum ratings last night.

WorldView Productions' three hour mid-season replacement *The Legend Of Dracula* became the stuff of legends when it topped the Nielsen ratings with a tale that proved both a critical success and an audience smash. Worldview Veep Arnie Feinstein attributes the hit to a new slant on a very old tale, and promises a series to follow the special.

Legend sees the familiar battle of light and darkness unfolding through the eyes of a teen adversary, and seems set to sweep the board at Emmy time.

Impeccable performances and stylish sets grace a powerhouse script of depth and subtlety.

Surprisingly for such an acclaimed project, the anonymous *Alan Smithee* tag conceals author credits, but with interest running this high, WorldView will have to name the source of their script to qualify for its inevitable awards.

Scene most singled out for praise features a struggle of wills in which the desperate Jonathan Harker is subjugated and lured to the brink of eternal darkness by his merciless captor. Given the fever pitch of worldwide sales interest, it looks as though the Prince of Night is once more set to reign — this time through the cable networks of the world.

Cooking The Books

Haldeman had left absolutely nothing to chance.

When he stepped out of his office on Friday evening, he walked through the restaurant instead of heading straight down to the garage, and stopped to talk for a few minutes with José and the head waiter, as if it were just the end of another quiet week. Sitting in his car on the way home he was surprised to find himself seizing up in a sweat, despite the fact that the air conditioner was turned way up high.

Haldeman ducked his gaze to the rear-view mirror, and what he saw disturbed him. It was the reflection of a forty-eight-year-old man at the end of his tether.

In the last six months, the roseate chubbiness of his face and neck had given way to the sickly pallor of a man eaten up with worry. His shirt collars were now a full size too big. Even his wedding ring was loose on his finger. The baggy serge suit lay too broadly across his slumped shoulders. It was years old, but how could he afford to buy a new one? His credit line was already extended far beyond his ability to ever pay it back.

When Mona left him, she said she would take him for every penny, but how could she take what he didn't have? He swung the Toyota into the driveway of his apartment building and turned off the engine. It was a beautiful evening. In Los Angeles the evenings were always beautiful because of the filth in the air, but this one held special promise. It held the promise of escape.

Haldeman climbed the stairs to his apartment and went inside, stopping in the kitchen to grab a bottle of José Cuervo. Then he sat down and opened the red financial folder, took a swig of warm tequila and began to read, not that he expected the figures to have changed from the last time he studied them, all of two hours ago.

137

The truth of the matter was, Haldeman was bankrupt. Worse than bankrupt, financially destitute. He had lost everything on a gamble, a calculated risk, and was about to lose even more. With each passing week the restaurant earned less and less. Who could say why? It had been a great idea, even Mona had agreed on that. With the small amount he had saved, plus the money he had raised from cashing Mona's share portfolio, he had managed to convince First Western to lend him an equal amount to invest in a theme restaurant.

The neon sign proclaimed the name in blue and purple. The RibTickler burst brightly into a burnished LA sky each evening at five-thirty. The location was perfect, or so it had seemed then, right on the corner of La Cienega and Santa Monica Boulevard. The decor was full of down-home charm. Rusting farm implements hung from the red-brick walls. A bare board stage stood before the tables. This was the first Bar-B-Q Comedy restaurant in Greater Los Angeles. Good ol' family cooking and stand-up comedy combined. The waitresses were clean-cut farm-girls in gingham shirts and boots. Everyone was eager to please, but something had gone badly wrong. First the food critics had given it a bad rap. Then the fickle and fashionable restaurant crowd who were supposed to have found The RibTickler a refreshing change had stayed away, preferring to haunt downtown eateries where the decor was post-modern, the chef was temperamental and the waiters were French and offhand. Haldeman was stuck with a restaurant that could not have attracted a less stylish crowd if it had been built in the shape of a doughnut. And without fashionable people to pay lunatic prices, how could he ever hope to cover his costs? Add that to his mortgage, his alimony, his gambling debts — yes, he had started gambling again — and you had a picture of a man moving fast towards the edge ...

*

Haldeman took a final slug of tequila and headed for the bedroom to pack. If he left in the next half hour, he would arrive in Palm Springs in time for a soak in the jacuzzi and a leisurely lobster dinner at the new Jap place on Highway 111. He knew it shouldn't take him more than two and a half hours to drive there tonight. After all, nobody else would be headed that way at this time of the year.

He glanced over at the typewritten figures again, silently thanking the gods for sending him someone as stupid as Larry Hyatt. Bumbling, well-meaning, never-say-no Larry was about to become the unwitting dupe in a plan so embarrassingly simple and foolproof that nothing — nothing — could possibly go wrong.

Haldeman loaded up the car and headed out to the freeway, turning on the 10 East and finding the traffic lighter than he had anticipated. Already he was beginning to feel better, although he would not have cause to celebrate until tomorrow evening, when he would arrive back in Los Angeles to find his poor restaurant a hollow, gutted shell of blackened timbers. Thank God so many of the uptown restaurants were wood-based.

Haldeman accelerated beyond the speed limit as he passed through the sprawling suburbs of Los Angeles County, past tyre factories and chemical plants and dere-lict drive-ins, beneath a vast clover-leaf flyover to the outer edge of the desert. Here the cloud-topped mountains glowed softly in the distance, and the monotony of the scrubland was only broken by glittering billboards announcing yet another golf course, retirement village or steakhouse to be built in Indio or Palm Springs.

Haldeman had only visited the desert resort once before, but had loved the serenity and strangeness of the area from the moment he had arrived in it. He could not have picked a better place to stay while his plan was being carried out by the fool Hyatt.

He turned up the air conditioner as the temperature

outside the car began to rise, and started watching for his turn-off. Coasting the Toyota from the freeway onto Bob Hope Drive, he headed for Rancho Mirage, at the far end of Palm Springs on One Eleven blacktop. Time to give the plan a final examination. Was there anything, anything at all he had failed to allow for?

The secret, he decided, was getting other people to do the dirty work for you. What you needed were employees of unswerving loyalty and supreme gullibility, and Larry fitted the bill on both counts. So for that matter, did José, the chef.

He had employed Larry as business manager, accountant and general runaround two years ago, when the restaurant was just a pencil sketch on a Denny's napkin. He had proven to be totally unsuited to the job, but thanks to his complete faith in his employer Hyatt had produced a set of completely erroneous books for the last financial year. It had been a simple matter to arrange. According to the computer in Larry's office, the restaurant was enjoying a record turnover, with custom this month building to an all-time high. Larry rarely came by the restaurant any more. He knew little of the Mexican staff who were paid virtually nothing for their services, or the nights when not a single customer crossed the foyer floor.

His records were based on false receipts and non-existent wage packets. Even once they had been logged into his computer they were far from safe, for Haldeman had subtly tampered with the figures, just a little at a time, and poor old Larry had never suspected a thing. The restaurant had to be shown in profit, in order to throw the insurance company off the track when it managed to salvage the books from the burned-down building. They'd be suspicious if business had been ailing, but not suspicious of a place with growth projections as sensational as this. They'd not be able to check the wages of the staff by talking to them, either. LA waiters were gypsies, forever moving on.

But the beauty of the plan was the way in which the restaurant was about to be destroyed. That was the real key.

Haldeman coasted the car into the forecourt of the Ranchero Motel and parked. Outside, crickets chittered noisily into the hot night air. The motel was a dump. Back in the fifties, when Palm Springs had become the hip new resort for city slickers to visit for a little R&R, it had enjoyed full residence for most of the year. Nowadays Los Angelenos were a little too slick for a rundown wooden building with ten rooms and a rarely cleaned pool. They wanted racquetball courts and jogging tracks, emerald golf ranges and crowded singles bars. They found all they needed in the impersonal new hotels downtown. They were turning the desert into a suburb of the city. But for Haldeman, there couldn't be a better place to hole up in.

The guy behind the check-in counter was wearing a sweat-stained vest and a full day's growth of beard, he noticed as he carefully filled out the guest slip, making sure that his handwriting was legible and the date was correct. The slip would be checked later. He just hoped that this guy wouldn't throw the damned thing away after he left. It was obvious from the outset that Haldeman was the only person staying at the Ranchero Motel. You had to be crazy to come to the desert in August.

Awful August the locals called it, when the relaxing warmth of the dry desert air turned to a scalding heat which could fry a cat alive on the sidewalk or melt a plastic toy left on the back seat of a car. For the duration of the month, even the locals deserted Rancho Mirage for the comparatively cooler temperatures of Los Angeles. Around here, the only bearable places during the day were the icy air-conditioned shopping malls and cinemas, buildings you could catch a cold entering. The streets were deserted and the pools were drained, and the only folks you saw were sealed behind the windscreens of their icebox automobiles. Haldeman checked out his chalet with a wary eye. In a place as rundown as this it wasn't unusual to find scorpions sleeping in the cobwebbed corners of the room. At night they beat the falling temperatures by nesting in your boots.

The desert was quick to reclaim its ground, shifting sand under doors and through windows, filling bedrooms with spiders, beetles and roaches, cracking stone and peeling paintwork with blistering blowtorch heat as fast as folk could repair the damage. The verdant golf courses, country clubs and vacation ranches existed courtesy of the day-and-night sprinkler systems that forced the desert back beyond pink-stucco walls and hedgework groves. The desert lapped the edges of these pastel oases, constantly searching for ways to re-enter.

After settling in, he drove into Cathedral City and ate a large, expensive meal in an almost empty restaurant. Returning from dinner, he went to his room swinging a six-pack in one hand and a bucket of ice in the other. Above him, as he crossed the crackling brown grass of the quadrangle and headed for his room, the desert air, rising from the cooling ground, had cleared away the clouds to reveal a spectacular view of the universe. Outside his room he stood and listened to the tall date palms rustling in the night thermals, their fruit wrapped in paper to protect them from rats. In a few hours his plan would be put into action. If he had any second thoughts, now was the time to call a halt to the whole thing.

But there was no alternative. There was no backing out of this particular dead end. He entered his room and started on the six-pack.

Haldeman felt the sun on his eyelids and turned over onto his stomach. His watch read six-thirty. It couldn't be this hot already, could it? He had somehow failed to leave the

142

air conditioner on last night, and now he lay tangled and sweating in the sheets. He crawled out of bed, clicked a switch, and the ancient unit began to hammer and gurgle. In exactly eight and a half hours José would light the burners beneath the barbecue pit in the kitchen, in preparation for the evening trade. At the same moment, Larry had instructions to call Haldeman from his office above the restaurant. Larry had been provided with the number of the motel. He had also been given an errand that would take him over to The RibTickler on Saturday afternoon. This ensured that he would be at the scene of the crime when it happened, and on the line to his boss even as the restaurant began to burn.

Haldeman hauled himself out of bed with a chuckle. He'd taken time out to study exactly how the kitchen burners worked. Before he left on Friday, he had jammed the gas valves so that when they were turned off for the night, two of the jets would remain a quarter open. Instead of the network of pipes in the pit being cleared, they would slowly fill. There would be no detectable leak to the outside air, but there would be a large, pressurised volume of gas in the system, just waiting for the touch of José's Zippo at three this afternoon.

Larry, calling from the floor above, would probably be far enough from the blast to be protected from major injury, and as José headed for that big taco stand in the sky, Haldeman would get an on-the-spot report from him as it happened.

Of course, he supposed, there was always the chance that José might decide to light the gas early today, but that was unlikely. If he did, Larry would have all the more reason to ring the motel, verifying his alibi. Whatever happened this afternoon, he was covered. He pulled on a pair of lightweight summer pants and opened the front door of the chalet. The heat hit him like a solid wall. He looked at his watch. 7.35 a.m. No wonder nobody came

143

here in August. A line of dusty lime trees stopped the pink cement strip of sidewalk in front of his room from becoming too hot to walk on. Even so, he slipped on his sandals and a baseball cap before venturing into the sun.

The second he cleared the shade of the lime trees, Haldeman could feel the harsh rays burning into his unprotected shoulders. He walked over to the pool and stared into its fluorescent indigo depths, watching the light crackle across its surface. Clusters of roaches and black winged insects clogged the water outlet. He dipped a toe into the water and found it almost hand-hot. All around the sunlight dropped palpably onto buildings and hedges, heightening colour and deadening motion, so that his surroundings appeared as flat and still and bright as a photograph.

He returned to his room and changed into more formal attire before driving to a nearby pancake house for a cool, leisurely breakfast. After waffles and eggs he felt uncomfortably full, and decided to take a walk around town before returning to his car. Everything was closed.

Shop windows were darkly shaded, their doors bearing signs which read SEE YOU IN SEPTEMBER. The mere effort of walking about in this ungodly, blasting heat was quite unbearable. Sweat trickled into his eyes. His shirt was stuck to his back. He bought a copy of the *Desert Sun* from a paperstand and returned to the car feeling drained of energy. The headline of the newspaper made an unsurprising reference to the temperature. Around here he doubted that there was much else to talk about. When he reached the motel he found the front office open, and entered.

'Howdy, Mr Haldeman,' grinned Ricky, the motel manager. His face still hadn't seen a razor. 'Y'all sleep well last night?'

'I guess so. Didn't expect it to be so damned hot this morning.' He dropped down into a cane chair by the door

144

and fanned himself with the newspaper. 'What do you think the temperature is?'

'Oh, a hundred ten, hundred fifteen 'round about now,' said Ricky, squinting out of the window as if he could see the heat. 'You wait till jus' after lunch, though, if you wanna feel some real heat. Be up in the hundred twenties by then.'

'Jesus,' muttered Haldeman. 'How come you stay around here?'

'I have to get this place fixed up for the season. Putting me some new roofing on, having the courtyards tarred and retiled. Damn' ground's cracked wide open in places.'

'By the sun, I suppose?'

'Hell, no. By the floods. You don't wanna be around here when we get those, mister, I'm tellin' yuh. We get three inches o' rain in as many minutes. Washes cars clean off the road, usually drowns a few fools caught out in it, too.' Ricky leaned across the counter in a cloud of sour perspiration. 'This ain't Los Angeles. The desert got no respect for people. Half of our lives is spent just keepin' it off our backs. I practically rebuild this place every summer. If I turned off the sprinklers for a couple o' weeks, the motel would look just like that out there.' He pointed from the window at the endless beige scrubland beyond the driveway. 'We get storms where the lightnin' strikes the metal ladders of the swimmin' pool so often that they get all bent outta shape. An' we get August heatwaves that damned near wipe out every senior citizen this side of Indio. You stay out here long enough and it fries your brains. You wanna beer?' He slid an icy can of Miller along the counter top.

A short while later Haldeman returned to his chalet and changed his wet clothes for shorts and a T-shirt. While he was waiting for the call, he decided to sit outside under one of the bleached orange sunshades surrounding the pool.

✳

145

The paperback slid to the ground with a thump and Haldeman jolted awake. He bent down to retrieve the book and a wave of dizziness swept over him. The baking air had been stealing his breath, willing him into a light, uncomfortable sleep in which fiery images danced across his eyelids. But now he was alert once more, and thirsty. Beyond the glittering pool rows of date palms stood as straight as prison bars, backed by distant slate-blue mountains. Somewhere in the middle distance a car was kicking up a thin trail of dust, its windscreen catching the sun as it coasted a curve.

Haldeman rubbed his hot eyes and reached for his wristwatch. The sun had shifted, exposing the metal band and causing him to drop it back onto the table with a yelp. Somewhere over towards the front office, hidden by lime trees, Mexican workers called to each other as they toiled on the new courtyard, heedless of the sun, stacking orange clay tiles in readiness for laying. How could they work in this heat? With the aid of a handkerchief Haldeman gingerly lifted his watch from the table and made his way back to the chalet.

Inside, the darkness cooled his skin, and polkadots of light danced in his sight. It was a quarter to one. Two and a quarter hours before Jose reduced the restaurant to a smouldering parking lot. He would have to make sure he was near the phone when the call came through.

It was at this point that he noticed the lack of a telephone in the room.

'No, sir, one thing we ain't got laid on yet is room phones,' said Ricky, picking his teeth with a piece of paper. He sat sprawled behind the reception desk with the remains of a plate of fried chicken before him.

'We ain't had no call for phones in the rooms. Folks come here to be left alone, if you know what I mean.' He leered, flicking a shred of chicken from his teeth.

'I'm expecting a very important call in a couple of hours,' Haldeman explained. 'I gave them the number here ...'

'Where'ja get that from?' Ricky stifled a belch.

'The directory. From your ad.'

'Oh *that* number, that's the old number ...'

'You mean I won't get the call?' Haldeman cut in.

'Oh sure, it still rings here, but it's out back on the old payphone now. We switched the numbers last fall.'

'Where can I find the phone booth?' he asked, trying to sound as casual as possible.

'Can't miss it. You jes' go out behind the workmen to the back pool patio, an' it's straight across from ya.'

'Thanks. I'll catch you later.' He rose from the whicker chair and headed out into the sun.

At exactly two-thirty, Haldeman left his chalet armed with a beach towel, a sticky bottle of Hawaiian Tropic and a jumbo polystyrene cup half filled with ice and half with vodka. He knew he probably shouldn't drink before the call, but the sun was dehydrating him and he damned well wasn't drinking Coke on a red-letter day like this.

At the end of the pink shaded sidewalk he rounded the corner and found himself facing a large rectangular courtyard. Along one side, a pair of battered loungebeds were propped in the shadow of the wall. In the opposite far corner of the courtyard stood a telephone booth, little more than a payphone on a metal stick. Below it, the faded remains of a Yellow Pages book hung on a chain.

The heat in the courtyard was astounding. Protected from the fickle desert winds, which could whip up a scouring sandstorm in seconds, it lay sheltered and silent at the back of the motel grounds. Haldeman tugged one of the sunbeds free and unfolded it in the shade. Several of its criss-crossed plastic straps had perished and snapped, but he managed to settle onto it comfortably enough, and

147

shortly fell into a light doze.

In this semi-conscious state, he imagined the chef coming into the restaurant, pausing by the door to remove his jacket. He would be surprised to find Larry in the building, and perhaps the two men would greet each other. José would make his way to the kitchen, don his chef's outfit and wash his hands. Meanwhile, Larry would head up to the office and sit behind the desk with his paperwork. Haldeman turned onto his side and drained the polystyrene cup before settling back into the sunbed. With the money the insurance brought in he'd have to be careful that Mona's smartass lawyer didn't find out and start bleating about the late alimony payments ... it was so damned hot here, almost hot enough to open up a barbecue restaurant that worked on the natural heat of the sun ... yes, maybe that was what he would do, pioneer a new kind of solar-powered restaurant, call it Natural Eating, something like that ...

The phone was ringing.

Haldeman sat up on the sunbed with a start and peered at his watch. It was exactly three o'clock. He must have dozed off. Jumping up, he looked around for his sneakers and shirt, then across at the ringing telephone on the far side of the blazing courtyard.

Four rings. He flicked away the sweat that had already begun to drip from his forehead once more. The shade from the building behind ended in a sharp line two feet from the end of his sunbed. The ground that stood between him and the telephone would be scalding hot, but he would have to run across. He couldn't afford to miss the call.

He launched himself towards the telephone booth on the balls of his feet, running as lightly as possible, but had only taken three strides before becoming aware that something was wrong. The searing pain which had begun to cut into his bare soles was obviously caused by the sunbaked concrete. But it did not feel as if he was moving across concrete at all. At the next step he faltered and screamed, as the sole of his right foot burned with agonising spears of pain.

In the distance, the telephone rang on. He looked down and saw the floor of the courtyard wavering and bubbling in the heat, and this time he was forced to wrench his left leg forward in order to keep moving. The sharp movement ripped the skin from the seared sole of his left foot away in a single broad strip, and he fell forward onto one hand and a knee, crying with pain.

Through the shimmering heat haze he saw the telephone, now no more than eight feet away, ringing and ringing. All around him the surface of the courtyard was boiling. The Mexican workers had only finished retarring the surface of the enclosure a day before. They had sprinkled its surface with sand to protect the finish, and had then moved on to refurbish another part of the grounds. But because of the heatwave, the tar had failed to set. Instead, the day's soaring temperature had brought the pitch back to a viscous state.

Unable to support his body on his burning hand and knee, Haldeman fell face down onto the courtyard with a scream. Molten knives of fire seared into his stinging flesh. He tried to turn over and pull himself free, but every time he moved more skin blistered and tore loose ...

Larry slowly lowered the receiver from his ear, then replaced it in the cradle. That was strange. Mr Haldeman had specifically asked him to call at this hour. As it turned out, he needed to speak to the boss anyway, because there was a problem at the restaurant. José the chef had called in sick an hour ago, and so far he had been unable to locate a substitute chef at short notice. It was beginning to look as if they would not be able to open at all tonight. Well, he'd try again in a few minutes.

Haldeman was stuck by his bleeding, raw face in the scalding morass. His chest, knees and thighs had become glued as well, and the more he struggled the more he stuck. His screams reached a new pitch as the molten liquid touched his right eye and boiled it white.

When the telephone rang again, Haldeman was in no position to answer it. Blood and tar had dried across his tattered back as he lay twitching like a fly in a honeypot. Though he had lost consciousness, he was still alive. Most of his scalp lay stuck in the tar, as did more than half the skin that had once been on his body, but still he twitched and flinched as the sun drilled its burning rays into his flayed flesh.

Altogether Larry rang four times, and for the first three Haldeman was still alive. But then the sun cruelly boosted the temperature a few more degrees.

Tomorrow the *Desert Sun* would announce that it was the hottest day of the year. But for now, the twisted red thing that had been Haldeman gave a final flop as the sound of the telephone bell lessened in its ears, and the chances of healing its seared body in the air-conditioned coolness of the motel's reception area vanished in the rippling, rolling heat.

The Vintage Car Table-Mat
Collection Of The Living Dead

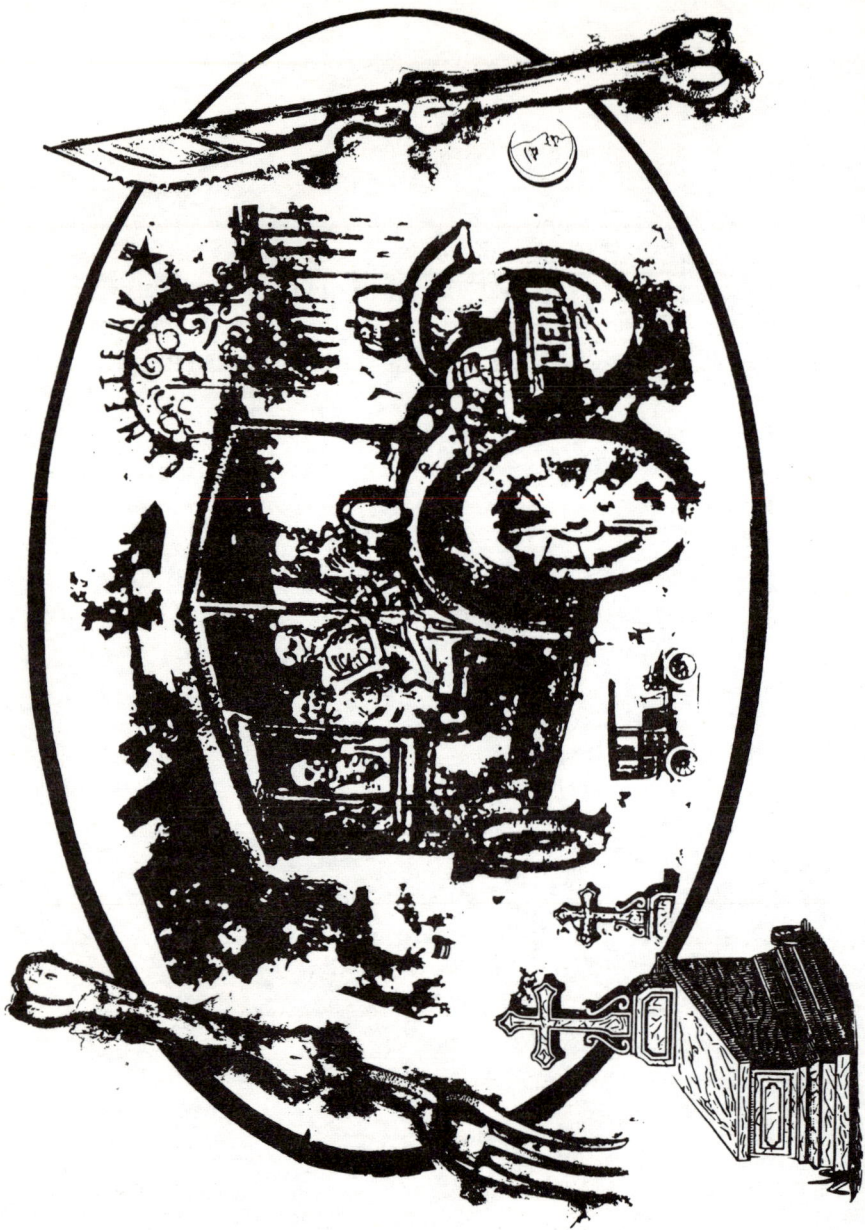

When Mark Houseman awoke in the middle of the night and found a shadowy figure standing at the foot of his bed, he screamed so loudly that they both jumped in fright. His first thought, naturally enough, was that he was being burgled. Somehow this intruder had entered his flat and was now preparing to bash in his head. Reaching under the bed, Mark's fingers fastened around the heavy chrome torch he kept there. In a single swift movement he raised, aimed and switched it on, only to find that the beam shone clean through the figure, as though it were made of smoke.

'Who the hell are you?' he asked, his heart thumping heavily beneath his T-shirt.

The figure raised its hands in a placating gesture. 'Oh, I'm sorry, I didn't mean to make you jump,' it said reasonably. 'I wasn't expecting to be here myself.'

Mark reached for the switch of the bedside lamp and flicked it on. The man before him was slim, pale and bespectacled, with a receding chin and hairline. He was in his early forties, and wore a cheap grey suit with a matching waistcoat, as if he had decided to detour here on his way to the office. More alarming was the fact that his body seemed transparent in the light. Details of the reproduction painting on the wall behind could clearly be discerned through his head and shoulders.

'Allow me to introduce myself,' said the opaque being. 'My name's Worthing, Owen Worthing.'

'You're a ghost.'

'No, I'm the assistant personnel officer for the second largest insurance company in Croydon. Or rather I used to be, because now I'm deceased.'

'How on earth did that happen?' asked Mark, incredulous.

'I was effectively demoted when they brought in a senior over my head.'

'No, I mean how did you die? Why are you here?'

'Well, that's the interesting thing,' replied Owen. 'I think I'm a revenant. I've been sent back to sort out a situation.'

'What kind of situation, for Chrissakes? It's four in the morning, and you're in my bedroom.'

Owen puffed out his cheeks and thought for a minute. 'Yes, I'm sorry about the inconvenience. It seems I'm a murderee. You know, I was, um —' He made a stabbing motion in the air and emitted a series of high-pitched squeaks reminiscent of the *Psycho* soundtrack.

'You mean you were killed?'

'Yes,' said Owen with pride. 'Brutally. The coroner said he'd never seen such a ferocious attack. In fact he said that in all the years he'd been a coroner —'

'Look, this is fascinating stuff,' interrupted Mark, 'but what have I got to do with it? I've an early meeting in the morning.'

'What, on a Saturday?'

'Yes, and I have to get some sleep.'

'What do you do for a living?'

'I work in the A&R department of a record company.'

'Oh, that must be very interesting,' said Owen, cheerfully jingling the change in his pockets. 'I had a cousin who worked in a record shop, and Sting came in once, but he was on his lunch hour and missed him completely. My cousin I mean, not Sting.'

'I think it's time you left my bedroom, Mr Worthing.' Mark smoothed his pillow and lay down once more. He was obviously having a hallucinatory experience of some sort; God's way of telling him to ease up on the party-going.

'I can't leave.' Owen shrugged apologetically. 'I think you're supposed to find my murderer.'

154

Mark sat up sharply and stared at the dead man. 'For crying out loud, why me?'

'You must have been a witness or something. Otherwise I wouldn't be here.'

'You seem very ill-prepared for this. Didn't anyone brief you?'

'No, not really. I came straight over.'

'How did you get here?' He had an image of a figure in clerical grey wafting down on a bed of phosphorescent dust.

'I caught a bus from Carshalton, then a Northern Line train via Bank.'

'You're missing my point,' said Mark, exasperated. 'What's the last thing you can actually remember seeing when you were alive?'

Owen rolled his eyes in an elaborate mime of abstract thought. 'Walnuts.'

'I'm not with you.'

'I had a bag of walnuts in my hand. I suppose I was looking at them when I died.'

Mark rubbed his tired eyes. 'I'm not going to get any sleep tonight, am I?' he asked.

'I could sit here quietly until the morning,' offered Owen. 'I wouldn't be in the way. I mean, I wouldn't haunt you or anything, if that's what you're worried about. I think that's what I'm supposed to be doing.'

'It's no good. I'd never get off knowing you were there.' Mark pulled himself out of bed and hunted for his slippers. The little clerk followed him out of the room. 'I'll have to stay in the dark after daybreak, otherwise you won't be able to see me.'

'Well, that's something to look forward to.' He donned his towelling robe and headed for the kitchen.

'Don't be like that,' whined Owen. 'We could be friends.'

'Listen, even if you were alive — which you're not — I doubt we'd be friends. You're not the kind of person I hang out with.' He filled the kettle and plugged it in.

155

'Oh, I'm sure we must have something in common, otherwise I wouldn't be here. Hobbies, perhaps.'

'Yeah, right. My "hobby" is checking out bands at rock venues. What's yours?'

'Table-mats,' replied Owen. 'I collect them, especially ones with vintage cars on. I have nearly a hundred various editions of the Ford Model-T alone, including one made entirely from watch parts. I also learned to make my own table-mats at evening class, while my lady wife was undertaking a course in the subtleties of the Bossa Nova.' He found himself a chair and sat, casting an envious glance at the teapot. 'I'd love a nice cup of tea, but I can't pick anything up. I have a feeling the afterlife's going to be a bit on the boring side.'

Mark snorted. 'Coming from you, that's really depressing news. You're sure you can't go away until you find your murderer?'

'Until *we* find him,' corrected Owen. 'You're in this too. I can't leave you.'

'What are you going to do until he turns up, just sit here in my kitchen?'

'No, I'll help you look. I'm familiar with Central London and parts of Croydon. I should imagine someone with common sense and a logical mind would be invaluable in a murder investigation of this nature.'

'I suppose it would help if you'd been beaten to death with a table-mat,' agreed Mark, pouring himself a mug of tea. Through the kitchen window he could see a faint glimmer of light above the rooftops. 'After I drink this I'm going back to bed. If you wake me up again, I'll kill you.'

'I just want to say how much I appreciate your cooperation,' said Owen, smiling tentatively.

'Right.' Mark turned in the doorway and regarded the clerk through half-closed eyes. 'We'll start looking for your murderer tomorrow. You'd better give me your wife's address in case I get killed as well, so I can go and annoy the shit out of her.'

When he arose at 8.00 a.m., Mark found Owen still seated in the kitchen chair with his hands tucked between his knees, in exactly the same position that he had left him. The revenant's eyes followed him pleadingly around the room as Mark made unconvincingly casual preparations for the day ahead. Without thinking he opened the blinds, and alternate strips of the ghostly clerk vanished in the sunlight.

'So, what great plan have you come up with then?' he asked, pleased to be able to discomfit his houseguest.

'I can't go out in daylight this bright,' Owen replied, wincing at the bands of light. 'We'll have to meet later, just before sunset.'

'Where do you think we should start looking?'

'I'm really not sure. I found this in my pocket, if it will help.' He handed his host a folded London Transport map.

'You're a bit useless for a spirit, aren't you?' Mark complained, examining the folder. 'You've come back for spectral vengeance armed with a bus map of Croydon.'

'I can't help it. I'm an ordinary person who's had bad luck. I'm not a victim of Jack the Ripper.'

'I wish you were,' said Mark, leaving. 'I'm already late for my meeting. I'll be back before sunset.'

The sun was sinking slowly behind the North London rooftops as Mark turned his key in the front door lock. Just as he was thinking that perhaps he'd been working too hard lately and had imagined the entire episode, Owen Worthing appeared in the darkened hall. He looked shabbier than before, as if staying around in the same clothes was having a deleterious effect on him.

'I ache all over,' he complained, 'and I feel so embarrassed, dragging you into this without an explanation. The truth is, I can't remember much myself. Murder victims must be prone to fits of depression, because I feel ever so peaky.'

'Stop moaning for a minute and listen to me,' said

Mark, ushering him out of the front door and down the stairs. 'I've had an idea. I think we should go back to the spot where you were killed. Perhaps we'll find a clue there, or your memory will be jogged, or some damned thing. On the way I want you to recall everything that's happened to you.'

The thought of this cheered Owen no end. 'Well,' he began as they walked to the car, 'I think I was on my way back from the sales. I remember seeing a particularly fine set of table-mats in John Lewis that I was thinking of purchasing as a gift for Malcolm.'

'Who's Malcolm?'

'The gentleman we bought our caravan from. His wife's in a wheelchair. He looked after our labrador when we went to Devon. He collects table-mats too.'

'If you could just forget about the fucking table-mats for a minute maybe we'll get somewhere,' said Mark, letting the revenant into his car. 'Try to remember where you were murdered.'

'This is nice,' said Owen, admiring the upholstery of the Saab. 'I had an Austin Maestro in the same colour, except it was more beige. Are you married?'

'I have a girlfriend who plays in one of the bands we represent,' muttered Mark, starting the engine.

'How exciting. I've always liked Neil Diamond myself.'

'So do a lot of dead people. Can we get on with the problem at hand? Where were you killed?'

Owen stared out of the windscreen at the darkening streets. 'I think if you just drive around for a bit it'll come back to me.'

'There must be a more scientific approach than this.' Mark turned the car in the direction of the city. 'Try to think. You must have been in a place where a man could get away with committing murder. Somewhere dark and deserted, somewhere —'

'Leicester Square,' said Owen suddenly, 'during the rush hour.'

'*Leicester Square?*' Mark braked the car to a halt. 'You mean to say you were brutally murdered in one of the most crowded places in the Western hemisphere? Christ Almighty, how am I ever supposed to find your assassin there?'

'I'm only trying to help,' said Owen testily. 'I'm positive that's where it happened.'

'All right, have it your way.' He released his foot from the brake and accelerated towards the West End. 'When was this?'

'Yesterday, I think.'

'That's impossible. You told me the coroner had never seen such a mess. The police would never have carried out your autopsy so quickly.'

'Well, I was pulling your leg about the coroner,' he raised his voice over Mark's protestation, 'but that's because I wanted you to help me.'

'Great. Have you lied to me about anything else?'

'No, I swear. Oh.' Owen pressed a fist against his stomach. 'I have a strange feeling.'

'What now?'

'I think this has to be sorted out within a certain time period, otherwise I stay with you forever.' He grimaced apologetically. 'Nobody explains the rules properly. I don't know how I'm supposed to manage in the afterlife without adequate training. Here, there's a parking space.' Owen pointed to the side of the road.

'We're nowhere near Leicester Square yet,' said Mark through gritted teeth, looking out at the lights of Euston Station.

'Better safe than sorry. It'll be impossible to park any closer. We never bring the runaround into the West End for safety's sake, but when we do we always park a good two miles away.'

He ignored Owen and drove on, finally hitting a traffic jam in Lisle Street, at the edge of Chinatown.

'I told you this would happen,' complained the ghost. 'We'll be stuck here for ages now. It's a good job we're not going to the pictures because we'd miss the beginning, and I never go in if there's a chance that I'll miss the beginning.'

They eventually parked in a tiny space between a pair of delivery trucks in Soho, Mark scraping the bumper as they backed in. Owen alighted and examined the damage, tutting and fussing over the cracked paintwork.

'Where in Leicester Square did you die, exactly?' asked Mark, as a startled stranger passed them.

'I think it'll come back to me when we get there,' said the clerk, looking around. 'Look at these sex shops. If I was on the local council I'd have them shut down.'

'Well you're dead, so just forget about it. Listen, what happens to you if we manage to get this sorted out?'

'How do you mean?'

'Well, where do you go?'

'Heaven, I suppose, if I've led a blameless enough life.'

Mark was walking so quickly that the spirit had to run to keep up. Each time they passed the light from a restaurant window, different parts of Owen disappeared.

'I wonder what Heaven's like.'

'It's probably just endless church services and a lot of standing around queuing for things, with the odd educational film thrown in on a Sunday evening. You know, *The Wonderful World Of The Worker Ant*, that sort of thing.'

'Oh dear.' Owen sidestepped a young woman who was about to walk through him.

'Did you have any enemies?' asked Mark. 'Anyone who might have wanted you dead?' He could understand the clerk annoying people, but not enough for somebody to take his life.

'Not really, no. Mrs Charkham wrote me a very nasty letter.'

'Who is she?'

160

'We met through the *Exchange & Mart*. I sold her my lawnmower after we lost Blackie, our cat. It was asleep in the long grass and my wife ran over it. I didn't want to keep the lawnmower because it, you know, held bad memories. So I sold it to this lady, but the blades never worked properly again.'

'So what did you do?'

'I bought a goldfish.'

'I meant after you received the nasty letter?'

'Oh, nothing.'

'*Then why tell me the bloody story?*' shouted Mark. Several passers-by turned and gave him strange looks. Presumably, none of them could see Owen. 'You're enjoying this, aren't you?' he snapped. 'You're spinning the whole thing out, pleased to have someone to talk about it.'

'Of course I am,' said Owen sadly. 'Being murdered is the only interesting thing that ever happened to me.'

They stopped before one of the illuminated entrances to the tube station. Some Chinese teenagers stood talking at the top of the stairs. A busker with one leg sat tunelessly gumming a harmonica. The little clerk partly faded in the overhead strip-lighting, and moved quickly back into the shadow.

'So what happened here?' asked Mark, already fed up. 'Some kid asked you for money, then stabbed you when you said no?'

'My head,' said Owen finally, reaching up to touch his brow. 'It's starting to come back to me. He hurt my head.'

'Try to remember. I'm freezing.'

'Last night, returning from John Lewis. I didn't have enough cash on me for the table-mats, and the store doesn't accept credit cards. We're on a tight budget at home, and sometimes ...'

'You arrived here at the station. What happened then?'

The revenant worried a cuticle between his teeth. 'I'm trying to think. It was raining. There were so many people.

161

I remember looking at my watch. It was nearly twenty to seven.'

'Wait a minute,' said Mark suddenly. Jesus, he must have been here at around the same time himself! After work he'd had a quick drink with Amber, his girlfriend, and had gone home to change before going out for dinner. The downpour had removed any possibility of finding a cab on the street, so he'd opted for the train. He was running late, pushing through the crowd. But he'd seen nothing remotely out of the ordinary. He must have arrived before the clerk.

'You said someone hurt your head.'

'That's right.' Owen pointed back at the entrance. I was just at the top of the stairs. It was very crowded — all pushing and shoving. I was thinking that perhaps I should have rung my wife. Suddenly this man shoved through with his brief case held above him.' He pointed down at the tiles. 'His elbow hit the side of my head as he pushed past, and I slipped over on the wet floor. As I fell I banged my skull on that steel rail there. Someone helped me to my feet, asked me if I was all right. I said I thought so. There were walnuts all over the stairs. The back of my jacket was muddy, and my head hurt. I fought my way out of the entrance and stood in the rain, trying to clear my mind. For some reason I decided that I wouldn't catch the train after all, that I needed more fresh air, and I set off towards Charing Cross.'

Owen stepped out of the shadow and crossed the road, walking away down the opposite pavement. 'I arrived at this point and stopped,' he called to Mark, indicating a damaged hoarding that concealed a building site opposite the Wyndhams Theatre. 'Then the pain began again. I raised my hands to the back of my head and felt around for a bump. It sounds so odd now but *it moved*, the bone moved beneath the skin. I remember thinking "hullo, you've done more damage here than you realised". And I began to pass out.'

Mark was horrified. He watched as the clerk removed his glasses and shook his head sadly. 'I leaned against the wall, and fell through the gap in the hoarding,' he said, pointing to a splintered hole in the plywood. 'Down into the mud. I must still be down there. The site doesn't open at the weekend, and you wouldn't see me from the road.'

Mark waited until the street was deserted, then leaned through the broken hoarding and looked down. In the sickly pallor of the cinema neon reflected from the square beyond, he could just make out the grey-suited corpse at the bottom of the pit. It lay face-down in a pool of mud, its soaked arms neatly at its sides, as if it had no desire to draw attention to itself in death.

'My God, Owen, I'm so sorry.' He could barely catch his breath. He pulled himself free of the hole and turned to face the revenant. 'It was a black leather briefcase, with gold corners, wasn't it?'

'Yes.'

'I was in a hurry. I just pushed through the crowd without looking. I knew I'd bashed against someone. I should have stopped. God, Owen, that's why you came to me.'

He should have been furious, but the clerk hugged himself sadly. 'So it was an accidental death. The only interesting thing that ever happened to me, and you've taken that away. I can't say I'm surprised. My life has consistently taken the least interesting route. I'm always the man standing next to the man with the lottery ticket. Not a natural winner. Not like you, all flash and dash and somewhere to go. Your flat looks like a nightclub. I bet your girlfriend's got cropped hair and long legs. I bet there's a bottle of champagne in your fridge. While I'm regrouting the bath you're probably sleeping off the effects of some designer drug.'

Mark looked down at his shoes, horribly ashamed. 'I'm sorry, Owen, I don't know what to say. I can't give you back your life.'

'No, I suppose not.' He shrugged, embarrassed. A gust of wind blew a fried chicken box through his legs. 'You can exchange your life for mine, though.'

'Look, I've already apologised. There's a limit.' The clerk was expecting too much from him. 'I can't live in a suburban semi-detached with carriage lamps and floral wallpaper, for God's sake. I'm not cut out for grouting, or collecting vintage car table-mats, or driving the kids around Whipsnade Zoo or whatever it is you people do at weekends.'

'Maybe not, but it's your fault I'm dead and that makes you my murderer, and you have to atone for your sin by taking my place.'

'Who said so?' asked Mark angrily. He felt himself growing queasy and faint.

'I told you, I didn't make the rules. I may not know much, but I know my rights. Murderers have to go to Hell. Which in this case is down there, in the mud.'

'Not me, Owen — no. I've too much to live for. I told you it was an accident!'

As Mark felt his spirit draining down to the sad corpse in the filthy pit below, his victim's soul filled his own body in an invigorated burst of energy. The reincarnated Owen Worthing walked quickly away from the building site, very pleased with his smart new appearance.

He was looking forward to his new life. An endless round of luxury and deceit, of seized opportunities and fashionable lies. He would start afresh, bringing nothing of his former ways with him. As he caught sight of his handsome new appearance in a supermarket window, he permitted himself a satisfied smile.

He had been given a second chance to live, and this time he would do so to the full.

As he returned to the tube station, his eye was caught by an attractive and reasonably priced table-mat in a shop window.

Persia

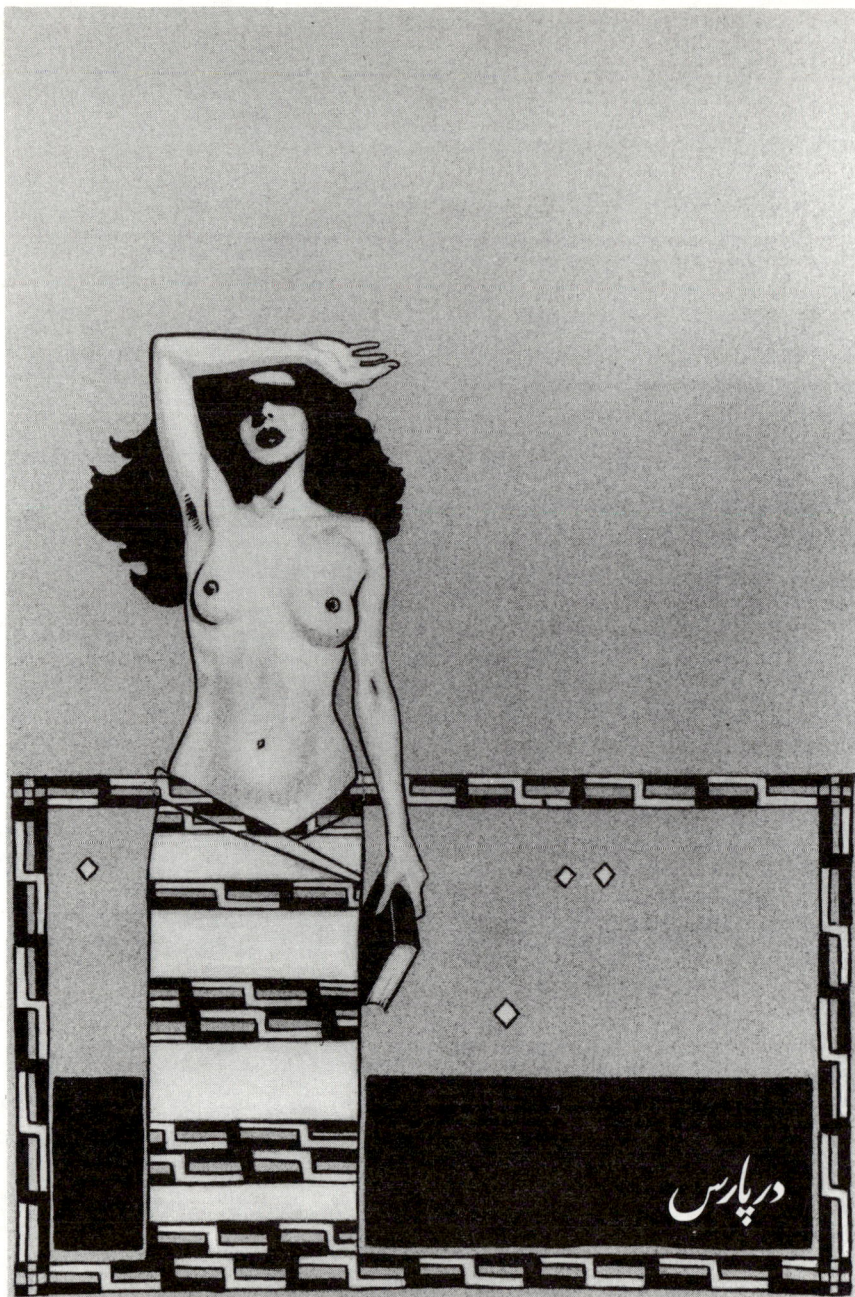

در پارس

And once again I am in Persia.

As always, the first sight which greets my tired eyes is the brilliant white colonnade of the harbour building twisting away in mad perspective, overrun with fleshy green cacti. The sapphire waters cast shimmering planes of light across the marble courtyard of the squares beyond. The jetty ends in smooth semicircles of warm stone, where young women sit in the blossom-crusted shade with open books in their laps.

As we tie up and begin to disembark, several of these girls rise and set aside their volumes. Gathering their robes below their bare pale breasts, they stand and shield their eyes from the sun as they watch us bobbing at the edge of the harbour wall. They turn excitedly to one another and reach for the rush baskets they had earlier settled at their feet. Delving into these containers, they fill their hands with rose petals and hurl them at us, pink clouds spiralling in the breeze which carries them to the sea edge, where they descend upon the jetty steps like falls of fragrant snow.

But of course, no one here has ever seen snow. If I could only have brought some from my travels, what a sensation it would cause! For here in Persia there are no seasonal changes, and nothing happens to disturb the pleasant, peaceful cycle of our lives. The sun-drenched sea laps against the white walls of the inlet, blossom-laden trees rustle faintly on the verdant hillside, swallows chase a path across an azure sky, and everyone is quite content.

It is good to be home.

The cabin-boys help me with the brass-handled baskets we have filled with the booty from far-off lands. As we set them on the dock, I see a distant robed figure shake herself from her dozing trance and leave the coolness of

167

her *exedra*, raising her arms in heartfelt welcome. The splendour of the scene overwhelms me, and I almost lose my balance as I seek to hold the moment in my mind. Everything is blue and white and yellow, the open saffron robes of the young women, the domes of the sea palace shining in pale alabaster, and in the distance the rich green hills still veiled by rainbow mists that will slowly dissipate as the trees unfold to the warmth of the day.

How I love this land! My travels are arduous and rarely pleasant. On every trip a smaller crew returns. I survive these brute excursions in the knowledge that at the end of each journey I will return to my true homeland, to the country I love so dearly. It is still early in the morning, and the air is filled with the freshness of a new day. As I fill my lungs I can taste the seasalt on my tongue. My nostrils detect the sharp smell of newly scythed grass, the sweet tang of cut nectarines.

The girls arrive in trains of rose petals, kissing us in welcome, their smooth skin warming our sea-chilled cheeks. Laughing, the bo'sun opens his bag and passes out gifts of scented almonds and painted beads, wrapped in multi-coloured parchment and tied with silk ribbons. He does this at the end of every trip, and the girls lead him on in an elaborate teasing charade that everyone knows and understands.

The happy crowd parts as my beloved approaches, her head shyly lowered, her dark hair garlanded with blue poppies and braided with gold at her exposed white bosom. As she raises her eyes to mine she smiles, and the world grows brighter still. We embrace, her arms linking behind my neck, and her lips touch mine as the warm breeze settles her robe around my thighs in silken folds.

We walk home towards the dazzling gold-roofed temples of the Handmaidens of the Sea Priestess, and I feel as if I shall never leave Persia again. High above us parrots are calling to each other, shocking vermilion flashes passing in high-looping rituals. I know their cries, and stop to watch, thrilled by the familiarity of their ascent. Their lovecalls counterpoint the distant chopping of the sea at the wall. Here everything has a familiar feel, the hand of my beloved pressed in mine, our steady rhythmic walk, the neatly cropped cyprus trees that line the pathway leading to our house, the Ionian blue of the mosaics that swathe the walls of the orchard.

Here in Persia, I am safe.

'You must tell me all about your trip,' she says softly, pushing back the gate that leads into the sunfilled court-yard of our home. 'I am so happy to see you safely returned once more. Did you encounter cut-throats, trolls, brigands, sea monsters?'

I laugh as I seat myself between the stone satyrs half buried in the ivy behind the white marble *lararium*. 'No, my dear, I encountered men, mere mortals only, but bad ones all the same.' My smile fades with the memory, and I turn my tanned arms over, revealing the tight red scars so newly healed.

'Tell me about these creatures,' she demands. 'Are they not like us?'

'Not at all. They are natural aggressors, broad men with red hair and red faces who would do us harm without a single prick of conscience. Anger is their natural state, righteousness and hatred their weapons. They are Christians, men who wish us to be like them, and who become dangerous when we refuse to exchange our gods for theirs.'

'What is their country like?'

'Cold, and brown, and wet, and harsh. Many thousands of them live there, many more than us.'

She passes me a pomegranate and I dig my fingers into the tough yellow hide, breaking the skin to reach the bitter scarlet globes within.

'Did these men attempt to capture you?' she asks, alarmed. 'What ever did you do to save yourselves from

169

such barbarians? Did you take their leader's life?'

'We fought,' I say, suddenly weary as my muscles loosen in the soothing heat. The sun is a wheel of flame, bleaching away my darkest memories. 'We fought and freed ourselves, and other captives too.'

'So there was no bloodshed,' she asks carefully, watching as I pick apart the globules, the crimson juice running between my fingers.

'I did not say that,' I reply. 'We lost several members of the crew, good men and true.'

'But you are here, safely returned home. I wish you would never leave Persia again. If only you would promise me to stay this time.'

'Yes,' I say, embracing her as tears break from my eyes, 'this time I will stay here with you forever.' As I bury my head in the honeyed perspiration of her breasts, I pluck open her robe, run my tongue across her sweet salt stomach, and know that nothing can ever separate us again.

By the angle of the sun in the copper sky it is far past noon when I awake. The shade has shifted beyond the sputtering green fountain on the far side of the courtyard, and my beloved is seated within the villa. Her silhouette is set within the window as she sews, slowly drawing the golden thread through the frame, her needle casting a spear of sun as it arcs above the cloth.

For weeks I have been without warmth, and now the suddenly renewed heat has awoken a restlessness within me. I stand and take an earthenware pitcher to the fountain, fill it to the brim and slowly allow the delicious cool liquid to trickle across my burning brow, my arms and chest.

'Are you hungry yet?' My beloved stands at the window batting at herself with an ostrich feather fan, watching as I rearrange my robes. 'I am planning a special meal in honour of your homecoming. Pheasant and partridge, marinated in nectar and roasted in roses.'

'In that case, I should take a walk to strengthen my appetite,' I say, and set off in the direction of the High Priestess's watergardens.

Here, passing between featherbeds of white and purple bougainvillaea, I see the familiar faces of friends and neighbours, all of whom pause to smile and wave, offering their pleasure at my safe return.

'Returned again, Franciscus!' calls a round-faced man on a mule. 'We had given you up for good this time!'

Before I can reply, my attention is distracted by the laughter of two young women who stand at the steps of the *tepidarium*. They are waving silken kerchiefs in my direction. 'We missed you, Franciscus!' they cry in perfect unison, for they are twins and share a common mind. 'You shall not leave again so easily!'

I pass my father's grey-haired servant at the garden entrance. He gives a toothless smile and doffs his woven sun-bonnet in respect. 'So glad to see you have returned, young master,' he says gratefully. 'May the gods always protect you.'

How could I not have returned to such a glad arcadia, where life maintains its pure and simple stride, passing each day in peace and harmony? Here amidst the fantastic buildings of the royal court, where children laugh and play below the flower-twined columns that surround the High Priestess's palace, where everyone is always happy, never sad ...

The watergardens are filled with flowers of every scent and variety. Pure stream-water from the hills is lifted and sprayed from a hundred fountains of varying sizes, filling the air with vaporous rainbows. Carp and angelfish flick and turn in the crystal pools below them.

At the farthest end of the parade is another sunlit square, larger than all the rest. This one is filled with tall bronze statues of our gods. Some are over thirty feet in height, and stand guarding the entrance to a sacred valley. I love walking between them, feeling their benign, imperious gaze upon my head as they reach out their arms to protect us, who worship and tend to them.

I step between the stripes of shadow, the fingers of a giant hand, and gaze up at these noble likenesses of our gods, filled with awe.

I would like to walk further, but know that if I do so I will be late for the evening meal which my beloved has painstakingly prepared for me. And so I turn, and retrace my steps to the villa.

By the time I return home the sun is setting in the hills, filling the distant woodlands with hesperidian fire. Lamps are burning in copper bowls within the garden, filling the air with a richly wooded scent. Off towards the harbour someone is singing, accompanied by *auloi* and *tympani*, a melodious sound that lightly drifts above the walls.

The cooked meats are quite magnificently prepared, as befits a homecoming meal. My beloved wears a revealing robe of peach chiffon, and golden bands of entwined snakes on either arm, gifts I have brought her from my travels. It is only after we have eaten that she says what I know she has been wanting to speak of since I returned from my walk.

'You were gone so long I had begun to worry.' She tears a mint-leaf from the fruit bowl and touches it to her lips. 'How far did you walk?' Her question is deceptively casual. I know that beneath the lightness of her tone there is genuine concern.

'As far as the Valley of the Gods,' I reply. 'Just to the entrance, you understand.'

'Darling.' She reaches across the table to touch the tips of my brown fingers with her pale hands. 'You have only just returned home, and you have made a promise to me.'

'I know,' I reply, chastened by my irresponsible behaviour. 'Sometimes I have to see.' Although I have to admit that usually the urge to do so does not seize me for many months following my return.

'This time, Franciscus, you must try to stay away.'

I agree, and the rest of the evening passes as it should do, in perfect harmony.

And so the pattern of life is restored. One day I visit the Royal Court, and I and my fellow shipmates gain an audience with the Handmaidens of the High Priestess herself. Another day I fish, and work in the courtyard, building a crib for the child we soon hope to have. And always I write, filling my journal with pages of inky scribble. My beloved cannot read, and so I am teaching her. Little by little we progress, question and answer, filling the days.

But my curiosity returns, and like a buried fire slowly builds.

On the day my beloved announces that she is with child, we celebrate by driving up into the hills. I tie a canopy of orange silk across the mulecart and load it with picnic provisions, although we will find all the fruit and fresh water we need in the woods. As the carts trundles higher and higher across the ascending pastures, bluebirds swoop about us like falling pieces of sky. Here the flowers grow in even greater profusion, tangled nests of poppies and anenomes hosting banquets for explosions of blood-red butterflies.

We seat ourselves in a grassy nook far above the distant water, where we can watch a flotilla of triremes setting off across the ocean like ponderous migrating seabirds.

The mulecart's canopy billows like a ship's sail, responding to the call.

'Do you think you will always be content here?' asks my beloved. She is facing away from me, looking out to sea. She tucks a strand of ebony hair behind her ear. I cannot see the expression on her face.

'I believe so,' I reply as honestly as I can. 'This is my

173

home. And soon we will have a child to consider.'

'Then why did you leave before? Your interests are scholarly, and yet you set sail with rough men for places I can only guess at, far-off lands, dark and terrible ...'

'Only one land, and that against my will, as well you know.'

'If only you never had to leave my side again. Everything you could possibly want is here for the asking.'

'Sometimes we discover things we do not want to know.'

'Then why discover them at all?'

'Because it is in our nature to do so. We are human and naturally inquisitive, and cannot help ourselves.' I reach over through lush talons of grass and still her questions with my parting lips.

Just two days later, I find myself back at the entrance to the Valley of the Gods.

The morning is crisp and still. The sun has only just begun to rise. I stand between the marble bases of the towering statues, which appear a hazy blue in the half-light of dawn. At home my beloved lies curled in slumber on a golden bed of swan-down. Unable to sleep, I have come here to visit the statue of the High Priestess. Few others ever do so, although it is not expressly forbidden. Nothing is forbidden here in Persia, so long as it is for the good. Here there is no crime, no jealousy, no hatred, no bitterness. Instead there is enchantment and endless joy, day upon day of peace and safety.

It is not forbidden to visit the statue of the High Priestess — but it is considered unwise to read the words she has had inscribed across the marble fascia at her feet. For so profound is her wisdom that it affects mere mortals like heady liquor on an empty belly.

As I approach the soaring figure I look up, becoming lost in the benificence of her calm gaze. She stands with

174

her head held high, her blind green eyes staring out across the harbour far below. Her feet are placed together, her arms outstretched. In the open palm of her right hand is a proffered laurel-sprig. On the back of her left hand stands a dove. Hers is the voice of wisdom, rationality and goodness. She is the representation of all I hold dear, the embodiment of all I value in my life, the shining symbol of Persia itself.

So why may I not read her message?

My eyes travel down from the verdured bronze folds of her gown to her sandalled toes. In the trees behind me, the first of the morning songbirds begins to trill.

Below I see it, the carved legend that has been inscribed across her base. My eyes alight eagerly upon each word, as with pounding heart and trembling breath I read: *What Have You Done With The Fucking Gun?*

At first I cannot comprehend. Is this some form of foreign language? A cryptogrammic reference, perhaps? I stand there frowning, attempting to decipher the puzzling message. Then a familiar roaring fills my ears and the pale dawn splinters into searing, soaring shards of light. My safe surroundings rush away from me and Persia vanishes, sucked into the darkness as I hear the anguished cry of my beloved replaced with the bark of my interrogator, pacing a room of corrugated tin.

'I said what have you done with the fucking gun?'

He hawks and spits on the hard clay floor, stepping back to allow the other American, the mad one, closer access. I smell the stink of their sweat, and my own fear. The wire tying my wrists together cuts white-hot bands of pain through my mind, and for a moment it is impossible to concentrate. My mouth is filled with blood and I find it difficult to speak. Earlier they loosened my teeth with a hammer.

'We know there was a gun, you little Iranian bastard,'

says the mad one. 'Your pal wouldn't tell us where it was so we blew his fucking head off.' I can see him from the corner of my remaining eye. He lies on the excrement-smeared floor like a flyblown sack. There is nothing solid left above the bridge of his nose. Insects are swarming in the glossy viscera which protrude from his gaping stomach.

'If you don't talk, you're gonna wind up like your little fuck-buddy here,' says the first one, leaning close. He waits for a reasonable period while I try to compose an answer, but I am still confused. Was there a gun? There had been rumours among the other students, but if there was a weapon I did not see it.

'This is a waste of fucking time, man,' cries the mad one, suddenly lunging forward. 'He ain't even in the room with us. Let me stick a knife in him.'

'Wait, he's trying to say something.' The first American raises his hand. He listens carefully. I bring burning air from my windpipe. I shape my lips. He leans closer as I try to say it again.

'*Persia?* What the fuck is that?'

'It's what they used to call this place,' says his partner, lowering the knife. He thrusts his head at me and grins. 'It don't exist no more, you dumb fuck,' he shouts, brandishing the blade again. 'It ain't nothing but a state of mind.'

He punches the knife into my shoulder with the heel of his hand, popping flesh. Blood sprays out like punctures in a hosepipe as he bumps the blade over my chest, jamming the tip against my ribs. The pain redoubles its assault and consciousness begins to slide away once more. The stench of shit and sweat is overpowered by the bitter fragrance of freshly opened lemons. The imprisoning agony of the abductor's knife is replaced with the freedom of the harbour winds. The men retreat. The tin walls fade. The sunlight beckons.

... And once again I am in Persia.

176

Black Day At Bad Rock

I have this irrational desire to kill Mick Jagger.

I've never told anyone about this until now. To explain why, I have to relate a story. Most of it is true, but one part isn't. Just for protection, you understand. You can figure it out for yourself.

At every school there's always one kid everyone hates and shuns. I was that kid.

Obviously I hadn't intended to be. It just worked out that way. It didn't help that I was stick-thin and wore glasses with sellotaped arms and hung out in the library when I should have been caving in heads on the rugby pitch. Pens leaked in my shirt pockets. I was born un-fashionable, from Oxford toecaps to short-back-and-sides. I still owned a clean cap. I was a classic hopeless case. Worst of all, I knew it.

The sporty set had a low tolerance level for kids like us. A boy called Bates in the year below me announced that rugby was for thickos and got hit in the face with a cricket bat. It knocked his nosebone right back into his skull.

This school was a posh school near posh Blackheath, the only posh bit of shit-ugly South London. I lived miles away, in chip-paper-strewn Abbey Wood, gateway to teen delinquency. The neighbourhood kids were neurotic, doped-up, walking scar tissue, groomed for early failure. Hanging out with them wasn't an available option. My mother, a study in thwarted gentility, faded, thrifty, lower-middle-class, never expected much from life and certainly didn't get it, but she expected more of me. My Dad was the Invisible Man. He left all the major decisions to his

179

wife, preferring to devote the whole of his adult life to revarnishing the doorframes, a job he had still not finished when I last went home. I got to the posh school because I got good exam marks. Most of the other kids were paid for by their parents.

School was a train journey to a different planet. Blackheath was full of dark antique shops and damp tea-rooms, and called itself a village. Ideally, the shopkeepers would have built a moat around the place to keep out the trash.

The timeframe may slide a little here, but I think this happened at some point in the very early seventies, when the 'village' was still full of crimson-painted boutiques selling lime-green miniskirts and military tunics. Trends weren't so nakedly motivated by marketing then. They seemed to evolve in a happy coincidence of mood and style. *Bonnie And Clyde* had been playing on and off at the local fleapit since 1968, and much to the horror of our elders everyone at school imitated the doomed gangsters as closely as possible. Me and Brian 'Third Degree' Burns, the kid I sat next to for eight years without running out of things to talk about, went up West and stole two guns from Bermans & Nathans theatrical costumiers with a forged letter purporting to be from the Dramatics master. The guns were fake, but were cast in metal and came in real leather holsters, like Steve McQueen's in *Bullitt*, which was good enough for us.

The music around this time was mostly terrible. Of course, now everyone thinks it's great. But it wasn't. Marc Bolan wanking on about fairies and stardust, Groundhogs and Iron Butterfly sounding like somebody masturbating in a roomful of dustbin lids, Jethro Tull hopping about on one leg playing a flute for Christ's sake. About the only bands I could bear to listen to were Mott The Hoople and — the great white god Jimmy Page – Led Zeppelin. *Whole Lotta Love* received some major suburban bedroom turntable time. It was an antidote to the local disco, where everyone sat at the corners of the room nodding their heads and grooving along with little spastic gestures of their hands. The girls wore floor-length crushed maroon velvet dresses and had long kinked hair, pre-Raphaelite virgins on cider and joints. The generally accepted idea of a good time was getting very, very stoned while carefully listening to the screaming bit from Pink Floyd's *Careful With That Axe, Eugene.* The sixties had finished swinging and the seventies hadn't started doing anything. My formative years. If my parents had only waited a while before having kids I could have been a punk.

I did have a few friends, but they were all like me i.e. shunned and/or regularly duffed up. The other kids had a collective noun to describe us. Weeds. We were the school Weeds. Do you have *any idea* how humiliating that was?

We mostly spent our spare time dodging our class-mates, revising Latin, sneaking into double-billed X movies like *Dracula, Prince of Darkness* and *Plague Of The Zombies,* and reading Ian Fleming novels. Everyone was talking about Bond having his balls tortured in *Casino Royale* I think it was, and Jane Fonda's see-through clothes in *Barbarella.* Also, there was this Swedish movie called *Seventeen* which had female pubic hair in, but some of us thought this was going too far. Nobody in my class ever got to speak to an actual live girl because it was an all-boys school where strapping chaps played lots of healthy contact sports in shorts. (I found out much later that those contact sports involving our revered head boy and the gym master extended to the shower room after games. Years later I heard they were running an antique shop together. A fucking *antique* shop. I'm not making this part up.)

Homework was four hours a night minimum, caps were to be worn in the 'village' on penalty of death and the boys from the nearby comprehensive, whose parents voted Labour and were therefore common, used to nightly pick fights with us at the bus stop. The one time we had a chance to meet girls was when our sister school teamed up for the annual joint operatic production, and obviously only dogs and germs signed up for six weeks of vocal strangulation in the company of *Die Verkaufte Braut.*

For the weaker members of the pack it's always a strange, cocooned existence on the sidelines of the action. We enviously watched the other kids as they honed their social skills, getting their hands into drunk girls' shirts while they danced to *Ride A White Swan.* We weren't like them. We were still making Aurora model kits of mummies and werewolves. None of us were rebels. The school had a good name. The head and his teachers, tall and stiff and imperious in their black gowns, stalking the corridors like adrenalised vampires, were grudgingly respected because they kept their distance and occasionally maimed their pupils. We'd seen the movie *If,* in which Malcolm McDowell machine-gunned his teachers, and it just wasn't us.

We spent our time discussing *The Avengers, Monty Python* and the lyrics to the songs in *Easy Rider.*

One day, all this changed.

Mike Branch, the relief art teacher, arrived.

He was about thirty years younger than any other member of staff, and came for the summer. Of course, everyone instantly liked him. He was handsome and funny and mad-looking. He let you smoke in the kiln room. His hair was over his collar. And *he wore jeans.* To schoolboys who were expected to wear regulation underpants, this was nothing short of frankly amazing. He asked us to call him Mike, and explained that as long as he was around, classes would be very different from what we were used to.

The first time I saw him, he was lounging with his brown suede boots on the desktop and reaching a long

182

arm up to the blackboard to wipe the masters of the Florentine renaissance away with his sleeve.

'I want you to forget the heavy stuff for a while,' he casually explained. 'We'll be concentrating on the Dadaist movement.' Then he wrote 'Rebellion in Art' across the board in red and threw the heavy chalk block clean through a closed window. There was a crack of shattering glass and we all came to attention, filled with borderline homoerotic admiration.

'Don't misunderstand me,' said Branch, sliding his legs from the desk and rising. 'We'll be working hard. But we'll be taking a new approach.' And with that he revealed the school record player — a big old wooden thing, never known to have been removed from the office of the headmaster — plugged it in, and began to acquaint us with his personal taste in rock.

Suddenly Art became the hot class to take.

Branch's periods were unpredictable and (something unheard of in our school) actually interesting. We created Anti-Meat art and Self-Destruct art and Death-To-The-Ruling-Class art. The other teachers tolerated our displays because technically speaking they weren't very good, which made them less of a threat. Besides, as pupils we were Showing An Interest, thus achieving a prime educational directive. The fact that we would have donated our kidneys for vivisection if Mike had asked us hadn't passed unnoticed, either. The other teachers realised they could learn something from watching the art class.

One day, Branch placed a single on the turntable and played it. I was fist deep in a gore-sprayed papier-maché duck when *Paint It Black* by the Rolling Stones came on. I'd never really liked the song. It already sounded dated when it was first released. Too dirge-like. It reminded me

183

of *House Of The Rising Sun.* But Mike had a special reason for playing it.

'For the climax of our season of Anti-Art,' he said, strolling between my paint-spattered classmates, 'you are going to Paint It Black.'

'What do you mean?' I asked. He turned to look at me. He had these deep-set blue eyes that settled on you like searchlights, looking for truth.

'A day of artistic anarchy. The idea is to take all of the work you produce this summer and paint it matt black. Then you're going to glue it all together, along with anything else that looks suitable, stick the record player in the centre, and stand it in the middle of the quadrangle.'

It seemed a bit stupid, but nobody argued.

'What if someone tells us to take it down, sir?' asked the pudding-basin-haircutted Paul Doggart, fellow-Weed, a boy who was born to say *sir* a lot in his life.

'You don't take it down. You don't obey anyone's orders until the stroke of noon. Then I'll appear and we'll play *Paint It Black* from the centre of the sculpture. The art will last for the duration of the song, and then we'll destroy it.'

'But won't we get into trouble, sir?' pressed Doggart.

'No, because I'll forewarn the other masters. They'll be turned on to expect some unspecified action of guerilla art.' (Yes, embarrassing as it may seem, people really spoke like this in the early seventies).

So, preparations were made, the date was set for the last day of term (third Tuesday in June) and we painted every-thing we could lay our hands on and added it to the pile. Clocks. Chairs. Tyres. Lampshades. Toys. Clothes. Tailor's dummies. Car exhausts. A washing machine. And all the time, the damned song played and played until it wore out and had to be replaced with a new copy.

Mike Branch strolled around the artroom, shifting from

184

table to table, stopping to watch as Ashley Turpin, a fat kid with almost *geological* facial acne attempted to get black paint to stick to a brass candelabra. The master nodded his head thoughtfully, running his thumb beneath his chin as he considered the sheer anarchy of his loyal pupil's work. Finally, with lowered eyebrows and a crooked smile, he turned his attention to the boy. 'Extremely groovy, Turpin,' he said. Turpin, who had previously shown no promise in any area of scholastic endeavour beyond 'O' Level Body Odour, was pitifully grateful.

Identified to other classes by our laminated badges, (black, circular, blank — oh, the *nihilism*) we suddenly found ourselves behaving like some kind of creative elite. Me and the other despised and shunned creeps had finally found our cause. For the first time ever we were part of a team, and the fact that the Sport Kings all hated us worked in favour of our anarchistic behaviour.

We began to be *bad*. I mean bad as in modern bad, good bad. By the week before end of term, we were discovering the non-artistic applications of *Paint It Black*. Minor league anarchy. Having pizzas with disgusting toppings delivered to masters COD. Gluing their wipers to their car windscreens. Brian 'Third Degree' Burns upped the stakes by removing the wheels from the French teacher's moped, painting them black and adding them to the sculpture.

Then someone found a masters' home address list. Crank calls to the wives, made from the caretaker's phone by the dining hall. Then obscene calls. Anyone who whined that it was wrong was ditched from the group and returned to the status of a Weed. His badge was ceremoniously taken back. To wimp out on the rebellion was to fail as a human being. The Sport Kings stopped thundering up and down the pitch to cast jealous sidelong glances at the Black Brigade. (Funny thing, we had only had one kid in our year who was actually black, Jackson

185

Rabot, and he wasn't interested in anarchy at all. He wanted to be a conservative MP).

Of course, the shit soon started coming down on us. Efforts were made to find the culprits. There were extra detentions, cancelled privileges. But end of term pranks were expected, and so far we weren't far beyond that.

On Monday, the day before term ended, the day before *B Day*, we stepped up the action and went too far. (You saw this coming, didn't you?) It's blindingly obvious now that some of the group didn't appreciate the subtleties of Mike Branch's orchestrated artistic protest, but had just joined for the party attitude. One of these B-stream hold-backs threw some kind of concentrated acid over the geography master's car. It stank and made an amazing mess, melting clean through to the chassis. Incredible.

News of the attack spread around class like wildfire. Paul Doggart blanched beneath his pudding-basin haircut and threatened to leave the group, but didn't because there was nowhere else to go, and even Brian 'Third Degree' Burns was impressed. Nobody dared own up. We were given until noon the next day to produce a culprit, or the whole brigade would be kept back while everyone else left for the summer. But by now there was an *all or nothing* atmosphere in the group, and we stayed solid. When the head took his record player back, someone brought in their own hi-fi system. The damned song played on.

There was never much studying done on the last day of term. Leisure activities were tolerated. We were allowed to bring in — wait for it — *board games*. I shit you not. And we could wear casual clothes, so everyone made an effort to look hip. Recently I found an old photograph of us Weeds together, taken on that final morning. You'd think we'd been dressed by blind people. Poor old Doggart.

Mike had arranged a double art period for his brigade of rebels. All of the black-painted stuff was arranged in

186

chunks around the room. The record was playing as high as the volume would allow, the sound completely distorted. The artroom was christened The Rock Shop. (I know it's embarrassing now but at the time you'd narrow your eyes and go 'Hey, if anyone wants me I'm at The Rock for a Study Period.' Highly cool) It was in a separate annexe of its own, and inside it seventeen maladjusted kids were free to do whatever they liked.

The party really started when Bates Junior brought in his mother's hidden supply of mixed spirits (the woman must have been an incredible lush, there was about six litres of the stuff). There were joints, courtesy of Simon Knight's brother, who was possibly the most corrupt customs officer in Britain, and there was acid, although I didn't have any. Everyone went into the kiln room to smoke (force of habit) and soon you could get high just by opening the door, walking in and breathing.

Everyone knew that the gym teacher was a queer because he brought this skinny hairless dog to school. A Mexican thing, big eyes, ugly little teeth. He never watched us in the showers or anything, (the teacher, not the dog) because he was too scared of losing his job, but he had this stupid mutt. *Had* being the key word, because Brian 'Third Degree' Burns came up with the great rebellious artistic act of luring it into the kiln room with a piece of bacon. The old art master had always warned us that the inside of the kiln, on full power, was hotter than the surface of Mars, so we decided to test it. A scientific experiment, like sending Laika the Alsatian into orbit with no hope of getting him back. The idea was to dip the dog in slip clay and bake it, then paint it black and add it to the sculpture.

The kiln was squat and wide, with these thick stone walls so you couldn't hear the dog whining once the door was shut. After about an hour we unsealed it and found that the only thing left was a small patch of blackened

187

sticks. Doggart started moaning about cruelty to animals, so we covered one side of his body with glue and pressed him against the artroom wall until his skin stuck.

Then we began to assemble the sculpture. Forming a chain, we passed the sections out into the school quadrangle, a pathetic damp square of grass surrounded by rain-stained concrete walkways. As the sculpture rose above the height of a man, an interested crowd gathered. The gym teacher asked us if we had the authority to do what we were doing and we said yes, so he went away. I figured he hadn't found out about his dog yet.

At a quarter to twelve the sculpture was fifteen feet high and we still had a load of stuff to add. Table legs, television sets and doll's arms poked out from the twisted black heap. The record player was wired up, but we were going to be late for our noon deadline, mainly because we were all so ripped that we were repeating each other's tasks. The assistant headmaster, a sickly wraith-like creature who looked as if he hadn't slept since Buddy Holly died, asked Simon Knight if he'd been drinking and Simon said no, which was true, although he had dropped acid. Behind his calm, reasonable, innocent exterior he was tripping off his face. Back then the teachers didn't really know what to look for.

The big moment arrived and we were still building the sculpture. Most of the school had turned out to watch. Everyone knew that something special was about to happen. The event had been whispered about for weeks. There were all kinds of rumours flying around — most of them far more imaginative than what was actually planned. Even the Sport Kings were here. Then the headmaster appeared to see what all the fuss was about. He stood in front of the crowd with his bony arms folded behind his back like the Duke Edinburgh, a look of thin tolerance on his face, tapering towards displeasure.

This was our brief flicker of fame. All eyes were on us. We were the kings. The *bollocks du chien*. The members of the brigade stood back while Brain climbed into the sculpture and started the record player. The opening guitar riff heralded Mick Jagger's voice, a voice which always sounded as if he was leaning obscenely into the mike mouthing distilled insolence. We looked around for Mike. Our Mike, the leader of the Black. No sign. Then we noticed the headmaster.

His displeasure had changed to — well, not pleasure but something sourly approximating it.

'If you're looking for Mr Branch,' he said in a clear Scottish Presbyterian voice that rang across the square, 'you will not find him here. He left the school last night with no intention whatsoever of returning today.' He pronounced the 'H' in whatsoever.

The headmaster triumphantly turned on his heel and led the other teachers back to the common room. And the record stuck. It stuck on the word *black*. The repeated syllable taunted, and the derision began. The Sport Kings just drifted away, snorting to each other, too bored to even beat us up. Suddenly we were Weeds again. It was as if the natural order had been restored, as if everyone had been returned to their correct status, with us back at the bottom, and the holidays could now begin.

'No intention whatsoever.' It was the *whatsoever* that hurt, as if he'd been ready to bottle out all along. The last of the Sport Kings were hanging back by the bike sheds watching us, evidently planning to crack a few Weed heads after all. We didn't care about them. We were too choked to even talk.

Brian ripped the plug from the record player, snatched off the record and returned to the artroom close to tears. He tipped over a table and threw a chair across the room, then so did a couple of the others, and suddenly we were smashing everything in sight. I guess none of us had expected to be betrayed at such an early point in our lives.

189

Perhaps if we could have had sex right then, nothing more would have happened. But we hardly knew any girls, so we had to make do with violence.

Paul Doggart was still stuck to the wall. We'd forgotten all about him. He started making a fuss about wanting to leave, but he couldn't get out of his clothes. His blazer and trousers were cemented fast to the white-painted concrete. So was his fat left cheek. His bellyaching went against the general flow of energy so we spray-painted him black with the leftovers in the cans, hoping it would shut him up. Of course this had the reverse effect, so someone (to this day I don't know who) finally obliged by putting a foot against the wall and tearing him free.

Doggart came away, but not quietly and not in one piece. His cheek left a grisly triangle of flesh stuck to the wall. The last time I saw him that day he was stumbling between the tables clutching his face, crying in hoarse angry sobs. By the time we had finished in the artroom, paint was dripping from the walls and there was broken glass everywhere. We knew someone must have heard the noise by now and didn't dare open the door, so we went out through the windows.

Our adrenaline was really pumping. Using the knives from the artroom we slit every tyre in the car park as we left. I cut the fingers of my right hand to the bone at the second joint because I was gripping my knife so hard.

That night most of us met up and went to see *Woodstock*, but by this time all those Country Joe And The Fish peace songs could only leave us cold. A bridge had been crossed. An unspoken bond had been forged between us.

It's funny how moments can change lives.

Doggart nearly died. The black paint infected his wound and formed some kind of poisonous chain re-action, so that the damage to his face became a whole lot worse. He had a load of skin grafts over the next seven

190

years. And his mind got all fucked up. Nothing he ever said again made much sense. I think his old mum tried to sue someone, but was forced through ill-health and lack of funds to give up the case.

I visited him in hospital once.

I remember walking along a wax-tiled corridor, shoes squeaking, pushing open the door at the end. He was lying in a darkened room, unfriendly eyes staring accusingly from a mess of taut shiny skin. As I made to leave, his right hand grabbed my wrist. I think he was trying to thank me for coming to visit him. I gave him a Get Well Soon card from the members of the B-Brigade. A fold of plain paper, blank shiny blackness. So hip.

The entire brigade was expelled, but the school took no further action. They had too many paying parents to risk getting a bad name. As I said, it was a posh school. Most of the Old Boys were masons. Money changed hands; word never got out. With the time I had spare I attended art college. Cue tears from mother.

Years later, someone heard what had happened to Mike Branch. It turned out that he never was an art teacher, relief or otherwise. He'd played in a band once, opening for the Stones. That was his sole claim to fame. He'd walked into our school with credentials that no one had bothered to check. Then, the day before our big event he'd simply walked away again, gone to the North to do something else. Somebody told me he's in property sales now. That sounds about right.

Still, I wonder if he had the remotest notion of the effect he had on us. He changed the lives of seventeen boys. Thinking about it now, I find it incredible that we trusted someone who regularly wore a turtleneck sweater and gold medallion beneath a brown patch-suede jacket, but there you go. I owned a mauve two-tone shirt with a huge rounded collar that fastened with velcro, a fashion crime I compounded with the addition of yellow hipster bellbottoms.

Personally, I blame Mick Jagger.

Revelation's Child

'I just can't believe it,' Amy said again. 'Six damned years I've been there, and the son-of-a-bitch says he isn't going to honour the lease because he knows he's got me on a legal technicality.' It was Max's birthday and they were all at the Italian restaurant on Bleeker, Max and Marsha and Howard, and some girl Howard was dating who hadn't said a word all evening but sat playing with his hair.

Marsha refilled her glass and passed the bottle. 'You said yourself he was a lousy landlord. In all the years you've been there, did he ever take care of the repairs on time? You'll be better off finding a new place than fighting for this one. Surely there must be something nearer town.'

'In Manhattan?' said Amy, finishing her wine. 'Are you kidding? There's nothing remotely in my price range. If there's an apartment that's halfway decent it never even gets advertised, you know that. And living here wouldn't be good for Simon. Besides, not that many places even take children.'

'It seems we know one that would,' said Max. 'We were just talking about it before you arrived. A converted town-house on West 44th. The area's a little rough but it'd be the prefect business location for you.'

'That's right,' said Marsha, 'and Simon could go to the same pre-school as Tommy. Howie, how much did you say the rent was?'

Howard thought for a moment and named a low figure.

'Wait, there's a catch,' said Amy. 'If this place is so great, why hasn't it been snatched up?' She gave a crooked smile and looked around the table. 'Is this some kind of Stephen King apartment? Did someone die horribly in it?'

'No, but you're right about there being a catch,' said

Max, lighting a fresh cigarette. 'The building belongs to a group of trustees. It's some kind of Christian fellowship, the CFF, and you have to satisfy their board. They're very moral, and very religious.'

Max didn't need to spell it out plainer than that. Amy was a single mother. Simon's father had left before she could even inform him of her pregnancy. Now her son was four years old, and the examining board would presumably want to know about the child's background.

'I knew it sounded too good to be true,' said Amy, throwing her napkin at Max.

'Sweetie, you could always lie,' said Marsha.

She could see the next question coming, and she dreaded it.

'Are you a regular churchgoer, Mrs Patrick?'

The three of them sat in a row like sanctimonious monkeys, their lips pursed, their eyes hooded. The oldest, Mr Whickes, was in his seventies. He was seated on the left with his chair tilted slightly back, carefully watching and waiting for an answer as she awkwardly folded her hands in her lap.

Amy Patrick looked from one to the other and swallowed audibly. 'I don't go quite as often as I'd like,' she lied. The room smelled of air freshener over damp carpet. A stern but lurid portrait of the Madonna stood above the mantelpiece like a blue-gowned dominatrix.

'But you are a practising Christian?'

The middle speaker was the tallest, a peppery orangutan of a woman, bony and thin. Her name was Mrs Forrest. She was in her early fifties, and wore round bottle-thick glasses. Her dry ginger hair was piled high on her head and held in place with a plastic slide. She seemed to be in charge.

'Well certainly, and you know what they say, practice makes perfect.' Amy gave a small, desperate laugh and realised that it was a mistake to try a joke with these people. *Stick to the script,* she thought, *for a two bedroom midtown apartment you have to make them love you.*

'Then you'll be pleased to know that there's a church at the end of the street.' The last speaker was fatter than the other two put together. She wore a badly-cut dress with a blue floral print, the petals slightly out of register so that she seemed to blur when she moved. Her face was smothered in broken veins. Her name was Miss Banforth, and she wore no makeup, even though it would have made her appearance more user-friendly.

'I noticed the church on the way here,' said Amy. 'It has a very, uh, striking appearance.' *In a decrepit, run-down, depress-you-to-death kind of way.*

'We don't allow pets of any kind,' said Miss Banforth, re-reading her application, although she had already examined it in detail. 'I see that you have a small child.' She sounded as if she regularly lumped the two species together.

'Yes, a boy, Simon. He's just turned four. He's very quiet. I have his picture here.' She removed a photograph from her purse and passed it across.

'And *Mr* Patrick?' asked Whickes, leaving the implication hanging in mid-air.

'I'm afraid my husband — died of spinal cancer two years ago.' *May God forgive me,* she thought, looking at the floor. She wondered what else she was capable of saying in order to obtain a lease on the apartment.

'You poor thing,' said Mrs Forrest consolingly. 'Too young for such a tragedy.' She looked at the others and smiled. Whickes harrumphed and dropped his chair down with a thump.

'About financial arrangements,' he began, tapping the end of his pencil on the desk. 'Without a husband, how would you propose to manage the deposit and the quarterly rental?'

'I have some income set aside for the deposit, Mr Whickes, and I make a comfortable living from the sale of magazine articles.'

'What sort of magazines?'

'That's quite enough cross-examining, John,' said Mrs Forrest, handing him the photograph. 'Isn't this child just adorable?'

I'm in, thought Amy. *I'm in.*

'If you don't sit still I swear I'm going to beat you to death.' She threw Simon a threatening stare but he just laughed.

'I want to go outside,' he said, 'It's boring.'

'It's still raining, darling.' She wiped condensation from the kitchen window and peered five floors down into the street. She had no intention of breaking the bad news to him for a while. Although she had dreamed of finding an apartment like this, Simon would never be able to play outside without the strictest supervision.

The building was located on a gentle curve of the road that allowed a distant view of the river, a dull grey band between the factories on the horizon. It wasn't, strictly speaking, an unsafe area, but how did you define the term 'safe' in a city where the junkies left infected needles in children's sandboxes?

'Marsha and Tommy will be here soon, so you'll have someone to play with.' She removed the last of the cartons from the work-top and placed it on the floor. Cutlery and crockery were all unpacked. Most of the furniture had been donated by her mother, and the delivery of the sofa had been delayed, but it looked as if they were in pretty good shape.

The apartment had high moulded ceilings and tall windows, an entryphone, a long gloomy hallway and walk-in closets that smelled of cloves. As yet, no cockroaches had made themselves discernible to the naked eye.

198

The carpets were old but clean, the kitchen 'quaint' in the sense that the splashbacks were covered with cracked tiles, the fridge rumbled ominously and the waste disposal sounded like an aircraft taking off. The rent had worked out to be upper-borderline affordable. Everything was painted in a lumpy eggshell brown that looked like the coating of a candy bar. It would be hell to remove. She was considering the problem when the entry buzzer sounded.

She successfully intercepted Simon just as he was reaching for the wall-receiver, surprised that his height would allow him to do so.

'Open the door, I'm carrying a chocolate pound cake and some bum is accosting me,' shouted a shrill voice.

Minutes later Marsha appeared at the front door laden with shopping bags. She was dragging her son behind her like a denim-clad sack.

'Jesus, this is some neighbourhood isn't it?' she gasped, dropping the bags. 'There's an extremely forceful home-less person on your front step and I couldn't get to my change-wallet. I nearly had to give him the kid.' She ruffled her son's hair. 'Just joking, Tommy. There's no light in your hall. I think the bulb's gone.' Marsha was one of Amy's oldest friends. The two women had attended the same journalism school along with Howard, and had given birth to sons in the same year. Now they both worked freelance, sometimes for the same publication, although Marsha mainly specialised in home economics copy. Howard had left journalism to work for the city, but they all still shared the same circle of friends.

The main difference was that Marsha was happily settled as a wife and mother. She and Max had an easy-going alliance that was more like a solid business partner-ship than a marriage, and struck just the right tone for living in New York. She was slim, dark and rather glamor-ous in a Manhattan Jewish way, while Amy was pale and freckled and a little heavy at the waist. Their children

199

behaved like brothers, which meant that they spent much of their time arguing with each other over Batmobile ownership rights.

Marsha removed a white cardboard box and set it on the kitchen counter. 'Hey, this is quite a spread,' she said, looking around. 'A little gloomy. It reminds me of something. I know, the apartment in *Rosemary's Baby.*'

'Thanks a lot, Marsha. Having met the members of the board, I figure we're pretty well protected from the forces of satanism. I still can't believe I'm in.'

'They say the church has all the best property in the city.'

'I don't think it's actually owned by the church. Mrs Forrest implied that the Christian Fellowship Trust is pretty well-off. They've got a couple of other apartment buildings on the Upper East Side. They organise a lot of high society stuff from what I can gather, gala dinners for children's charities, church funds for abused kids.'

'At least that means your rent is probably doing some good for once.'

'Maybe. Miss Banforth called by yesterday with the welcome wagon. She told me I should visit this store in SoHo that sells religious artifacts, went on and on about it. I think she gets commission from the owners for every 3-D Last Supper painting she offloads. On the way out she said to remember that God was watching me all the time.'

'Cute. The apartment next door to you is playing hymns. I could hear *Onward Christian Soldiers* coming through their door. Have you met them yet?'

'No.' Amy's forehead furrowed slightly. 'I'm not sure I want to if it means getting Sunday school lessons every time I try to borrow a cup of sugar.'

'We should go and say hi, check 'em out.' She reached over and touched Amy's arm. 'I can't get used to the idea of you living so close by. It always took us an hour to get to your old apartment. Did I tell you Howard has a new girlfriend? Do you have a knife?'

200

Marsha unwrapped the cake and licked her fingers as the boys chased each other in the direction of Simon's bedroom. Amy pulled over a stool and stood on it, feeling around at the top of the cupboard. 'I'm keeping the sharp stuff up here where Si can't reach it,' she explained. 'Just until I can get the drawers unstuck.'

'Looks like you can't reach, either,' said Marsha. 'I love these tall rooms. So what was the board like?'

Amy passed her a knife and climbed down. 'Just as I imagined. No, worse. Creepier. I had to lie myself blue in the face. They asked questions about my religion . . .'

'You were warned about that.' Marsha slid two thick chocolate slices onto paper plates and began to search for coffee cups. 'So you told them you're thinking of becoming a nun.'

'Practically. And I showed them the picture of Si on the swing.'

'That was sneaky.'

'I think it won them over.'

'I'll bet it did. So what are you going to do now?'

Amy looked at the walls with distaste. 'Paint it, of course,' she said.

The next morning, she paused outside her neighbour's door and listened. Handel's *Messiah* boomed from within. She wondered whether to knock and raised her hand to do so, but faltered at the thought of being drawn into a religious discussion, and timidly crossed the shadowed landing back to her own apartment.

The wet, warm weather had made the flat unbearably humid, but several layers of eggshell paint prevented the window jambs from being parted. The kitchen panes were running with condensation. 'Okay,' thought Amy, 'this is where I declare war on the decor.' Structurally, the apartment was perfect, but it needed a coat of paint in a late twentieth-century colour. She switched on her portable radio and tuned in a rock station to counteract the music from next door. Then she adjusted a paint-spattered bandana on her head and produced a hammer and chisel from the toolbox beneath the sink.

Twenty minutes later she had succeeded in freeing the upper half of the largest kitchen window and sliding it down. Pleased with herself, she unwound the flex of the hot-torch and plugged it in. Modern technology had aided Amy in her determination to be self-sufficient. They didn't exactly replace a husband, but the power saws and sanders she had bought at least took some of the strain out of being single. She watched as the paint bubbled and lifted from the sill, trying to calculate how long it would take her to strip so many windows. As the cream paint fell away, something else appeared.

'Max, come here.'

She led Marsha's short-sighted husband across the room and waited for him to adjust his glasses. 'There,' she said, pointing at the windowsill, 'what do you make of that?'

Max leaned forward and examined the ledge. He had come over to check out the new apartment, and to take Simon to the park for a while so that Amy could set up her word processor in peace. Now he rose and turned to her, scratching at his goatee beard. 'I've heard of this before,' he said slowly. 'They're supposed to be on every building in the city, if you look carefully enough.' The word PRAY had been carved deep into the wood in letters over an inch high. The command was repeated all around the frame in a frieze.

Amy dusted away the paint-chips to reveal more carvings. 'Who could have put them here?'

'Evangelists offering some kind of talismanic protection, I imagine. These look different to the ones I saw in the newspaper. I've only ever heard of them on the ground floors of buildings. Sometimes you'll find them scratched into the metal doorframes of an office block while it's still under construction. They just appear in the night. The new mediaevalism. Very interesting.' Max gave lectures on social history, and found all urban legends interesting. He had married Marsha during her sabbatical in London, and moving here had allowed him to continue his studies with a vengeance. Still, his gleeful descriptions of New York as a *fin de siècle* plague pit unnerved her.

'There you are, you little monster.' Simon swung easily into his arms with a scream of delight. He'd been waiting for 'Uncle Max' all morning. 'So,' said Max, struggling with the boy's jacket, 'apart from being protected by the power of prayer, how do you like the apartment?'

'Well — I'm really grateful to have gotten it.' She turned about, smiling and shrugging her shoulders.

'But?'

Max could always read her. This time she was amazed, because even she wasn't sure of her reservations. 'I don't know,' she said finally. 'The water pipes make funny noises at night. The woman next door plays hymns all the time. The lights never work in the hallways. I guess I'm not settled yet.'

'It's bound to take a while. The neighbourhood must seem pretty strange. You're probably just not used to having hookers on your doorstep. Try and remember that we're only a few streets away if you need anything. Take a leaf from Simon's book. He's at the adaptable age, just moving right along with the change. Do you like it here, Simon?'

'I like the elevator. Can we go to the zoo?' He was waiting to be zipped into his hooded jacket.

'With you?' He looked at Amy. 'Is he kidding? People will think I'm divorced and didn't get custody.' They joked about such things now, but at the time of Simon's birth Marsha and her husband had seen her through a

203

terrible time. 'I have a better idea. What say we go pick up Tommy and have milkshakes?'

'Yaay.' Simon led the way, tugging his 'uncle' from the room.

'We'll be back at around five,' called Max as he vanished around the door. 'Make sure you get some work done.'

Amy spent the next hour unpacking and wiring up her new IBM PC and printer. She was just loading the last part of the word package she had customised when there was a smash of glass on the landing outside the apartment.

She ran to the front door and opened it to find a heavy-set black woman bending over a shattered bottle. A smell of sweet, dark rum filled the air. The torn brown bag under her arm was threatening to release a carton of eggs.

'Here, let me help,' said Amy, stepping forward.

'Jeezus, honey, don't creep up on me like that.' The woman looked up at her just as the bag split wide. They managed to catch everything but the eggs.

'I'm so sorry, I didn't mean to startle you. I'll get a brush for this.' Amy scooped the broken shells into her hand.

'It wasn't your fault, I overloaded the damned bag. I'm Betty Jarrold, I live next door to you.' She held out her hand and smiled. She had a broad, friendly face, a double chin and straightened swept-back hair held in place with a black velvet ribbon. Amy guessed that despite the smoothness of her skin she was in her early forties. Betty looked towards the open door of the apartment. 'Can I smell coffee brewing in there?' she asked innocently.

After they had cleared up the mess, they sat together in the lounge.

'Great little machine,' she said through a mouthful of chocolate cookie, walking around the lounge to admire her computer. 'The same model as mine.'

'What do you do?' asked Amy, seating herself on the newly delivered sofa.

'I'm a legal secretary. I sometimes bring work home, so the office pays for a console in the apartment. I listen to music while I work. Do the hymns bother you? I play 'em real loud sometimes.'

'Uh, no, that's fine. I mean, I can hardly hear them.' Amy shifted uncomfortably.

'Now you're just being polite. I don't want you getting the idea that I'm like, a religious nut or anything. To tell the truth,' she lowered her voice, 'I just started playing them 'cause of Mrs Forrest. You know her?'

'I met her at the interview.'

'She lives right above me. They all do, all three of them. They have the whole of the top floor.' Betty pointed at the ceiling as if it was about to fall on her. 'You should see the place. All crucifixes and religious paintings, it looks like part of the church across the street. When I moved in I told Mrs Forrest I was real religious, otherwise they'd never have given me the apartment. I went out, bought a whole bunch of religious records an' started playing them loud. Then one morning Mrs Forrest stopped by and said 'I didn't know you were Jewish', 'cause it turns out I was playing all this Jewish music without realising it. Now she checks up on me all the time, so I keep the music going. I've kinda grown used to a good male chorus in the background.' She laughed mischievously. 'Sure beats having a real one about the house.'

'How long have you been here, Betty?'

'Three years or so.' She set down her cup. 'There aren't too many friendly faces here, I'll tell you that. The couple who were in this apartment before you were yuppies. He had an obnoxious kid by an earlier marriage. The bottom fell out of the stock market and they just took off overnight. Broke the lease, didn't even say goodbye, which suited me fine.'

'Do you see much of the trustees?'

'Oh, they come down every Sunday and try to get me to

go to church. I've given them every excuse under the damned sun but they still don't give up. They run this thing called the Crusade For The Unborn. It's a right-to-life group with some heavy political clout. Old Man Whickes knows some pretty powerful pro-lifers on Capitol Hill. There was a big scandal here a couple of years back.' She edged herself forward on the sofa. 'Did you hear about that?'

'No, I didn't.' She felt sure she was about to, though.

'One of the ground-floor tenants got herself pregnant. She was a pretty little thing, curly dark hair, couldn't have been more than twenty-two. Alice somebody, I can't remember her name now.' She tapped a scarlet nail against her thigh. 'Wait, Alice Mayer, or Myer — that was it. Anyway, her boyfriend took a hike when he found out she was going to have a baby, and he left her no way of contacting him. A real charmer.

'But the real problem was that she had been diagnosed HIV-positive. Well, she wanted to have an abortion, but the trustees stepped in and tried to put a stop to it. They argued with her doctor, who was in favour of a termination, but finally they managed to persuade her that all human life was sacred and she should have the child.' She paused to drink her coffee. 'Anyway, there were complications in the pregnancy, and Alice got frightened. Finally she heated up a steel clothes hanger and tried to terminate the baby herself, in the apartment. The whole thing went wrong, and she haemorrhaged and died. We had the newspapers in and everything. It was so cruel and sad, to think that the tragedy could have been prevented.'

'But that's barbaric,' said Amy, appalled. 'Couldn't anyone do anything to help her?'

'None of us knew what she was going through until it was too late. Now you know why I don't do much socialising with Mrs Forrest, Mr Whickes or Miss Banforth. They're always so high-minded about protecting the

206

children from Satan, but anyone who can do that to a young girl in the name of God — well, they're not my kind of people.' She looked up and smiled benignly. 'Do you have any more of these cookies?'

After her neighbour had left, Amy seated herself at the IBM with the intention of annotating ideas for future articles, but found it impossible to concentrate. Betty's story had depressed the life out of her.

She needed to jump-start herself into some work. The trouble was, none of the magazines she sold articles to wanted investigative journalism. They were looking for movie gossip, TV trivia, and to excel at that kind of assignment you had to be close to the handlers at the major PR companies. Besides, gossip didn't interest her. She wanted a real story, human interest with wider implications, like the one Betty had told her today. Unfortunately, an investigative article on that kind of angle could get her kicked back into the street. After fighting so hard for the apartment, she was determined to keep it.

That night she went to bed early, soon after she had tucked Simon beneath his Batman blanket. As she lay listening to the water pipes creaking and the distant rumble of traffic in the street, she made out another sound: quick footsteps pacing the stone-floored landing, back and forth, stopping each time outside her door. Then Betty's hymns began and she lay back on the pillows, happy in the knowledge that her neighbour was playing them in a deliberately sacriligious show of protest.

Amy stood by the open front door and examined the object again, running her fingers over the pressed tin crucifix that had been nailed to the wood like a mazuza. She shook her head in disbelief. What was it about these people, that they had to try and shove religion down your throat? Why couldn't they simply respect the beliefs of others? She knocked on Betty's door. Her neighbour answered displaying a frightening array of multipastel hair equipment.

'Hi, honey, what's up? Excuse my appearance, I'm expecting my fancy man tonight.'

'Do you know who could have put this here?' Amy pointed to the cross. 'I'm sure it wasn't there last night.'

'Y'know, that's really strange.' Betty unplugged something in the skirting board and stepped out into the hall trailing electrical leads. 'The Yales had exactly the same thing happen to them.'

'The Yales?'

'Sure. The yuppies I was telling you about who had your apartment? *Dick Yale*, don't you just love that name?' She gave a light, wheezy chuckle. 'Somebody put one on their door, too. Dick took it off and complained to the superintendent.'

'Do me a favour, Betty,' said Amy. 'If you see anyone else hanging around out here, let me know. This is too weird for me. I love your hair by the way.' She returned to the apartment, puzzled. Perhaps she would leave the cross there. After all, what harm could it do?

Two days later, Simon started attending Tommy's pre-school and she sold the first article she had written since she had moved in. Okay, it was a shopping feature, price comparisons at Fifth Avenue clothing stores, but at least the money was good. She would save her investigative powers for the next piece that was starting to formulate in her mind.

That morning the sun emerged from a fortress of stormclouds, and the breeze through Central Park was bitter with the smell of spring. She collected the novel she had ordered from Coliseum Books and headed downtown to pick up Simon, who had taken his first step into institutional life with alarming ease.

Later, as they approached the building along West 44th, Amy watched their new home appearing above the rise. She admired its age and dour solidity. The brown bricks and shuttered windows, the tall dark halls and steep staircases were unmistakable marks of an older, more puritanical New York. It was a pity that the elevator was so slow and the trellis door left grease on your clothes if you brushed against it. The word PRAY had been carved several times on the metal struts.

She arrived on the fifth floor to find a folded sheet of paper, personally addressed on the outside of the page, sticking out from under the apartment door.

The series of typeset biblical quotes was vaguely familiar to her. The handwritten message which accompanied them was not. Near the bottom of the page the author's obsessive zeal reached a lunatic pitch with warnings of sin, judgement, eternal damnation and solemn repentance. A pencil illustration showed the devil biting off some poor sinner's head. As she began to ball the sheet in her fist, she heard a voice behind her.

'I wouldn't do that if I were you.' Betty was standing at her door, holding a similar leaflet. 'Miss Banforth goes to a great deal of trouble printing this stuff up.'

'Do you think she was the one who put the cross on my door?'

'I hope not. I don't like the idea of her walking around with a hammer in her hand.'

Amy looked up at the darkened floor above. 'I guess they really practise what they preach. I always thought religion was supposed to be comforting, but this is kind of scary. I wonder if I should have a word with her.'

'If you do she'll think you're a sinner, and God knows what she'll stick under your door then. How's the writing going?'

'Okay.' She hesitated for a moment, unsure whether to broach the subject. 'Listen, I'm thinking of doing a follow-

209

up story to the Alice Myers case. Can you remember any dates for me?'

'Do you think that's such a good idea, living here and all?'

'I've thought about that. It'll be a balanced piece. I mean, I'll let the reader decide what's right.'

Betty shrugged. 'That sounds fair enough, but you'd better be careful. Mrs Forrest will find a way to break your lease if she doesn't like what you're doing. I can recall when Alice died, if that's any help. It was the last weekend of October, two years ago. I remember 'cause I had my folks staying with me. They always visit at that time of the year.'

'Thanks, Betty.' She unlocked the front door and shooed Simon in. 'If you remember anything else that might be useful, let me know.'

If Alice Myers had decided to protect the life within her, her baby son would have been born on approximately 17 June. Instead it died just twelve weeks earlier, when a desperate attempt at self-termination went tragically wrong. It was a death the authorities could have prevented if only they had set aside their personal differences.

She read the piece again. It was an odd coincidence, she had to admit. Her son shared a birthday with Alice Myers' unborn child. This coming 17 June he would be five years old. Well, with just 365 days in a year the odds were long but maybe it wasn't so odd. The *Times* carried the only halfway-decent report of the tragedy. Amy had been surprised to find how badly the story had been covered by the press. As she ran through the library microfiles, she saw that much of the reportage was sensationalist and inaccurate.

There was definitely a story here. With so many violent crimes occurring daily in the city, no one had taken time to recognise the possibilities of this particular case. She pushed back her hair and stretched her legs beneath the table, feeling for her shoes. She had uncovered the basis of the investigative article that would make her name.

Mrs Forrest's glasses were so thick it was a wonder she could see anything at all. She peered around at the walls approvingly, nodding and smiling. 'Oh, you've done a lovely job, just as I knew you would,' she said, stepping forward as if walking on ice. 'These pastels are so tasteful.' She found a safe path to the sofa and seated herself next to Mr Whickes as Amy poured them coffee.

'Hello there, little man,' boomed Whickes, opening a freckled paw to reveal a squashed-looking peppermint. He held it out for Simon, who had appeared at the edge of the sofa. His eyes glinted at the boy as if he was thinking of eating him. Simon took one look at the avuncular old man and raced off for the safety of his television chair in the next room.

'He's a little shy around strangers,' said Amy.

'Oh, we're not strangers, we're *friends*.' Mrs Forrest gave a broad smile. Receding gums had left her with teeth like book-matches.

'Praise the Lord,' said Whickes, returning the elderly sweet to his pocket.

Amy listened as the TV went on next door. Her son had taken to hiding whenever any of the terrible trio from upstairs put in an appearance. He seemed genuinely scared of them, which was kind of understandable. Mrs Forrest's perfume smelled like Airwick.

'And how are you finding our church?' asked Whickes, running an exploratory thumb around one nostril. 'Does the standard of the service meet with your approval?'

'Oh it's — fine,' she replied, caught unawares.

'It's just that I haven't seen you there.'

'No — I tend to go at odd hours. My writing.' Whickes was probably a verger or something, knowing her luck.

But he seemed satisfied with the explanation, and settled back with his cup while his partner finished acknowledging the furniture.

'Dick and Sarah Yale were a nice enough couple,' said Mrs Forrest, who had not volunteered a switch to first-name terms. 'They had a lovely little boy about the age of yours.'

'Betty next door told me they left very suddenly,' said Amy. 'Why was that?'

'Dick changed — didn't he, Luke?'

'Oh, sure,' Whickes confirmed, 'he changed a lot.'

'How do you mean?' asked Amy. Through the wall she could hear the bangs and crashes of a Batman cartoon.

'When he first came here he told us he was a godfearing man, and we believed him. In fact, when Mr Whickes asked if he and his wife would like to help in our part-time volunteer programme, they happily agreed. Later on, though, he was most rude to us, wasn't he?'

'Extremely rude.'

'And him a so-called practising Christian.'

'What kind of volunteer programme was this?' asked Amy, sipping her tea.

'The CFF has a number of associations that it uses to help children who have been abused, sexually or satanically.'

'Oh?' Amy lowered her cup. 'I thought that whole scandal about satanic child abuse turned out to be a myth. Didn't they discredit the cases that came before the courts?'

'Oh, they tried to say that the children had made things up, but I ask you, does it sound likely that a little child, a child like your own perhaps, would lie for the sake of pure mischief?'

'Well,' Amy began, 'children have very vivid imaginations at that age and are just learning to use them —'

'Children are the vessels of God's will, and quite

incapable of lies,' said Mrs Forrest sternly, looking towards the next room. 'You should always bear that in mind.'

'Betty, do you know if the Yales left a forwarding address?' Amy stood in the doorway, dressed in a smart black business suit. She was on her way to lunch with Marsha, and it occurred to her that she might put her fears to rest by calling the former tenants.

'They left one with me, so's I could send on their mail. We weren't too friendly with each other, to tell the truth. It's probably in one of the kitchen drawers. Come on it.'

Betty's apartment was clearly planned for comfort. Everything seemed to be designed around a huge, tartan-covered sofa, which in turn faced the television.

'You haven't heard too many hymns from me lately, have you?' she called out. 'I've had enough of them. Gone back to my Easy Listening station. Jesus versus Elvis, no contest. Here you go.' She extracted a slip of paper from the envelopes in her hand and passed it to Amy.

'I don't know if they're even there. I've never needed to use the number. Oh, my.' She looked back at the envelopes. 'These must have been for the little boy's birthday. I guess I forgot to forward them.' Amy took them from her hand and studied the postmarked dates.

15 June. 15 June. 16 June.

'Well, these people sound nuts,' agreed Marsha, half of her attention still on the menu. 'Do they bother you in any other way?'

'No, not really. Well, I think I can hear someone walking around on the landing some nights, pacing back and forth, but maybe I imagine it. I don't know.'

'Listen, you can't stop someone from being friendly.'

'No, but I can't discourage them from calling around without making them suspicious.'

213

'Does it really matter if they find out you don't go to church?'

'Oh, absolutely. You know, there are all these crazy biblical tracts flyposted in the basement. Real fundamentalist fire and brimstone stuff. They're very — zealous. They said something about the previous tenant, how he'd disappointed them.'

'You think they kicked him out?' Marsha closed the menu and set it aside. Lately they had taken to meeting in a small French restaurant frequented by several of their mutual clients. In theory it was supposed to help them drum up work, but it hadn't happened yet.

'Betty says Yale and his family left pretty suddenly. In the middle of the night. Simon's scared to death when Mrs Forrest comes around. She's always talking about him, how it's my duty to train him as one of God's "vessels".'

'Let me guess,' interrupted Marsha. 'You think they're witches, and they're going to kidnap your kid.'

'No, of course not, but — I don't know. I feel like they're watching me all the time. Mrs Forrest always seems to be on the stairs when I'm going out.'

'You've probably been seeing too many late-night horror films,' said Marsha. 'You know how obsessive some religious people get. It can be unnerving.'

'I guess you're right,' agreed Amy. 'I'm being stupid.' But she'd seen the way they looked at her child, and she couldn't forget it.

'There's something I've never told you,' she said finally, looking up at her friend. Marsha's interest was piqued. She thought they knew everything there was to know about each other.

'You remember what a state I got myself into when I found out I was carrying Simon?'

'Sure. You were a little wacky for a while, but you got through it all right.'

'Well, there was a time when I wanted to have an

abortion. I had a preliminary appointment with the doctor, but I never showed up for the main event.'

'Is this what it's all about, this business with the apartment?'

'I don't know. Maybe they found out somehow and they're trying to reform me.'

'That's completely ridiculous and you know it. Besides, you changed your mind and had Simon.'

'Alice Myers tried to terminate her pregnancy and she died.'

'So?' Marsha threw her hands in the air. 'What the hell has that to do with anything? Amy, are you familiar with the word *paranoia*? I think you're just being overprotective about your boy. When he's sixteen you're still going to be threading his mittens through his coat.'

'You're right, I'm sorry,' she apologised. 'Over-Protective Mother. Forget it.'

'I will if you will,' said Marsha. 'Let's eat. Hey, waiter.'

A pony-tailed young man approached the table and produced a notepad, licking the end of his pencil. He gave them his sharpest smile. 'Are you ladies ready to order?'

'Tell me,' asked Marsha, 'how's the cheesecake?'

'Better than sex.'

'With you or with my husband?' She turned to Amy. 'This could be a long lunch.'

'For you, maybe,' said Amy. 'I have to go and work on my article.'

But Amy went to the library instead.

Under the computerised business directory listing for CFF, she found the following:

CHRISTIAN FUNDAMENTALIST
FOUNDATION
*Group of Church Charities/ founded in Alabama 1896/
includes the World Committee For Christian Children/*

Protect The Children Trust/ first established in Wisconsin 1978.

She keyed into the file details of the latter.

The PCT is a fundamentalist trust which targets young people with leaflets and holds seminars to alert teenagers to the dangers of occult involvement and the power of Christ's deliverance on the Day of Revelation.

That was it, the verses on the leaflet had been taken from the Book of Revelation. So they bombarded their tenants with inspirational literature. Where was the harm? Perhaps the Yales would be able to tell her more.

After the library, she collected Simon from Pre-School. The boy was anxious to be allowed to play at Tommy's house, but as he had complained of a sore throat that morning, she was reluctant to allow him to do so. Instead, they shopped and returned to the apartment, Simon heading off to catch up with his pal Batman while she called the number in her pocket.

A woman's voice answered on the third ring, identifying herself as Sarah Yale. Amy quickly explained that she was renting their old apartment, and began to ask a question when she was interrupted.

'Wait,' said Mrs Yale, uncertainty sounding in her voice. 'I'm not — I think you'd better speak to my husband about this. He won't be back from work until late tonight.'

Behind Amy, the doorbell sounded.

'Can you hold on a second?' She placed the receiver on the kitchen counter and ran down the hall. She opened it to find Mrs Forrest standing in the doorway with a covered baking dish in her hands.

'I was just on my way to Bible class and I thought little Simon might like some of the pecan pie I made . . .'

'Hi, Mrs Forrest, uh, come in, I'm just on the phone.' She turned her attention back to the receiver and lowered her voice.

'Listen, Mrs Yale, it's not a good time for me either, but I was wondering, well, I have to ask you this —' She peered back at the hall. Mrs Forrest must have shown herself into the lounge. 'It isn't my business, but I'm living here with my son and something doesn't feel right, and I was wondering why you left the apartment so suddenly. I wouldn't ask, only —'

'Oh, you can ask, because I'll tell anyone who's prepared to listen why I left,' said Sarah, her voice suddenly sharpening with sarcasm. 'That sanctimonious bitch wanted to take my child. Nobody would believe me, but I knew then and I know now, only I'm not allowed to say it anymore. Nobody ever believed me, not even my husband.'

'Who are you talking about —?'

'The Forrest woman, her and those religious freaks, the Crusade For The Unborn. They're looking for a child.'

'I don't understand what you mean —'

The voice on the end of the line sounded weary with repetition. 'They need a child to fight their battles for them. One they can train to take on Satanists or whatever the hell they believe is out there. That's what she told me. They're looking for a child they can indoctrinate — a vessel to fill. Born on a certain date and accidentally conceived. Born without love — so that God would allow it to be taken.'

Amy felt the receiver slide from her hand. She turned and ran towards the TV room, only to find it empty. The front door was wide open. The landing was deserted.

'Simon!' She ran back into the flat and saw the baking dish upturned on the hall carpet, the cotton wool that lay beside it, sweetly reeking of chemicals, a thin smear of blood on the door jamb.

She took the stairs to the sixth floor three at a time and began to hammer on the door, shouting for someone to open up.

But no one came. The darkened landing at the top of the house remained completely silent. She pressed her ear against the door and listened, but no sound came from within. She began to scream, and her cries attracted Betty, who called the police.

Eventually the door was broken down, but the apartment was neat and tidy and empty. It had clearly been vacated and locked up, as if its owners had gone away for the summer.

Amy was sedated and attended by her friends, but refused to leave her own apartment in case word came via the telephone. The police treated the case as a kidnapping and called Mrs Yale, who simply reiterated the story she had told many times before, adding 'I warned you this would happen'. Vindicated, she refused to help any further with their enquiries.

On the following evening, Amy grew suspicious of Marsha and Max, because they had told her about the availability of the apartment in the first place. She said nothing, but watched them from the corner of her eye as they fussed around the sofa where she lay. Max could sense the change in her attitude towards them, and confronted her.

'Surely you don't think *we* had anything to do with it?' he asked, sitting on the edge of the sofa, facing her back.

'They must have had inside help,' said Amy softly. 'Someone gave them information about Simon and me.'

'But it was Howard who told us about the apartment.'

She turned to face him.

'Don't you remember?' Max was distraught. 'That night at the restaurant? He'd been telling us all about the place, how perfect he thought it would be for you. I took it upon myself to tell you when you arrived, but I had to ask him how much the rent was. I swear it's the truth.'

She remembered. He was right. He hadn't known about the rent.

They called Howard but there was no answer, which was odd because he had a machine. The police found his apartment empty, too. Suitcases were missing. His girlfriend hadn't seen him for days.

Like Mrs Forrest, Miss Banforth and Mr Whickes, he never returned to New York.

Amy's days are different now.

She traverses the South and the Mid-West visiting Fundamentalist groups in sun-bleached tents and cool church halls and rowdy temperance meeting rooms, hoping to catch sight of a small boy in robes standing on the platform, a boy being taught how to fight the Devil with the power of prayer.

She travels alone. She trusts no one. She keeps faith only in herself.

She is frightened that if she doesn't find her son very soon, his eyes will be clouded to the truth. He won't see his mother standing before him.

Only an agent of Satan.

Can't Slow Down
For Fear I'll Die

The ground rushed by beneath his pounding feet, tarmac and concrete, grass and brick, passing ever faster. Blood had soaked through the canvas of his once-white jogging trainers, blossoming crimson flowers from his torn toenails and blistered heels. Sweat poured freely from his forehead and shoulders, his stinging armpits and back. His heart, pumping harder to maintain its racing circulation, was inflating and contracting at such a pace that weak spots were developing in its walls, like metal fatigue in an overworked aeroplane. It seemed impossible that the searing agony caused by the stitch in his side could grow any worse, and yet it continued to mount. As each damaged sole connected painfully with the ground, another judder flashed through his wracked body.

The scenery changed constantly, shops and offices flashing by, drycleaners and supermarkets and pubs and butchers, trees and traffic and people crowding closer, making it ever harder to maintain his speeding course. On and on he ran, through the miles, through the pain, and through the years.

When he was a child, he had been part of a baby boom that had seemingly provided every house on his street with a howling infant. As the mothers compared notes on the progress of their offspring, he delighted the family by learning to walk some weeks ahead of all the others. But that wasn't enough for him. More than anything else he longed to run. Sadly, his earliest attempts brought cuts and bruises from all manner of unexpected obstacles. His mother purchased a harness in powder-blue leather, with little bells adorning the front panel. Embarrassed, he galloped around like a demented reindeer. But he soon

223

learned how to navigate, and so avoided disaster. Without realising it, he had begun his training.

In his teens, desperate to behave in a manner that would have him accepted by his schoolfriends, he concentrated on his walk. He developed the right kind of swagger, the correct level of attitude, the perfect amount of disinterest. Occasionally it left him stumbling into potholes and looking like a fool. Walking like the others was harder than he had realised.

At the end of his teens he was anxious to start running seriously. He just couldn't wait. Others of his age were already off from their blocks, and time was wasting. Every second was precious. He was young and strong, and knew he could be fast. He looked at the older men and women jogging around like ponderous beasts of burden, and couldn't believe that they had chosen to set so slow a pace. Schooldays ended and he was out of the gate at a sprint, setting off at a speed he could never hope to maintain. He had forgotten that he was entering a marathon, and was running with an energy more suited to a hundred-yard dash.

The thrill of those early days was unforgettable. There were only highs and lows, ecstasy and misery and nothing in between. The road was clear and his heart was a powerful machine. Beautiful women ran with him in serial stretches, like relay runners, then waved farewell as they sprinted away. Buildings and fields flashed by, and he was the fastest man in the world. But when he looked up, he saw that the sky remained unchanged. That was his first warning of the vastness of the race.

He was in his mid-twenties, working all hours for a tough new company, when he began to notice the other runners. People of his age in the same trainers and jogging suits, equal and identical in appearance. Sometimes he would look across at them and they would smile knowingly at each other like vintage car owners passing each other on the road, proud of their fitness, their

224

bearing, their neatly matched speed. But there were others who had set themselves a more deliberate pace, their dry limbs moving rhythmically alongside his, their faces bearing a look of great determination. Covertly he watched these others, never letting them gain too much ground, and never allowing himself to forge too far ahead of the pack.

Then when he was in his thirties, his formerly successful business began to suffer in recession, and the path around him became overcrowded with runners. Some had decided to become gold medallists, and were running ahead with pounding hearts and ragged gasps of breath, risking all. Every once in a while one of these would suddenly drop to the ground, or veer from the road and expire in the dirt. Not our hero. He learned to control his movements. He was determined to finish the course. He ran on alone.

At some point, he couldn't quite establish when, he was no longer running for fun but just to stay alive. Easing up and slowing down no longer lessened the pain but actually increased it. Now everyone was trying to lead the pack. They fought for space, elbowing each other from their determined paths. Tempers flared and teeth were bared in ritualistic behaviour, dogs snapping and snarling to protect their territory.

And on he ran, smeared with blood and sweat, the price of overtaking others, the pace always increasing by measured increments, like a ratchet marking notches on a rack. Never to slow down, never to stop, he could only gain momentum in his rush towards the end. Quicken or die.

As he looked down in agony at his stinging blood-soaked shoes, he wondered. Did every life turn into this? Could it only end this way for others? Nothing sensual, nothing beautiful, nothing peaceful left. No birdsong, no harmony, all sacred silence drowned in the sound of screaming traffic. The smell of the sea and the sky and the

225

grass swamped in the stink of engine fumes. Only the distension of his aching veins and the pounding of his engorged heart, only the flashing scenery and the blurring road beneath his burning feet. And he so wanted to stop. He was so very tired of being a runner.

God, how he wished to walk.

Outside The Wood

And now, here's some good news for the dead, he thought moments before losing consciousness. Kevin O'Neal won't be joining you after all. He was lying on the floor of the ballroom covered in blood and brickdust. His left arm was broken, his right ankle was chipped and sprained, he had three cracked ribs, a broken nose and heavy facial bruising. But he was still alive.

Inches above his head the thin slabs of concrete, a load weighing nearly three quarters of a ton, had exploded after tearing loose from their mooring on the gantry. When the rope had broken, Kevin had been thrown over the tube-steel walkway to the floor fifteen feet below. The lethal cargo that had followed him down had looked set to crush him flat, but the remaining guyrope had pulled it askew so that it missed him, shedding and shattering on the ground instead. The god assigned to protect Kevin that day deserved a bonus for putting in overtime.

They kept him in Lewisham Hospital overnight for observation, and ran checks to make sure that there was no hairline fracturing of his skull, but the following morning they needed the bed, so he was discharged into the waiting arms of his wife. His ankle was splinted, and the doctor had provided him with a metal crutch. His peppery cropped hair had been cut even shorter for cranial examination. Violet patches concealed one eye, and his nose was stuffed with bloody cotton wool. His arm had been set in plaster at a right angle to his body. When Linda saw him she started laughing, then burst into tears. She talked incessantly as she drove home, describing the details of their single evening apart in the grateful manner of one who knew that a loved one's life had been spared.

Kevin had to admit that he viewed the surrounding grey streets through his unclosed eye with a new-found sense of joy. He had not imagined that his perspective could shift so dramatically. Now every corner store and poster hoarding seemed bursting with vitality and interest. Yesterday morning he had argued with Linda, complaining about their lot; today his complaints had paled in comparison to the importance of his continued survival.

At home she made him soup and set him in front of the television while she fixed supper for Ivy. The old lady asked her daughter what had happened, but quickly lost the thread of the conversation. At the age of eighty-three, Linda's mother was growing too physically and mentally frail to be left alone, but neither of them thought it proper to place her in a home. Since the death of her husband she rarely left the confines of her gloomy bedroom. She spent her life apologising for being a burden, as if her continued presence in her own house was an imposition. She had been born here in the little terraced house that backed onto the railway line. In the summer she warmed herself in the garden, but travelled no further, and so was spared the sight of boarded shops and derelict houses patrolled by bellowing, mindless youths. Perhaps she had retreated to her room because she sensed that she lived in an age she no longer cared for, an age that did not care for her. The prim Victorian houses of her childhood had rotted like decaying teeth, and no one bothered to halt the canker.

In bed that night, Kevin watched as his wife arranged the pillows behind his back and lightly kissed his damaged flesh, needing to feel the heat of his skin, as if reassuring herself that he was still alive. He loved her more than ever, because he had been spared to do so.

The morning cast cold light on familiar financial

problems. Two years earlier, Kevin had graduated from university into a job-market flooded with overqualified applicants. He had a new wife, no job and nowhere to live. Eventually they had come to live in Ivy's house, in the littered cul-de-sac just south of Vauxhall Bridge. Kevin had found himself work on upscale building sites, supervising the restoration of the few Victorian buildings that could be saved from the clutches of the city's developers. The salary was minimal but the work was regular. There were a few organised benefits, but decent sick pay was not one of them, and from the look of him Kevin would not be restored to full health for several weeks. It was not an ideal time for Linda to be carrying her first child, but who knew if that fabled moment of financial stability would ever arrive? At least it was spring, and the baby would be born into a summer world where even the city trees managed to hide their dusty limbs.

'I've been thinking of going back to Mackley's,' said Linda, clearing away the breakfast china. 'Phil says I can have my old job on a part-time basis. I'm not due for four months.'

'I thought he used to drive you mad.'

'Only until I got married, then he gave up. Anyway, the money's good, and it wouldn't be forever. So long as you don't mind looking after Ivy.'

'I'll be back on my feet long before the baby arrives,' said Kevin absently. He sat propped in a kitchen chair, watching the budded garden branches crazing across the windows. 'I could still work as an adviser. And there's bound to be some kind of compensation.' He fell silent, the shadow of the swaying trees webbing his pale features.

'What are you thinking about?' She stopped drying her hands and came around to study his face.

'Oh, you know.' He turned to her, embarrassed. 'What if the second rope hadn't caught, what if the load had swung two inches further down, that sort of thing.'

231

'Well, it didn't and you're still here, thank God.' She gave a brisk smile and hung up the teatowel. 'Take your tablets and stop thinking about it.'

'They make me drowsy. I slept like a dead man last night.'

'Please be a good invalid and finish the course.' She shook two pills from the bottle and handed them to him. 'I'm going to see Phil, find out how long he'd be prepared to employ me with this sticking out in front.' She patted her heavy stomach. 'I don't suppose you'll see Ivy much before one o'clock. She usually comes down for a while and eats something light.'

'Just as well.' He smiled up at her. 'I don't think I'd be able to manage the stairs.' If only it had been his left ankle instead of his right. He was forced to walk by placing the crutch beneath the joint of his broken arm. 'You want me to cook you dinner?'

'No, you go ahead,' said Linda, slipping into her over-coat. 'I'll get something for myself on the way back.' She sounded confident about finding employment, anxious to begin. He sat back, wincing in pain, frustrated by his enforced inactivity.

He ate a quiet lunch with Ivy, who sat half-heartedly picking at an omelette with her fork, unwilling or unable to enjoy her food. Kevin could not help thinking that she seemed to be merely marking time until her death. Little pleased or interested her, and their conversations together were uncomfortable and trivial, as though they were both avoiding some ever-present subtext. Following her meal, the old lady returned to her room and the house resumed its silent status.

The neighbourhood was populated largely with working couples, and remained silent and empty between rush-hours, like a deserted film set. Tired of his book, he watched the street from the ground-floor window. The house opened directly onto the pavement. Outside the door, a labrador lay on its side, asleep in the dead after-noon sunlight. At the end of the street some Asian children were mapping out the rules of a complex game, their brows furrowed in deadly earnest as they surrounded their hieroglyphs with chalk-lines only they could under-stand.

He was supposed to have taken more tablets, but knew they would only send him to sleep. Even without them his eyelids were closing, and he was starting to drift. He was standing on the vertiginous scaffold when he felt the planks shift beneath his feet, the air displacing around him. Slowly he raised his eyes to the grey bale of concrete slabs as they broke free and swung lazily down. The gantry trembled and began to buckle from the redistributed weight, throwing him against the tubular railing. His hand came out to steady himself, but already he was sliding over the top of the bar and falling backwards towards the ground.

His left arm took the full weight of his body, and he clearly heard the bone splintering above his elbow.

He looked up to see the concrete slabs cascading down on him, but this time they were not above his head. No, this time the lethal shards thudded into his body, shat-tering his ribcage, puncturing his throat, smashing open the eggshell plates of his skull.

He awoke with a start, sheened in sweat.

The kitchen clock read 3.05 p.m. The street was still bright and silent. But there was something else. A shadow dancing in the corner of his eye, a group of half-seen figures in the road that vanished when he looked at them directly. He shook his head, refocussed, and the shadow reappeared. Something whispered to him beyond the windows, shifting back and forth with impatience. This could not be a side-effect of his medication; he had failed to take his tablets.

He closed his eyes and rubbed the sore lids with his

forefingers, but the whispering stayed. No individual words could be distinguished in the susurration, but there was a spiteful tone that filled him with a growing sense of discomfort. With the aid of the crutch he hobbled to the sink and filled a kettle, refusing to acknowledge the hallucination.

The effect suddenly faded as a group of noisy children ran into the street, a sign that school had just ended for the day. The ticking of the kitchen wall clock reappeared, and with it came the sound of a distant ice-cream van. The fabric of normality was restored.

He did not place enough importance on the incident to mention it to Linda when she returned. His wife had arranged to resume her old position, sorting out accounts in one of the furnishing stores in the high street. The hours were short, and she would be able to come home for lunch. The role of breadwinner appealed to her; they would get by.

That night he lay in bed listening to Linda breathing lightly beside him, and watched the light from the street lamp ripple with rain on the patterned wallpaper above the bedhead. Thunder rolled faintly in the distance. Sleep was impossible. Sleep harboured dreams darker than any night. Better to lie awake. Awake was alive.

The following morning, one of the boys from the site called around bearing Get Well cards and flowers from his friends at work. Kevin asked about the accident; how had it happened, did anyone know? A pipe had fractured in the wall, the boy explained, soaking the brick and plaster in which the cargo rope's lynch-pin had been anchored. A chance in a thousand that the wall should soften at that precise spot. Although no one had been at fault there was talk of considerable compensation for his accident, because after all he was very nearly killed.

That night Kevin imagined a depleted double bed, his wife a grieving widow, the old lady with no one left but her pregnant daughter, and was chilled by the thought of what might have been. Without the tablets he found it impossible to sleep. A little after 4.00 a.m., just as he was finally starting to doze off, a thudding sound in the hallway outside roused him back to wakefulness. He raised his head from the pillow, listening intently. There it was again, a wet thump, like someone dropping a pile of soaked laundry on the floor. Careful not to wake Linda, he slipped from the sheet and opened the bedroom door.

Further along the hall at the head of stairs stood a black figure, barely discernible in the dark. As he approached, it turned and slapped a wet hand against the bannister. It was impossibly gaunt, thinner and less substantial than any human being could be, and stood awkwardly, as if in danger of imminent collapse. Kevin could feel the hairs lifting on the back of his neck as he stood within the creature's reach, waiting for it to make its move. He sensed an air of desperation about it, as though it had been goaded and starved into appearing before him.

Suddenly it lurched forward and seized his wrist, the slippery bone and sinew of its fingers digging into his palm, and in that instant Kevin saw that it meant to drag him to the head of the stairs. Revolted by its touch and the smell of corrupted tissue he snatched his arm away and lost his balance in the process, falling backward onto the landing carpet.

'What on earth is going on out here?' Linda had snapped on the hall light and stood looking down at him. The stairs were clear. There was no sign of any disturbance on the landing.

'I was going for a drink of water and slipped,' he said lamely, pulling himself up.

'You look like you've seen a ghost,' she said, unaware of the irony. 'You're as white as chalk.' She offered her hand to him. 'Honestly, what a pair we make, me with the baby

235

and you with your bandages. Ivy's the only fit one left in the house.' She had meant to lighten the moment.

The day was passing with agonising slowness. Linda, reinstalled in her old job at Mackley's, checked flickering green strings of computerised digits. At home, her mother put in an even shorter lunchtime appearance than she had the day before. Any attempt to draw her into conversation was met with fatigued indifference. Kevin watched as her dry hands clutched the knife and fork, unable to decide what to eat. After a few laboured mouthfuls she pushed back her chair and left the table, smiling wanly at him, apologising for her lack of appetite.

Later he lay in the lounge listening to the quacking of talk shows on television, trying to understand what was happening to his mind, wondering if he was suffering from some kind of concussion brought about by the accident. By day the house and its lone upstairs occupant drained away his energy, forcing him to stillness.

In the early evening the rain returned, and so did the shadowy figures in the street. Tired of reading, he had been watching the dark clouds lowering over the factory when he once more became aware of their presence. It seemed that there were three or four of them loitering within his peripheral vision, emaciated men and women constructed of blurring shadow and soot. He hobbled to the front door and looked out as the first large drops spattered on the pavement, expecting the figures to have fled the deserted dead-end street.

Instead he found them standing no more than three feet away. He fell back against the lintel in shock as they angrily raised their wet hands at him. They shook with tiny vibrations, shedding particles of black into the air, as if they were bleeding darkness. One of the women snatched at him, her nails leaving thin red scratches across the back of his wrist. The crutch slid from beneath his arm and

236

clattered to the pavement.

'What do you want from me?' he shouted, backing into the doorway.

'Your life,' they seemed to reply in ragged unison. 'Your life.' They were still hissing their demands as he slammed the door against them.

'You're very quiet,' said Linda, watching him. 'Your face is looking a lot better.'

He made no reply.

'Is there something you want to talk about?'

He gazed at her steadily, unsure of raising the subject. She looked well, ripening in health along with her child. Work had provided a direction for her energies. Linda was never idle, always in movement. Around the house she would tidy up, make small repairs, add little touches, always looking for improvements.

'When I was a child,' he said distantly, 'I had a linen-bound book, an Edwardian children's book that belonged to my grandmother. I remember it clearly. It was called *Where The Rainbow Ends*, by Clifford Mills, full of jingoistic cruelty, the stuff of nightmares. Of course I loved it. The illustrations were horrendous. I remember one vividly. "Rosamund Outside The Dragon Wood." A prim little girl in a floral dress and white socks, standing at the edge of a sunlit meadow.' His hands traced the air, recalling the scene. 'Before her is a dark thicket leading to the wood, and from this thicket hundreds of tiny black imps are emerging. In the picture they're swarming all over the little girl, pulling at her skirt, tearing her flesh, trying to lure her into the darkness. She's leaning back, digging in her heels, holding her ground, but the fight has already been lost. I used to have such nightmares. My father eventually took the book away and burned it.'

She looked down at her hands, folded in her lap, patiently waiting for him to finish.

'I'm having some — visual — problems,' he said, 'since the accident.'

'What sort of things? Seeing double? Blurred vision? Is that why you fell the other night?'

'Not exactly. I've been seeing things. It sounds so stupid.'

'Kevin, you were hit in the face. It doesn't sound stupid at all. Do you want to see a doctor?'

'I just want to know if the imps are real or not,' he said, sliding his hand over the scratches on his wrist.

'There's nothing on the scans,' said Dr Jahbata, unclipping the transparencies and returning them to Kevin's file. 'That's good. It suggests that what you're experiencing will prove to be a temporary effect.' He turned to the prescriptive dictionary on his overflowing desk and began thumbing through it. 'The human brain is built on a suspension system of fluid to prevent it from suffering damage in the case of a jarring blow. But this safety mechanism sometimes backfires, and when your head is struck it can cause the brain to bounce against the inside of the skull and become bruised. This may have a variety of olfactory and visual side-effects.'

'Could it cause me to hear things as well?'

'Most certainly. But I'm afraid we won't know how or why this happens until we discover exactly how the brain works. I'll write you out a prescription, but these tablets will only act as tension-breakers. They'll reduce the symptoms, but they can't stop them until we know the cause.' He tore off a slip of paper and passed it across the desk. 'You should find the problem easing as your body copes with the shock of the accident and heals itself, but if the visions continue or worsen, come back to me, and we'll talk about seeing a specialist.'

Kevin rose to his feet, folding away the prescription. He instinctively felt that the doctor was wrong, that the visions would not end until some kind of demand had been met, and a price paid. As he stepped back into the noisy street, he resolved to confront the conjurings of his mind. He would understand their anger, and if necessary negotiate a solution.

He did not have very long to wait.

As he coughed in the billowing exhaust fumes, searching for a gap in the heavy Lewisham traffic, he felt hard hands slap his back and propel him from the pavement into the road. He fell slowly, so that he could see the lead-laden air of the intersection coalescing in the shimmering darkness of their forms. Lying on the warm tarmac with the alloy crutch wedged beneath him, he watched them gathering around his head, sucking form from the airborne waste, their claw-like hands seizing his arms as they tried to pull him beneath the huge wheels of passing lorries. Their shrieked demands were drowned in the thundering suction of traffic, the air jittering with shockwaves as he fought to free himself of their grip.

He tried to cry out, to tell them that he could not understand their rage, when comprehension dawned on him. He was unable to thank the two men who hauled him to safety. His only conscious thought was that he would confront his nemeses again on quieter ground.

'Can you see anything?' He lay on his side in bed, naked, looking back across his shoulder. Linda carefully examined the centre of his spine.

'There are a couple of small bruises, that's all.' She pulled the sheet up. 'How did you get them?'

'I don't know,' he lied. 'How was work?'

'Their accounts are in a total mess, and Phil's desperately grateful to have me back.'

'I bet he is.'

'He's already talking about a permanent position. I've told him it's too early for me to decide. How was the doctor?'

'He couldn't tell what was wrong. He gave me some tablets. I didn't get the prescription filled.'

She returned to the mirror and began combing her hair. 'You really must. They might make a difference.'

He watched her brushing out the day. She smelled warm and milky from her bath, like a child. 'What do you want to call the baby?' he asked.

'A strong name,' she replied, watching him in the glass. 'Jack, if it's a boy. And if it's a girl, Hope.'

He lay awake with Linda beside him, awaiting their return. He was convinced that he knew what they wanted. He had not been familiar with the jealousy of the dead. From their vantage point on the other side they had seen a human essence, fresh and filled with life, moving close towards them, only to be snatched away. Through the accident they had intended to breach his physical shell, transferring his spirit to their starved forms. But the calamity had misfired, leaving them with nothing but an unquenched envy for his continued existence.

How much energy had it taken from them to touch the living side, to pull the pin from the wall, to twist the rope? And why had they chosen him? He would never know. Perhaps the dead engineer many mishaps in our world, he thought. This one failed, and I live on. No wonder they feel cheated. He rose from the bed and descended naked through the darkened house, clutching to the bannister, sure that they would be summoned by his heat.

In the kitchen he turned on the light to find them waiting like stubborn pockets of night, flickering sickly figures, damaged and desperate and unsatisfied, lurking by the walls with no more substance than the charcoal drawings of a child. One of them, a female, divorced herself from the blurring group and approached, her thin red eyes shining like embers in a draught. She grew clearer as she drew near. It was time for them to talk.

'I won't die for you,' he told her. 'You had your chance.'

'It makes no difference,' said the woman, desperately hovering near his warm skin. She spoke as if it caused her pain to do so.

'When a human being sees a wild animal, the animal is changed. Even if it doesn't see the watching human, it loses something of its spirit. It can no longer be called wild. You have glimpsed death, and part of you has been lost to us. We can see you now. And we cannot leave until the rest of you follows.'

'But you intend to make it follow, even though I'm happy here.'

'There is no happiness in our world, only need.'

He could sense their dreadful, bitter longing. Behind the blackened woman the rest of the group skulked, reluctant to negotiate. One of them had found a matchbox on the stove, and was flicking pellets of flame at the gas jets.

'That's true for you, perhaps,' said Kevin, edging closer to the others. 'But I won't come without a fight.'

'Then we'll take your wife and child. We sense her when she is near you. Sense enough to catch.'

He sprang at them then, swinging his good right arm, shattering one into a miasma of burnt sticks. The others screamed thinly, regrouped and dropped, the last burning match harmlessly igniting a gas ring as it fell. He limped back to the bedroom as fast as he could, but Linda was still asleep, curled undisturbed beneath a blanket striped with lunar light.

That morning, as he lay awake in his wife's embrace, he watched them creeping through the door beside the bed, preparing to seize her hair and pull her away from him. Linda drew his lips to hers, kissing him lightly, but his eyes watched the bobbing figures at her back.

He broke prematurely from her kiss and painfully jumped from the bed, ignoring her puzzled look. He knew they could not follow her to work. They were tied to him, and that made him dangerous to her.

As he watched Linda leave from the ground floor window, saw her turn at the corner and wave, slowly smiling, he wondered how he could ever touch her again without placing her and the life of her child at risk. Two unthinkable solutions presented themselves. He could leave her, or sacrifice himself.

The morning passed. The light shifted. He made tea, skimmed through a book, retaining nothing, sat in his armchair and watched from the window. Outside a pair of schoolboys loped back and forth, mindlessly kicking a piece of brick against a wall.

At noon he began to dread his wife's return. Linda had promised to look in after lunch. He had no protection against the forces that would gather at her presence. They had found his weakness, and would exploit it to the fullest extent. Absently he heated the casserole she had left them, and summoned Ivy to the table. Ten minutes later the old lady had still not appeared, and he climbed the stairs to check on her. The bedroom door opened at his knock, and she beckoned him in, indicating a chair where he could sit. As always, her curtains were drawn against the sun, keeping the world at bay. She waited for him to settle himself, then walked to his side. Her clothes smelled of time, of happier days. Photographs filled his vision, brown figures on streets without traffic, framed along the mantel-piece and dressing table, stacked in piles along the sills.

'I know, Kevin,' she said softly, in a voice as dry as sand. 'I know about them.'

He affected a look of puzzlement, unable and unwilling to acknowledge her.

'You think they want to take you because of the accident,' she continued. 'You may be right. People talk of lives cut short, but sometimes a short span is all that God intends. To live too long is just as sad. Look at me: I

expected to be long gone by now, and yet here I am —
with all of this.' She tugged the curtain back a foot and
gestured at the world beyond the window.

Downstairs he heard a key enter the front door lock.
She touched his shoulder with a creased hand, gently, with
affection. 'I've listened to you arguing with them in the
night, but that's no use at all.' Her voice was no more than
a whisper. 'They don't understand what you're saying.
They can see you, taste you, and it drives them insane.'

'I don't know what to do.' He looked at her in surprise.
'I always thought I was strong enough to protect my
family.'

'You are,' she said, smiling. 'Perhaps I can help you to
see that. These things are nothing new. They fight for our
loved ones through all of our lives. I think it's time to fight
them again.'

Below, a door slammed.

'Hello?' His wife called up to them. 'Anyone home?'
Instantly he heard the urgent whispering, the sounds of
darkness gathering. Ivy grabbed his hand and made him
rise, pushing him across the room to the bedroom door.
He stepped onto the landing with her at his back. Linda
was standing at the foot of the stairs, about to ascend. As
she pulled off her jacket a look of puzzlement crossed her
face.

'What's the matter? Is something wrong?' She took the
stairs quickly, moving towards him.

'Stay where you are, Linda. Don't come up.'

In frenzied anticipation the denizens of the night
coagulated about him and the old woman, whispering
excitedly as his wife continued her ascent, frightened now.

Ivy thought back to the nights she had sat in silent vigil
beside her dying husband. She had watched the gathering
of these wizened creatures as they tried to claim his wasted
body. She had stayed awake beside him, rocking her
young daughter in her arms, holding them at bay beyond

the circle of light that bathed the bed. She had been determined to ensure the safe passage of her life-partner from this world to the next. When he finally left her side, he did so alone and unencumbered, free of their parasitic embrace.

Linda had almost reached her husband. Death moved around him like a sparkling shroud. Now was the time. Ivy stepped into the darkness with a willing smile, happy in the knowledge that her own death could fulfil a service. Moving swiftly into place between her daughter and her son-in-law, she drew a sharp breath, then fell at once as if she had been struck. They absorbed her soul before any contrary action could be taken, and so were forcibly appeased. It was not what they had wanted, and they were not pleased for being cheated. As their sated darkness retreated, balance was restored.

Kevin and Linda both cried out as the old lady fell. Now her carcase lay at their feet, the dead beneath the living, as it should be. Even as he wept, he saw the wisdom of her choice. Within his wife, their child's heart grew stronger.

Chang-Siu And The Blade Of Grass

Long, long ago in China, at the time of the Sung dynasty, a poor farmer named Chang-Siu lived with his daughter in the bleak hinterland of the Hopeh Plain near the city of Ch'in-huang-tao. Their home was as barren and austere as the dark mountains at their backs, but Chang-Siu was content in the knowledge that he would one day be buried beside his ancestors, most of whom had expired after lifetimes spent breaking the hard dry soil by day, and shielding themselves from the bitter winds which crossed the plain at night.

Chang-Siu's frail wife had died giving birth to their only child, and the farmer had been left to raise his daughter, whose name was Ti-Pu, alone. Ti-Pu's beauty was as flawless as polished chalk, and Chang-Siu's love for her had the strength of the sky. Nothing grew on the desolate land which surrounded their house, not even a blade of grass, so each morning, while the misty sun was still low beyond the plain, Chang-Siu would take his daughter to the sluggish river at the base of the mountains where they would gather rushes. After this, they would return home to place them in racks for drying, and Chang-Siu would empty the old racks so that his daughter could begin to weave the hardening stalks into matting. From this simple trade they were able to buy the few necessities they required to silence their bellies and keep them warm.

Half a day's walk from Chang-Siu's modest house, a village sat sheltered in shadow at the base of the mountains. Although small, it was situated at the edge of a much-used trading route, and it was here that the couple were able to sell their wares. On the few warm days of late summer, when the sun cut free from the towering horizon

247

and shadows withdrew from the village like a retreating grey tide, Chang-Siu would sit in the square and play checkers with the merchants, while his daughter remained seated obediently beside him, and the old hound that lived in the square slept with its tail gently twitching. On these days their life together gained a pleasurable respite from eternal toil, and Chang-Siu felt the fleeting luxury of leisure.

As the years passed, Ti-Pu's beauty grew until it exceeded her mother's, and as Chang-Siu escorted her through the town he saw heads turn and men whisper as she passed. The old rush-farmer knew that their hard life on the plain would soon rob his daughter of this delicate beauty, and because they spent almost every waking moment of their day together, he turned his admiration of her golden days into a fear, and then an obsession. He knew that unless a good marriage could be made for her they would die without advancement, as poor as they had been upon their arrival in the world, with nothing to show for their lives of labour.

There lived in the next village a handsome young merchant named Wang-Lin. At an early age he had inherited a fortune from his father, who had once been a painter to the Emperor Chao Hsu himself at the Imperial Palace. Wang-Lin's father had fallen from grace after painting a picture that was wrongly interpreted, and had expired in comfort and regret at the house of his son. The young merchant was barely older than Ti-Pu, and although he had no need to work, did so in order to contribute to the fortunes of his village.

To strengthen his family following its depletion by the sudden inertia of his father, Wang-Lin was rumoured to be searching for a wife. It became Chang-Siu's deepest wish to see his daughter married to the merchant. All who had met him spoke of the boy as kind and noble, the perfect partner for a girl as beautiful as Ti-Pu. Soon, the residents of both villages had linked the couple's names in anticipated harmony. The arrangement of their meeting and subsequent marriage were regarded by all as an occurrence as inevitable as the rising sun.

For his part, Chang-Siu let it to be known that he would allow his daughter to meet with Wang-Lin, to discuss the details of the impending nuptials. Ti-Pu's dowry would be her beauty, a gift more precious and fleeting than summer rain. Accordingly, Wang-Lin replied that he would consider it a great honour to receive a visit from Chang-Siu and his daughter.

Just before dawn on the day they were to travel to Wang-Lin's village, Chang-Siu was seized with a terrible foreboding, and leapt from his rush bed with a fearful cry. As soon as he saw that his fears were founded, fingers of ice began to close over him, and in an instant he sensed that his dreams for the future would never be fulfilled. Ti-Pu, who always faced the day with clear eyes and a hopeful heart, was crying. Between her sobs she explained that despite his desirability as a husband she had no wish to marry Wang-Lin, for she loved another, a scholar who lived in their own village, and that worse still he was penniless.

'How could this be?' demanded Chang-Siu, for in all their years together his daughter had never been left alone in public. Ti-Pu explained that she had fallen in love with the scholar, whose name was Liu-Yen, in the square while her father played checkers.

'But surely this means you have never even spoken,' Chang-Siu gasped, unable to believe his ears. Ti-Pu explained that they had no need for words, and that all was understood between them. Chang-Siu considered his afternoons in the village square and recalled the scholar, who was as thin and pale as he was poor.

249

'It is out of the question for you to marry this man,' he cried, quite enraged. 'Does it mean nothing to you that we have slaved and sweated to survive on this land, where not even a single blade of grass will grow? Why should you seek to destroy our family's only chance to change our lives for the better? I am your father, and it is right that I decide whom you should marry. I will not countenance the idea of your betrothal to a pauper. I forbid you to ever look upon this man again. Furthermore, today we will journey to the house of Wang-Lin to formalise the forthcoming nuptial ceremony.'

At this, Ti-Pu cried anew, and her misery was deepened by a dark cloud passing above the house, which Ti-Pu took to be an omen of death.

Chang-Siu sought to console his daughter, and tried to explain that his actions were compelled by his concern for her happiness, but Ti-Pu was deaf to his entreaties, and ran from the room in tears.

As the day passed, she refused to go with her father to see Wang-Lin, insisting instead that her suitor be informed of the situation. When he saw the pain in his daughter's amber eyes, Chang-Siu set off alone, and with every step he took towards Wang-Lin's house, he watched his dreams slip away. Wang-Lin was disheartened when he heard that Ti-Pu loved another, but Chang-Siu was sure that there was still time for his daughter to admit her folly and return to the marriage he so desired for her. Love was more powerful than Chang-Siu's anger, and although he forbade the girl from ever seeing her lover again he took her back into his heart, hoping that she would quickly see the error of her ways.

Several nights later, there arose a terrible thunderstorm. Lightning cracked the sky in two and filled the great plain with fire, and the rushes beside the river clattered like the bones of the returning dead. Hail hammered over the little house so that it sounded as if a flight of stallions was riding across the roof. Inside, Ti-Pu's misery broke like a dam, flooding into anger. Bitterly she begged her father to allow her a single visit to the man with whom she had fallen in love, but Chang-Siu furiously refused. His rage against his daughter followed the course of the storm, finally blowing itself out when Ti-Pu threw open the door of the little house and fled into the rain.

Chang-Siu's weeks of loneliness were preceded by the knowledge that he had lost his only child. The storm abated and the bare plain dried, but Ti-Pu did not reappear. The rain channels which had been carved into the hard earth slowly dried and filled, and the pale sun climbed to the sky once more, and Chang-Siu no longer dared to leave the house for fear of missing his daughter's return.

Finally, when he was forced to venture into the village for supplies, he heard the women gossiping outside the teahouse. In truth he wished to overhear, for he had no other way of discovering the whereabouts of his child. In this way he ascertained that Ti-Pu had become the wife of the scholar Liu-Yen, and that they lived in a tiny hut beside a rocky outcrop at the foot of the mountains, in the place where her new husband had been born. The one thing that marred Ti-Pu's happiness was the loss of her father's devotion. It was only her fear of his wrath, said one of the women, that kept her from calling on him. Sadder by far, said another, was the news that the heart-broken young merchant, Wang-Lin, had arranged to marry another for the favour of financial convenience, and not the grace of love.

That night the old farmer raged around his threadbare home, greatly vexed. Eventually exhausted by his rage, he tried to sleep, but the cold air which invaded his bones seemed the coldest air that had ever been, and the darkness which filled the room was darker than the blackest night that had ever fallen on the plain.

The next day, Chang-Siu arose with a stubborn ache in his heart, and bitterly returned to the routine of his daily business, resolved that he would never set eyes on his daughter again.

For six days and nights Chang-Siu saw no one. He made war upon his work, using it to combat the enemy of his memory. His gnarled hands had not the dexterity of his daughter's, so that the mats he wove were imperfect and unfinished. On the seventh day he returned to the village, but managed to sell little more than a third of his wares, and those out of pity for his loss. The merchant, a man whom Chang-Siu had known for most of his life, seemed uncomfortable talking to him, and was relieved to conclude business so that the old farmer would finally leave his store.

Chang-Siu returned home, to his work, to his empty house, and to his rancour, which ate into his chest like a deep-rooted poison, and clouded his every waking thought. At the end of the week he returned to the village, but now the merchant said he could not take even a few mats, for he had found a more reliable supplier.

Disconsolate, Chang-Siu sat in the square and searched for challenges. He tried playing checkers, but his friends all drifted away from him shaking their heads, refusing to be drawn into a game. Everywhere he went it was the same. Those who would once have cheerfully passed the day with him now lowered their eyes and searched the ground, anxious to be gone. Even the ancient hound in the square slunk guiltily from his presence, preferring the company of flies.

Chang-Siu knew he had done nothing wrong, and could not understand the behaviour of the villagers. Was it not

252

the lot of man to better his station, and marry his daughter to the best advantage of his family? One old friend, an elderly merchant full of travelling tales, now pointedly refused to sit with him. Another refused to eat with him. Chang-Siu sensed that something terrible had occurred, but could find no one to tell him what had passed. And so, as his melancholy deepened, his life took on a pattern quite empty and devoid of meaning. His house, uncared-for by any human hand, accepted the embrace of nature. What little savings he had accrued in a lifetime of toil were soon exhausted in the purchase of provisions. Each trip to the village was filled with dread as children darted from his sight, and even the birds refused to alight on the ground where he walked.

One morning, Chang-Siu arose with the familiar ache filling his chest and stinging his joints, and resolved to visit a physician, a kindly old man who lived on a windswept hilltop. The physician held his hands across the farmer's heart, then stared long and hard into the pupils of his eyes. Finally, he told him that he had discovered the root of the problem. He asked the farmer how long he had been suffering from aches and pains. Chang-Siu explained that his health had begun to fail after the terrible fight with his daughter which had resulted in her departure from the family home, and that the moon had passed three times since.

'Well, that's it,' said the physician, nodding sagely. 'I'm afraid I have some bad news for you. You are dead. Your demise most likely occurred on the night that your daughter became lost to you. Your ill-humour overpowered your heart. You have been dead since that time, but neither you nor your friends can see your death, only sense it. The light of life has been extinguished from your eyes, but your angry spirit is unwilling to leave your body.'

'What will become of me?' asked Chang-Siu, appalled.

253

'Unless you find a way to make your spirit leave soon, your body will start to corrupt even though it continues to perform its normal duties,' said the physician, 'and although the chill winds still sweep our village, summer is coming.'

Devastated by this news, the old farmer returned home and sat alone in his hovel. He looked out on the bare plain where nothing grew, remembering the death of his lovely wife, and the departure of his beautiful daughter. It was as if the land itself had taken a hand in robbing his family of life and happiness. Chang-Siu grieved for the end of his line. Dead! How vastly the grim truth of his mortality differed from his imagined demise! Instead of exhaling on silken cushions, to perish in such dismal penitude! Finally, his self-pity was usurped by the search for a solution to his problem. At first light the following morning, he began the journey to his daughter's house.

As Chang-Siu reached the end of the rocky promontory above his daughter's home, he looked down and saw that the tiny shack had been painted vermilion, and was surrounded by small plants that bristled with blossoming pink buds. As he watched, Ti-Pu appeared at the door, and he saw that her waist was thickening with child. When she saw him she ran to his arms, and it was as if they had never been apart.

They walked together beside the house and spoke softly of the past. Chang-Siu decided not to mention that he had died, for he did not wish to alarm her. Ti-Pu told him how Liu-Yen had gained a position teaching, and although their income was modest it would be enough to support their child. Chang-Siu fought his natural indignation, but still he found his daughter's choice hard to understand. For it seemed to him that even if he worked as hard as the old rush-farmer had done all his life, Liu-Yen would still have nothing to leave his wife and child.

'It wasn't as if I attempted to wed you to an ogre,' he said. 'Wang-Lin was a fine catch, but you refused to even meet him. Our family owns nothing, not even a single blade of grass. How could you think of marrying this man?'

Instead of being hurt by his words Ti-Pu smiled, and took her father by the hand. At the back of the house she knelt in the small green garden, then arose with her fist closed. 'This is where my child will play,' she said, slowly unfolding her fingers. 'It is more than we have ever had. Look at our riches now.'

In her palm lay a single blade of grass.

At the end of two days, Chang-Siu took his leave of Ti-Pu and her husband. As he walked back along the rocky path of the promontory, he felt the warmth of the setting sun slowly fill his limbs, soothing away the soreness in his joints and the ache from his heart. His body fell softly, fading away in the gentle spring breeze. Last of all to disappear into the earth was his closed right hand, and the slender emerald treasure it concealed.

The Words

Some straight answers about where these Sharper Knives really came from. Tales sometimes emerge from a single thought or feeling, and gather detail like poisoned candy-floss around a stick. Others are the result of the odd *odd* experience.

On Edge stems from the surreal melding of drills and decor mags that is a dentist's waiting room. Perhaps dentists assume that reading about the grotesque houses of the hunting set will have a zen-like calming effect on your fear of pain.

Norman Wisdom And The Angel Of Death reached me from two routes — discovery of Asperger's Syndrome, the 'train-spotter's' disease, and the awful realisation that I still find Norman Wisdom and Charlie Drake funny.

Dale And Wayne Go Shopping wrote itself after I witnessed a drunken fist-fight at the cheese counter of Camden Town Sainsbury's, Home Of The Shellsuit People.

Mythology can always provide inspiration, and I was thinking that if the Phrygian king, Midas, existed today, he'd probably be forced to work for the CIA. Hence, **Contact High**.

Last Call For Passenger Paul — a flight attendant told me that people really do overshoot their destinations. Now I jab myself with cocktail sticks to stay awake on multi-stop journeys. And it's said that troublesome passengers have their luggage chalked with a code ...

The Legend of Dracula ... was born of a desire to approach the original gothic in a fresh manner, and if you've ever pitched to a TV executive you know you're battling the Forces of Pure Evil.

Cooking The Books is a morality tale begun after watching sales staff shovelling sand from a fur-and-diamond store in the desert. I remember thinking that this was another creepy frontline in the war of Man against Nature.

The Vintage Car Table-Mat Collection ... came from a sneaking thought that although the living dead always return to cannibalise and wreck venegance on the living, they might really prefer a nice cup of tea and a sit-down.

Persia grew from thinking that such a beautiful word should be a synonym for something which doesn't exist, and from looking at the paintings of Sir Lawrence Alma-Tadema.

Black Day At Bad Rock is largely, alarmingly, true (I still have my Black Badge). Aren't schooldays great? Like *Lord Of The Flies* with detention and homework.

258

Revelation's Child stems from reading an exposé of the so-called satanic child abuse investigations, and wondering if US evangelists cause more harm than their counterparts. The bit about the PRAY carvings is absolutely true, by the way.

Can't Slow Down . . . is a warning.

When I was a boy I owned a copy of the book mentioned in **Outside The Wood**, and the illustration discussed still bothers me (along with 'Uncle Two-Heads Sinks Slowly Into The Quicksand' and 'Karik and Valya In The Lair Of The Water Spider' from other forbidden books).

Finally, I love the formality of Chinese ghost stories, and **Chang Siu And The Blade Of Grass** is my lowly attempt at the genre. So now you know.

The Illustrations

Some of the artists who provided these lovingly rendered illustrations are seasoned veterans. Others are in print for the very first time. All of them believe that books should be treated as desirable objects in their own right. They are:

John Bolton

'Norman Wisdom And The Angel Of Death', 'Last Call For Passenger Paul', 'Persia'

John's vast body of stylish work includes graphics for *The Vampire L'Estat*, *Someplace Strange*, *The Books Of Magic*, *Man Bat*, *Army Darkness*, and *Menz Insana*. His interest in the bizarre can be seen in the extraordinary objects filling his North London studio, many of which are dead or asleep.

Graham Humphreys

'On Edge', 'The Legend Of Dracula ...', 'The Vintage Car Table-Mat Collection ...', 'Outside The Wood'

Graham is a master of music and movie macabre, having painted outrageous posters for cult bands like *The Cramps*, and horror films like *The Evil Dead I* and *II* and *Santa Sangre*. He created designs for the movie *Dust Devil*, and

261

the lethal robot in *Hardware*. He remains a very nice person, which is odd, really.

David Lloyd

'Revelation's Child', 'Chang-Siu And The Blade Of Grass'

David needs no introduction to anyone who enjoyed *V For Vendetta*, an electrifying graphic novel for people who don't switch off the news. When he's not teaching comic strip illustration, he's producing graphic tales for *ESPers*, *Slaine* and *Crisis*, among other pursuits. He currently resides in Brighton.

Martin Butterworth

'Contact High', 'Black Day At Bad Rock'

Martin left New York to continue graphic design in his native London, and now works in Soho creating provocative poster images for art-house movies like *Toto The Hero*, *Night On Earth* and *Prospero's Books*. His enthusiasm for the fantastic is positively creepy.

Lee Brimmicombe-Wood

'Dale And Wayne Go Shopping'

Lee is a newcomer to the graphic field, but someone we'll be seeing more of. He fills his spare time drawing Japanese-style comix, and possesses a sense of humour normally found only in exotic root vegetables.

Martin Smith

'Can't Slow Down For Fear I'll Die'

Although a first-timer in book illustration, Martin's large-scale paintings and drawings of athletes are much admired by collectors. He's currently experimenting with new graphic styles.

Richard Parker

'Cooking The Books'

Richard's interest in natural studies surfaces in his stunning ceramics of British flora and fauna, currently available in London. His paintings of birds, beetles and butterflies admirably suit the illustrative medium.